TALISMAN

GIFTS OF
THE SHAVTAL

BOOK 1

TALISMAN

GIFTS OF
THE SHAVTAL

BOOK 1

TONI YAP

atmosphere press

For my husband James Dixson III
in making this book a reality.

CHAPTER ONE

THE PHONE CALL

Gripping the phone receiver as it almost slips from my grasp, I wait for the phone line to be answered. Beads of sweat break through my pajama top, so I'm nervous.

"C'mon, C'mon, answer!"

A woman's voice on the other end breaks my train of thought.

"Nine-one-one operator. What is your emergency?"

Tears continue to run down my face as I wipe my runny nose with my left pajama sleeve. My mouth is dry, and my throat is tight; I answer with a stutter.

"H-hello? M-my mother needs h-h-help!"

The 911 operator replies with a steady voice. "Sure thing, Miss. What's your name, age, and address?"

I take a deep breath and let it out.

"I'm Georgina Trabeck, twelve years old, and my address is 121 Greens Road, Lot 23, Waitborne, Ohio. It's the Western Estates mobile home park."

"Can I speak to your mother?"

"She's not conscious. She might be asleep. Her face is

3

swollen, and she might have a broken nose, but it's hard to tell since it's badly bruised."

I look over to Mom and then back on the phone.

"There's a lot of blood lost from her nose."

"Can you wake her up?"

"Hang on."

Tapping Mom's shoulder, I lift my mom's head and gently plead.

"Ma ... Ma, you need to wake up!"

Her head tilts back, and she's still breathing through her mouth, but her eyes are closed, and her body is limp.

"Please, Ma! Wake up."

I gently move away from Mom to return to the receiver I left on the floor. I put the receiver to my mouth.

"She's having trouble waking up. I-I don't know what to do. How much longer before someone shows up?"

"Just a few more minutes. Is she sitting up at least?"

"Yes ... I just want to let you know she's nine months pregnant."

"Can you tell me what happened?"

Fear is rising in my chest; this is the part I've been dreading. The silence feels like forever.

"Hello? Georgina? You still there?"

I don't know what to say; this is the first time I've ever called 911. It's a big no-no because Stepdad won't allow it.

"Uhhh ... I think she fell or something. She's been kinda clumsy with her tummy and all."

My right eye catches an image at the front door. I had forgotten it was still wide open. Stepdad took off. I don't know where he went.

The two paramedics standing in the doorway startle me. The receiver slips from my sweaty hand and lands on the kitchen floor.

One of the paramedics gives me an apologetic look.

"Sorry to startle you. Are you Georgina Trabeck?"

"Yes, I'm Georgina." I point towards Mom.

"That's my mother, Rosaria Trabeck."

The paramedic with short curly black hair and hazel eyes asks sincerely.

"May I take a look at your Mother?"

His head motions towards my sleeping mother. My head nods in agreement as he motions to the other paramedic, a gentleman in his twenties, with a thin frame, brown crew cut, and brown eyes, carrying a med kit across his right shoulder; he walks towards Mom.

They immediately go to work on my mom. The first paramedic checks her pulse and breathing.

"Mrs. Trabeck? Can you hear me?"

He gets down on his knees next to her and taps her on the shoulder. She jolts awake and looks around while blood streams down from her nose. She looks around, confused. Her shoulder-length black hair is matted to her head and neck. Her bloodshot eyes look empty; her face has no expression. I'm tired of seeing her like this, same thing, different day.

I'm still standing next to the phone on the kitchen wall, just realizing that I've been crying. My urine-soaked pajama top feels chilly against my bare skin, making me shiver. The smell is noticeable as I look down on myself. Parts of my pajama pants are soaking wet.

"GEORGINA!"

Reality jolts me back to the phone receiver on the floor.

I snatch up the phone to my mouth.

"Yes, ma'am, I'm here. Sorry about that. The paramedics have arrived. We're okay now."

I hang up the phone, not giving the 911 operator another opportunity to ask more questions.

Mom doesn't fight too much when they put her on a stretcher; she has a respirator strapped gingerly to her whole face so she can breathe. I approach the curly-haired paramedic hesitantly.

"Excuse me, what hospital are you taking her to?"

He smiles at me. "I was about to get to that, Miss Trabeck."

He hands me a business card printed in black ink, "Waitborne Regional Hospital," with the street address and phone number.

His kind smile fades as he keeps his gaze on me.

"What happened here? I need to know so we can give your mother the proper treatment."

He motions for me to sit on a chair across from him at the table.

My wet top clings to my chest like a cold blanket as I sit in the chair.

"Did you wet yourself?"

I couldn't look at him, so I kept my gaze on the floor. The light blue hue of his aura tells me that he means no harm and that maybe he's a caring person. I answer his first question.

"I-I don't know what happened. I was in my bedroom sleeping. I found Mom like this."

Telling him the truth will have consequences in the next few hours. They don't know about Stepdad.

Scratching the back of my head, I twitch my feet together. My arms automatically cross, signaling that I was no longer comfortable with this situation. I look down again.

"And no ... I didn't pee myself. M-my little sister peed on me while ..."

His hazel eyes widen.

"You have a little sister? Is she here?"

"Yes, she's changing into some dry clothes. She's only three years old, so she has had potty accidents. I took care of her while my mother was in the kitchen."

"By the looks of things here in the kitchen, it looks like there was some sort of skirmish. Did someone hurt your mother?"

His face darkens with concern while his aura turns a darker blue. He's getting suspicious; I've seen that look before. He looks at me for a long time, waiting for me to answer him.

"I-I don't know what happened ..."

He leans in closer with the same concerned look in his eyes.

"Do you have a father?"

Leaning back in my chair with reservation, I lie.

"My Stepdad went to the store for some more milk. He'll be back."

He stares at me for a long time, then gets up.

"Well, you have the card. Give that to him as soon as he comes home."

I didn't say anything more, just nodded my head in compliance. He joins the other paramedic who was waiting by my mother's stretcher.

The other paramedic seems impatient as his eyes dart between the first paramedic and me. He stares at me for a good moment, and I stare back.

I've seen his type before ... one who has no tolerance for people who aren't like him: light skin and only speaks *American, not English but American.*

His drab green-and-brownish aura confirms what I see in his eyes.

They hoist her stretcher out of the house and walk towards the ambulance. I follow them out the doorway and stop to watch. The curly-haired guy looks at me and nods. His frown is all too familiar, like the one doctors and nurses give my mother when they don't believe her excuses of being too clumsy, and that's why she has so many bruises on her arms and legs. Most of the time, all I could do was look away to hide my expression of disappointment and sadness.

The ambulance's flashing lights are turned off as it backs out of our driveway. There were a couple of neighbors hanging around watching.

Mrs. Jenkins from next door runs over to us. She's a middle-aged lady, big boned, with broad shoulders, and very tall.

Her stocky frame makes her look masculine even though she likes to wear a house dress with yellow and pink flowers, even her ankles look thick in her black socks cradled in flip-flops. Her dirty blonde with lots of gray hair is piled on her head like a messy bun and loosens as she runs towards me.

"Gi-Gi! Are you okay? Was that your mom in the ambulance?"

Her five-feet-nine-inches frame stands before me, shadowing me as she looks down with kind, blue eyes. Her smile is sincere, but her facial expression is riddled with curiosity. Motioning her to come inside, I look at the nosy neighbors watching. I give them a dirty look. Mrs. Jenkins takes notice and yells at them.

"DON'T Y'ALL HAVE LIVES?! GO HOME!"

She steps in without any hesitation as I slam the door shut.

"Would you like some tea, Mrs. Jenkins?"

She waves her hand as if swatting away a fly.

"Nah ... I'm all right, drank too much coffee, so now I can't sleep."

I motion for her to sit at the kitchen table with me.

"I need to make some hot cocoa ... I hope you don't mind."

I grab a saucepan from one of the drawers.

She grabs the saucepan from my grip.

"How 'bout I make you my famous hot cocoa. It's my niece's favorite. Got any milk and cocoa powder?"

I point to the fridge, then to the pantry.

"Yeah, milk is there, and cocoa powder there."

She quickly mixes the ingredients in the saucepan and turns on the stove burner, stirring while heating the ingredients slowly.

Sheer exhaustion hits me as my eyes scan the black and white cat clock with roving eyes that move rhythmically to the hanging pendulum tail. I can't believe it's past 1 a.m.

I'm so not looking forward to going to school later. Mrs.

Jenkins notices my silence as she quietly pours a cup of delicious cocoa into a cup on the table. The sweet chocolate aroma dances under my nose, so I pull the cup closer. The warm liquid soothes me as I sip it slowly.

Mrs. Jenkins sits across from me, waiting patiently as I begin to relax. Her aura resembles my mom's when she's in loving mother mode with hints of cotton-candy pink and shades of faded orange. I stare back at Mrs. Jenkins and study her a bit longer. Her intense blue eyes don't miss a thing.

I wouldn't be surprised if she's aware of what goes on at my home. Her face softens to a warm smile as she reaches over to hold my hand. It feels warm and dry but firm.

"You know if you and your mother ever need anything, you only need to ask. It's the 1970s and women need to stick together. Okay?"

I grip her hand back with an affirming squeeze.

"Thank you, Mrs. Jenkins. You're a good friend to our family and a kind neighbor. I noticed nobody else came over to help except for you."

Her smile continues, but her eyes moisten with tears.

"Is your mom gonna be okay? Were you the one who called the ambulance?"

I nod my head.

"That was very brave of you. Probably saved your mother's life."

Tears flood my eyes, and my stupid nose is runny again. She got out of her chair to hug me; I didn't object. Her hug comforts me. As she presses against me, she feels my cold, damp, urine-soaked pajama top, and I pull away.

She looks at me with the same pitiful look doctors, nurses, and recently, a paramedic gave me.

"Sorry, Chrissy wet on me while, while … I'm gonna change before bed. It's nothing."

She pulls me to her and looks into my eyes.

"Listen, let your Stepdad know I can watch little Chrissy

while you are at the hospital. She'll get to meet my niece, Danae. She just moved in a couple of days ago. I'd also want you to meet her too."

"I would love to meet Danae. Is she about my age?"

"Yep! Don't be surprised you two might be in the same class together!"

I hug her back and look at her.

"Thank you. I'll leave a note on the table before I go to bed."

Mrs. Jenkins took the hint and let go. She quickly put my empty cup in the sink.

"I'm glad you're all right. So, is Chrissy asleep? I haven't seen her."

She notices the surprised look on my face.

"Oh my God! Chrissy!"

She pulls my right arm as I am about to run to the bedroom.

"Shhhh! She's probably asleep!"

I calm down, and she lets go of my arm.

"See you in the morning!"

She lets herself out of our mobile home. I quickly get a broom and dustpan to sweep up broken glass on the floor. In the middle of the kitchen table, I leave a note about Mrs. Jenkins and the hospital address card the paramedic gave me. Hopefully, Stepdad sees it when he gets home. Then I turn off the lights to walk towards my bedroom.

As I walk into my dark bedroom, the moonlight beaming through my window illuminates the little bump under my bed sheets. Relieved to hear her breathing calmly under the covers, I pull it down to see Chrissy sound asleep. I tiptoe to my dresser to grab a pair of pajamas. I quickly dress and quietly slip into the covers next to my sleeping sister. Holding onto her comforts me as my eyelids slowly close.

I'm lulled by a sweet humming sound. This soft, soothing voice doesn't sound like my mother, and besides, she never sang a lullaby to me, even when I was a baby.

She whispers to me with an unusual accent.

"Shhh ... child, tomorrow is another day, and you'll be much stronger. Rest now."

The sweet melodic humming is too tempting, and it's frustrating. On the one hand, I want to be lulled by a high-pitched voice soothing me, but on the other hand, I'm angry about what happened today. I shouldn't be surprised to see my tiny mother used as a punching bag by Stepdad, but today, he went just a little too far.

Seeing Mom with a bruised face and a bloody nose, then passing out and becoming limp scared me. I've done something I've never done before, and that was to call for help, knowing I would face some serious consequences from Stepdad.

Saying a prayer to myself, I hope Mother Mary watches over Mom. The singing continues; it's worked its way into my troubled mind.

I can't fight it off; I'm just too tired. Who is this woman in my head? Sleep takes over me.

CHAPTER TWO

A NEW DAY

I must've slept past my alarm clock on my nightstand, and I don't remember pushing the snooze button. It doesn't matter since a set of heavy footsteps approach outside my bedroom door.

Bang! Bang! My bedroom door slams open against the wall. Stepdad, with his bloodshot eyes in his air force fatigues green uniform, stands over me with a hateful glare. A loud, thundering voice fills my bedroom.

"Get out of bed! Damn it!"

He pulls my bed covers off as the cold, crisp air startles me awake. Like a bucket of icy water dumped over me, I'm back to the brutal reality of my life.

My body shoots up in bed while he stands over me with his cold, bloodshot eyes and messy hair. There's a black cloud aura coiled around his neck. I know he can't see it, but I can tell he senses it because he keeps scratching his neck.

This coiled black aura reminds me of a snake tightening around his neck. He talks with a gargled voice.

"You have exactly thirty minutes to dress, clean up, and

eat before I drive you to school! Get your lazy ass moving!"

He turns away, walks out of my room, and slams the door.

Little Chrissy, still sleeping next to me, stirs and lets out a little whimper. I stroke her back to calm her; she stops whimpering and sticks her right thumb in her mouth. She falls back to sleep.

Whispering under my breath, staring at the shut door, I wait for my nerves to calm.

"Good Morning, Gina, how are you doing? I'm fine, thank you. Do you even care that my pregnant mom, your wife, could've died by your filthy hands? No? I didn't think so ..."

No longer startled, just angry, I kick off the covers and slip out of bed.

Great! The day hasn't even started, and I'm already in a bad mood! Screw my life!

If I hadn't called 911 and stayed in my bedroom like Mom usually tells me, I don't know if Mom would've pulled through this ordeal. I must hurry, get dressed, brush my teeth, comb my hair, and make my lunch pronto.

Then a song pops into my head: Yes, it's that freaky but cool guy David Bowie. My imagination conjures him dancing around and singing to me his latest song I heard on the radio.

I hum the tune now while grabbing a pair of jeans, a T-shirt, socks, and underwear from my dresser drawers. My nervousness is still hanging on as I try to drown it out with my humming.

Stepping into the bathroom, I close the door and lock it with a loud click on the doorknob. I lean against the locked door, take a deep breath, and let it out. I swallow hard to keep the bile down, a wave of exhaustion plagues me.

Doing my best to recall what to do when I feel nauseous, I lean down and breathe slowly. My brain is still in panic mode.

What the heck are you doing? You don't have time!

There's that anger again as I yell to myself.

"Shut Up!"

I'm vigorously brushing my teeth by the faucet.

While doing that, I notice how tired I looked in the mirror. My bloodshot eyeballs have bags, and my face looks almost green or sallow. I'm lucky if I even got five hours of sleep; sadly, this is nothing new. I've become such a light sleeper; I'm sure it's stunting my growth.

I swear to God I'm already looking old, like my thirty-year-old homeroom teacher, Mrs. Young. Fighting to put my long, black, wavy hair into a ponytail is a regular morning challenge. The circles and bags around my dark eyes are something else. I press a rolled-up hand towel soaked in cold water under my eyes, wishing I didn't have to look so different.

I'm the only one in school who doesn't look like the others; the kids make fun of me because my eyes are too squinty or I tan easily during the summer, so when I come back to school in the fall, they call me the black Jap girl or the red chink girl.

I can't look in the mirror anymore—it's disturbing—so I focus on rinsing my mouth. Picking up the pace, I quickly change into my clothes.

Back in my bedroom, little Chrissy stirs. Somehow, she managed to pull the covers back over her while I was in the bathroom. It's hard to believe she didn't wet my bed because of Stepdad's yelling.

Pulling off the covers, I nudge her to wake up.

"Hey, Cookie Monster! Wake up! You gotta go over to Mrs. Jenkins today!"

That works; she pops up with a big smile on her face.

"You tink Mrs. Jenkins has pancakes?"

I smile back at her.

"She might if you ask her politely. Come on, get dressed. Your father is waiting too."

Her cute little smile fades, and her light pink aura turns red in seconds. She jumps out of bed and leaves my room.

As I grab my school bag and a sweater out of my bedroom, Chrissy is in our parents' bedroom, just a few doors down.

We live in a two-bedroom mobile home that Grandma May (Stepdad's biological mom) bought for my parents when they first moved into Waitborne, Ohio, three years ago.

Some days I wished we lived in an apartment near the air force base; at least I would be going to a school nearby where many of the kids come from mixed-race families that speak more than one language. It would be neat to see other Filipino kids or Korean or German—anything. I don't think I would run into so much prejudice against me for just existing with a different skin color.

Walking into the main bedroom, I see Chrissy rummaging through her little dresser for something to wear. She pulls out a light blue, flimsy nightgown with a picture of Cinderella on the front. The soft, powdery blue color reminds me of Mom's favorite house dress. I can't help but think about her. I hope she's doing all right. Chrissy distracts me from my sad thoughts.

"I'm goin' to be a princess today! I must wear my gown."

We laugh, then I grab the nightgown from her.

"How 'bout something warm, okay? I'll put your nightgown in your diaper bag. You can wear it at Mrs. Jenkins' for nap time. All right?"

She frowns for a second but then beams a big smile when I show her a cute yellow dress with long sleeves, ruffles on the skirt, and a picture of chicks on the bodice.

"How about your little yellow dress, yellow tights, and your pink boots?"

She happily grabs the clothes, and I hand her some underwear and training pants.

She runs to the bathroom to change.

"Don't forget to use the potty too!"

"I will!" She closes the bathroom door.

She pops her head out of the doorway after a few minutes.

"Okay, can you help me brush my teeth and comb my hair?"

"Sure thing."

She leaves the door open and waits for me to help comb her hair and brush her teeth.

We walk into the kitchen where Stepdad sits at the kitchen table, drinking black coffee from a mug and reading the morning paper.

Mrs. Jenkins is already knocking on the front door and walks in. She doesn't wait for anyone to answer. Chrissy lets go of my hand and runs to Mrs. Jenkins.

"Good morning, Mrs. Jenkins!"

Mrs. Jenkins can't help but give her a big smile and leans down to pick up Chrissy.

"Look at you! All pretty with your lovely dress and ponytails!"

Chrissy hugs her for a moment and beams in Mrs. Jenkins' face.

"Ya! I dressed all by myself!"

Chrissy giggles, sticks her tongue out, and makes a goofy face at Mrs. Jenkins, who, in turn, lets out a boisterous laugh.

I hand the diaper bag to her; she gives me a big smile while Chrissy's legs wrap around Mrs. Jenkins' waist.

Stepdad puts down his coffee mug and newspaper; he doesn't even acknowledge Mrs. Jenkins and yells at me.

"You've got exactly five minutes to make your lunch."

She waits for him to greet or notice her, and he returns to reading his newspaper. She stares at him for a long time with narrow eyes and a frown on her face.

Looking nervously at Mrs. Jenkins and Chrissy, I decide to break the uncomfortable silence.

"Have a good day, Mrs. J! Love you, Chrissy!"

Mrs. Jenkins nods, gives Stepdad a bewildered look, then replies to me with a painted smile. "You have a good day at school, young lady."

Chrissy blows me a kiss as Mrs. Jenkins carries her and her diaper bag out the front door.

Walking past Stepdad while he's sitting makes my heart beat harder. Sometimes he'll give me a swift kick in the ass when I take too long to get moving. So, I run past him to access the fridge behind him. I let out a deep breath as soon as my hand grabs the refrigerator door handle.

Fortunately, some cold, fried chicken legs were wrapped in foil, an apple, and a cheese slice in plastic wrapping. I grab my metal lunch box and my thermos located on top of the counter. I throw in all the food I found in the fridge and manage to pour some punch into my thermos.

Packed and ready to go, I turn around and walk towards the front door.

My stomach grumbles while I sit in our station wagon's front seat; it is too tempting to just get into my lunch box to eat some chicken.

Hold on! If you eat your lunch now, what're you gonna eat for lunch?

My thoughts ask me questions even though they already have the answers.

"What in the world is taking him so long?"

He storms out of the mobile home, slamming the front door shut. He has something in his hand, a little brown pouch. It looks familiar, but I can't recall where I've seen it before. He must've seen the confused look on my face as he opens the driver's seat door and gets in.

"Whaddya lookin' at?"

He throws the pouch on the dashboard in front of him. He starts the engine and backs out of the driveway. I don't answer him; I never do. He's sitting too close to me, and there's no place to run away if he gets the urge to slap me.

I can feel the sweat on my upper lip and wipe it off with my sweater sleeve. Sticking my face out the open window to daydream is my only refuge.

He takes a different route instead of the usual straight path out of the mobile home park. So, I sit up, look at him, and then look out the window again. My heart is pounding loudly, drowning out any other sound. Stepdad's aura changes to something like pinkish-red while the black cloud that won't go away coils itself around the pinkish-red hues.

His face turns beet red, avoiding my direct stares. He keeps his eyes on the road in front of us.

"Making a pit stop."

The station wagon pulls up in front of a run-down mobile home; the peeling white paint reminds me of when I let some glue dry on my fingers. It cracks and rips, tempting me to peel the dried layer. When I showed my fingers to Chrissy, she thought my skin was peeling off.

Why won't you ask him what he's doing? Are you a scaredy cat? Get a backbone for once!

Shoving the negative thoughts away, my fear is too great, and I'm too ashamed. I decide to slink down into my seat and pretend nobody can see me as I peek over the car's dashboard.

A woman about five-feet-five-inches tall comes out in anticipation of our arrival. Her appearance reminds me too much of her tattered mobile home with her wiry, auburn hair piled on top of her head and her gray, dingy bathrobe and blue, rubber flip-flops. She sees him come out of the car and walks toward him.

Her aura is a mixture of pink swirled with some olive green. Her face lights up to a schoolgirl smile as she takes a final drag from her cigarette before she puts it out with her flip-flop foot. I've never seen this woman before, and yet there's something about her I don't like.

Stepdad is quietly talking to her; he's standing too close. Strangely enough, the little black snake of an aura wrapped around his neck since yesterday's incident loosens up and then fades away. She tilts her head back and laughs out loud at his conversation. He hands her the pouch; she takes it. She leans closer as if she is about to kiss him, but he gently nudges her away. He whispers something in her ear.

His back is facing me so that she can look around his shoulder. Her eyes lock with mine. We both stare at each other for a few seconds. He turns around to walk back towards the station wagon. He stares back at me with cold, menacing eyes.

He scratches his neck again, and the black aura reappears and tightens around his neck again. He subconsciously rubs at his neck like he's trying to loosen a constricting necktie. I can't help but smile at his misery, and this time I don't care what he thinks.

He puts the car in drive and backs out of the woman's driveway. He gives me a quick look, sensing my curiosity.

"Not a word to your mother, you hear?" I give him a dirty look.

You should! Tell her everything! Scream it from the rooftops! God, that would feel so good!

He parks the car again and grabs my face, pulling me closer.

His breath smells of coffee, last night's beer, and rotting stench.

"Did you hear me?"

Tears run down my face, and my body shakes. I pull my face away from his grip. Like a frightened baby, I cry with my face buried in my hands.

"Shut up!"

Crumbled up in the front seat, there's nowhere else for me to run. I shake in fear as I convulse and blubber.

I'm so tired of feeling like this! Tired of feeling fear and cowering in my imaginary corner.

I think it makes him happy to see me scared, suffering, and full of fear.

Then it dawns on me. The woman I saw was the "other woman" my mom accused him of running around with during last night's argument.

How could he do this to my mom, and she's pregnant? He runs around on my beautiful mom with some dirty dishrag of a has-been woman? Pig!

Try as I might, it will be difficult to erase this moment from my mind. Glancing over at him driving, I feel nothing but total disgust and loathing.

Did you think he would have any kind of loyalty towards your mother? You've seen how much he's talked bad about her whenever she steps out of the room or out of the house. He never stops talking about how stupid she is because she can't speak English without an accent or puts her down because she doesn't have a driver's license. His goal is to put her down to keep her down! And you too.

I grip onto the door latch just in case I need to throw myself out the door. His behavior towards me can be like rolling a die and seeing what happens. Sometimes he ignores me and pretends I don't exist; other times, he'll take a swing at my face without any warning.

God, I'm tired of living the fight-or-flight life!

Feeling like I was going to come down with a fever, I can feel my aura emanating from me. Moving on its own, flowing like a red ribbon, and dancing in the air. Watching my aura float above me and dancing toward Stepdad, I think maybe this is what it feels like to have an out-of-body experience.

My thoughts creep into the darkest corners of my mind, envisioning my ribbon-red aura sliding around his neck, tightening again and again. Smiling, I know it's only a dream, but I can't stop thinking about it.

I open my eyes again to see if it is real—it's there, choking off the black snake-like aura that's become a regular feature around his neck. My aura is now a maroon red, like that of fresh blood. The black aura mixes with my aura, and now it's formed a deadly noose around Stepdad's neck. Not taking my eyes off this new fascination, I want so much to take his life away. Just then, a familiar voice, the one from last night, is in my head telling me:

"If you do, you won't be any better than him!"

"I won't go to jail! I'm just a kid!" The voice counters with me.

"If he loses control of the car, you will go down with him!"

Gasping at the thought of being in a car accident with this horrible excuse for a human being, the words fall out.

"No! God, No!"

Stepdad turns his head and gives me an annoyed look; the invisible noose quickly chokes him.

"Aargh!"

He's gagging with his tongue hanging out. He lets go of the steering wheel, and the car swivels left, right, and left.

"Ahh! The car!"

I'm screaming at the top of my lungs while Stepdad clutches at his neck. His face turns into a bloated, purplish-blue bulb while he tries his best to gain control of his driving.

Regretting the consequences of my action, I close my eyes, wishing for the choking to stop.

Please, no more! I don't wanna die! Not today!

Opening my eyes again, the maroon aura noose loosens its grip and recoils away from his neck. Naturally, he goes into a coughing fit. He can't stop coughing.

"Please pull over!"

As I'm shouting at Stepdad with sheer panic, he surprisingly does what I ask. He pulls over to the side of the road and puts the car in park. I wait for him to stop coughing so he can drive again. He clears his throat several times. He stops, looks out ahead, then looks around. I stare back at him. He won't look at me. He puts the car back into drive, steps on the gas pedal, and drives silently.

Did I do that? Do I have that kind of power? This is crazy! God, I wish I could talk to someone about this, but who?

The cold spring air blowing into my window feels so cleansing to my face. The sweet smell of roses lingers. My eyes scan for any rose bushes nearby. There it is, a handful of pink rose bushes blooming in front of a tiny silver, bullet-shaped trailer.

Time seems to slow down as we pass by this trailer. I love everything about this area, with just-trimmed grass in the yard, a couple of tall oak trees towering over the trailer, a swing set just to the left of the rose bushes, and a beautiful lady coming out of the trailer.

She reminds me of an angel visiting us mere mortals. Her tall, lean physique, pale skin, and long, silver-blond hair flows over her shoulders. Her long, white gown looks like it was made in heaven instead of on earth. She sees me and waves. She mouths something, but I can't hear her words. We're too far away. Then I hear her words in my head.

"We'll meet again."

Time catches up with us; we're no longer driving in the mobile home park but on a farm road. I'm unsure how I feel about the strange, angel-like lady. I can't keep her words out of my head.

Am I going crazy? Have I finally snapped? It's bad enough my aura can do bad things, I think. Maybe I just imagined her talking to me. She does sound like the voice in my head from last night.

My eyes well up. I'm trying my best not to cry. Honestly, the lady wasn't frightening, but she was certainly strange. Who comes out of their trailer in nothing but a see-through nightgown to water her flowers? Especially in a low-income neighborhood such as Western Estates Mobile Park. Fat chance I'll see this lady again. I guess it takes all kinds.

We pull up in front of Waitborne Elementary School. This big, red brick, one-story building in front of us is the main building that houses the principal, vice principal, school counselor, and school nurse, as well as the attendance office and the auditorium that doubles as the school cafeteria in the back of the main building. All the classrooms are divided into the lower elementary buildings for kindergarten to third grade. There is also a big, red brick building with three stories to the left of the main building.

Since Stepdad dropped me off and quickly drove off, I must sign myself in at attendance office. The school secretary, Mrs. Snodgrass, is too busy going through some paperwork. It looks like all the buses have left; everyone is in their proper classrooms. I'm late for the first-period class. *Sigh.*

CHAPTER THREE

HOME ROOM HELL

Getting dirty looks from Mrs. Snodgrass is a typical thing. She stops typing and looks toward me; the front counter is the only thing separating us. I pull the clipboard and the pen with a metal chain attached towards me. I start signing it.

"Miss Trabeck, you've been warned about signing yourself in!"

She snorts while looking over her typewriter, her glasses sliding down her pointy nose.

"I'm sorry about that, Mrs. Snodgrass, but my stepfather didn't want to trouble himself with signing me in, so I have no choice."

Mrs. Snodgrass rolls her eyes and goes back to her typing. Pffft! She's unbelievable; blame the kid, not the parent, why doesn't she?

Principal White walks past me towards his office, a tall, burly man in his forties with balding white hair, a potbelly, and a warm smile.

I acknowledge him because Mom taught me good manners.

"Good morning, Mr. White. How are you doing today?"

"Quite well, thank you! Everything okay at home?"

His hazel eyes darken while his aura swirls with strips of light blue and smoky white, which is typical for him.

"S-Sort of. We had to call an ambulance last night. Mom's having some medical problems. T-that's the reason why I'm so late this morning."

He walks up and puts his right hand on my shoulder to show concern.

"Is she gonna be okay? I heard she's expecting ..."

I take a step back, so his hand falls to his side.

"I-I hope so. Maybe I can see her later this evening."

Of course, Mrs. Snodgrass, who was busy typing up attendance forms, stops and gives me a frown.

Goodness, she's one busybody. She takes her heavy bottom, orange, polyester pants, and tree trunks for legs from her desk and swishes herself to the counter to stick her nose in my business.

Mr. White gives her a disapproving look from the opposite side of the counter. She leans over the counter, looking squarely at me. She reminds me of a nosey goose with a white bouffant hairdo that looks like a helmet.

"So, what happened to your mother? Did she lose the baby? What hospital is she at?" I give Mr. White an exasperated look.

"Can we leave Miss Trabeck alone? She's already gonna miss first-period class. I'm sure we'll find out more later."

He pulls a pad of paper from his left shirt pocket, scribbles some words, and hands it to me.

"Here, give this permission slip to Mrs. Young. This will excuse you from the first period. I hope your mother recovers soon."

Fighting back the tears, I gratefully accept the note with a forced smile.

"Thank you, sir. Have a good day, you too, Mrs. Snobgrass."

God, it was satisfying just butchering her name.

I run out of the front office with my sneakers squeaking down the hallway toward my homeroom. I don't bother to look back and see if she noticed how I addressed her as Snobgrass. It would've been better to use Snob-Ass but not gonna push too many buttons today.

Stepping into my homeroom is like dodging land mines and stray bullet fire, from my idiot classmates' feet sticking out to make me trip to stone-face stares from Mrs. Young. She never pays attention whenever I need help from her. The bullies know it.

Fortunately, everyone has their heads down, reading and writing in their assignment books. Surprisingly enough, Mrs. Young sitting at her desk, looks up and smiles at me. I give her the permission slip from Principal White, and she takes it from me.

I wait for her reaction. She's a quiet teacher, petite but slightly plump all over. She's only in her thirties but being a teacher for the past decade has aged her quickly. Hence the creeping gray hairline growing from her roots out, over-whelms the efforts of her dyed brunette hair. Not to mention the wrinkles etched deeply at the corner of her eyes. Mom calls it "crow's feet." That's supposed to be a bad thing for adult women.

Her smile fades, and she looks up at me.

"Sorry to hear about your mother. I hope she recovers soon."

She searches my face for a reaction while her aura exudes a light blue cloud. That surprises me because her typical aura is usually a mud brown but, today, she seems nice to me. She looks somewhat bewildered by my stone-face expression.

"Thanks for your concern." Her smile disappears.

"You may go to your seat now. Please open your home-room assignment book and follow the board's instructions."

I respond with a nod. "Yes, ma'am."

Anxiety creeps up again as I walk toward my desk; it

means I must pass by one of the bullies in my class. A ginger hair, freckled face Robert O'Malley in a desk in front of my desk on the farthest left column of desks.

I can't stand this idiot. He's four inches taller than most of the students and me too. He has no qualms reminding all of us short kids of his towering stature. On the playground, he and his sidekick, Walter Smith, the shortest and chubbiest kid in class, is always willing to help Robert in his bullying quest.

Hoping that Robert is too busy with his assignment to notice me walking by, I cautiously take a couple of steps. Like usual, he doesn't miss this opportunity and sticks his tattered tennis-shoed, left foot out at the perfect time.

Usually, I would avoid it in time, but not today. His foot is too elevated for me to step over, and his ankle is at the perfect angle to catch my ankle.

In split seconds, I feel myself falling forward and I hit the cold tile floor with a hard slam. With the wind knocked out of me, I must take a deep breath. I feel my left side, bruised from last night's fiasco, flare up with a fiery red shot of pain. It doesn't help that my book bag strapped over my right side puts more pressure on my bruised left hip.

I lie on the floor in extreme pain. I can hear the rest of the class giggling and snickering under their breath, with Robert looking at me with a smirk.

"Stupid klutz!"

I slowly get up, but the pain on my left side is still throbbing. A small, tan hand emerges in front of my face, so I look up to see who it is. She doesn't look familiar, but her kind gesture moves me. She bends over to pull me up.

"Hey, you okay? You look like you're in pain."

Finally, on my feet, I let go of her hand.

"I am. My left side is bruised pretty bad, but I'll be okay."

Shrugging off her sympathy, I give her a grateful smile.

Mrs. Young, who's still sitting at her desk, yells at us. "Okay, ladies, take your seats!"

The girl ignores our teacher, holds out her right hand, and introduces herself. "I'm Danae, and you're, you're ... uh ..."

"I'm Georgina Trabeck, but you can call me Gina for short. Thank you for helping me up."

She's a couple of inches taller, with light tan skin and sun-kissed honey highlights in her long brown hair. Her hazel eyes seem kind. Her aura emits warm lemon tones with strips of sky blue, reminding me of cotton candy.

Mrs. Young yells at us again, "I said take your seats!" Danae gives her an annoyed look.

"Aren't you concerned for Gina here? She's in lotta pain. Maybe go and see the nurse?"

Mrs. Young rolls her eyes and gives me an angry look. Her aura is back to that muddy brown cloud. She shows no concern for my well-being.

"I'll be okay. I was tripped by Robert, though. He needs to stop doing that."

Giving Robert a dirty look, his freckled face contorts into a prune. His brown eyes turn dark as he stares me down while sitting in his seat. He makes a "gun" gesture with his right hand, points it at me, and acts like he's shooting me. It's funny how both Robert's and our teacher's aura match - both have that same muddy brown hue.

Mrs. Young gets up in exasperation, yelling in Robert's direction.

"Robert, go to the principal's office now!"

She raises an arm and points towards the door.

She stares him down until he gets up from his desk. Danae quietly returns to her desk in the middle rows while I gingerly sit at my desk.

When Robert leaves the room, Mrs. Young looks in my direction. She doesn't bother to ask me if I am okay, nor does she tell me to go to the nurse's office to double-check my condition. She doesn't waste any time humiliating me.

"Miss Trabeck, have your parents signed your math test

yet? I've only been waiting for a week now."

I look around the classroom; all eyes are on me, waiting for a response.

"Well?"

Mrs. Young crosses her arms in front of her chest, keeping her eyes on me. My brain scrambles around for an answer.

Think, Gi! Quick! Mom, hospital, pregnancy! Something!

"My apologies, Mrs. Young. I'll have it to you by Friday. Hopefully, my mom will be out of the hospital by then."

She gives me a guilty look, her eyes darting around the room.

"Uhh ... yeah, that's fine, or next week will work too."

Yes! Saved by the "my mom is at the hospital" excuse, I'll take it.

Feeling satisfied, I take out my assignment book to start writing.

The classroom is quiet again until a crumpled piece of paper hits me on my arm. I looked around to see who threw it.

Fat face, rat fink Walter is looking straight at me. His tousled, curly, brown hair looks like it's never seen shampoo and water, his beady, tiny, brown eyes remind me of a rat, and of course, his crocodile smile makes my skin crawl.

He makes a slicing motion across his neck with his left finger and points at me. I want so much to flip him off, BUT I will be the one to get into so much trouble with Mrs. Young and not him.

His aura is also a muddy brown. Opening the crumpled paper to read its content, it says, *"Stupid Chink! You flunked your math test—maybe you should learn some Engrish! You dumbo!"*

I crumple up the paper again while I hold back the tears. Shoving the piece into my jeans pocket, I focus on my assignment. My only response to Walter is no response at all. Don't look at him or react to his stupid note that will only give him the satisfaction of hurting me.

Then again, choosing to ignore people like Walter only means I will have to answer to his retaliation during recess. I can't seem to win in this crap game of racism and xenophobia. Some new words I learned from reading a lot in the library.

Concentrating is difficult when dealing with an insensitive teacher and bullies in my classroom. I hate living in this god-awful town; everyone is so lily-white and not friendly towards kids like me.

People like Walter, Robert, and others from many generations of farmers in this community only associate with their kind. Mrs. Young brags about being born and raised in Waitborne as if it was some lottery she won. She wasn't thrilled about having a little Filipina girl born in another country and from a mixed cultural background. It's too much for her to realize that other places on earth are way more interesting than Waitborne, Ohio.

I switch my gaze to my right so I can see Danae. She has her head down and is busy writing in her assignment book. She must be the new kid and maybe Mrs. Jenkins' niece. It's funny how she doesn't look like the other kids; she's tan but with brown hair. She's certainly a lot nicer than the other kids in class. Maybe she's from a mixed-race family like me.

I'm looking forward to lunch and recess today.

Lunchtime, sadly enough, is also my favorite subject in school. Walking into the auditorium that doubles as the whole school's lunchroom, also connected to the industrial kitchen, students stand in line to order their hot lunch meals. Sometimes, if I'm lucky, Mom has a spare dollar to give me so I can go and get a hot meal. That usually happens occasionally, so cold sack lunches from home are what I typically do.

Springtime is here with the sun shining into the auditorium, and the large windows have been rolled up like garage doors to let in the warm breeze. Many students have already picked the prime sunny spots on the long benches, and the only spaces available are in the dark, shaded areas. Exasperated with the seating choices, I just sit outside the auditorium.

Looking around to find a quiet place to eat my lunch is still challenging. The picnic tables are filled with students, so I choose to sit on a soft grassy patch under a nearby tree.

I can finally relax by popping open my metal lunch box on the grass beside me and enjoy my current book. The sun shining on my legs feels good as my back leans against the tree trunk. Startled by a female voice, I turn to see who it is. Danae stands over me with a big smile.

"Hey there! Thought I'd find you here."

"Wanna join me? It's the best seat on the lawn."

We both laugh and giggle to ourselves.

"Scoot over. I wanna sit under that tree too!"

"Yes! Your Highness!"

I give her some room to sit next to me.

She opens her sack lunch and tears into her peanut butter-and-jelly sandwich while chewing loudly. I can't help but stare at her and laugh.

"Are you hungry?"

Her face turns red, and she giggles along with me. She takes one last swallow of her sandwich.

"Sorry 'bout that, just a long day and starvin' to death."

I smile back, taking a big bite of my chicken leg and chewing it quickly so I can swallow it.

"Me too." Danae burst out in laughter.

"I like you! So glad you live next door."

My smile freezes. ... *what was she talking about? Wait! Mrs. Jenkins' niece! Dum! Dum!*

Danae reads the confusion on my face, but I reply quickly.

"You're Mrs. Jenkins' niece. That's so cool!"

"Nice to meet you! Again!"

She pulls the spout from her milk carton and takes a long, gulping drink.

I point to the second carton of milk next to her lunch sack.

"Are you thirsty too?"

She shakes her head. "No! Silly, that's for you." She trails off into a giggle.

That's a first! Someone is doing something nice for me.

"Aww! You shouldn't have, but I thank you truly."

Danae's smile beams wider as she responds by shrugging her shoulder. "You're welcome."

I pick up the closed milk carton, but someone else grabs it from my hand.

"Well, whaddya know! A half-breed and a chink together under a tree."

A freckled, lizard-face Robert stands over us. He tosses my milk carton between his hands. His aura spews a nasty mud brown and shades of olive and mustard.

He's looking for trouble, and he's coming after you girls.

I stand up on my feet. Just having him stand over us only tells me about his dominance in this situation.

"Give me back my milk carton."

I can feel sweat building up under my nose.

"OHH! Do you mean this milk carton?"

He tosses it up in the air, then places the carton in the palm of his hand. He offers it to me.

"Want it?"

I quickly try to snatch the milk carton back, but he is too fast for me. His ugly smirks make me so angry; I wish I could punch him in the face. Danae stands by my side; her hazel eyes turn into dark coals. Her aura matches her angry voice, dark violet with red streaks.

"You heard her. Give it back and leave!"

Robert's smirk falls off his face as his freckled cheeks turn red while his lips tighten into a thin line.

"You want it back, here!"

He smashes the milk carton against my chest with a sharp thud. The wind is violently knocked out of my chest as I double over from the intense pain. It happens so fast; I'm floating over my body as I witness myself screaming in pain. Danae doesn't waste a second as she punches him in the stomach.

The children who are sitting nearby gather around us. Robert yelps in pain as he clutches his stomach area.

"You'll pay for this, you stinkin' half-breed."

He struggles to stand up, tears running down his eyes. Rat-faced Walter pushes his way between the students crowding around us.

He sees Robert standing with tears running down his face. Walter looks surprised at Robert's crying, then gives Danae an angry look.

"You stupid little twit!" He lunges forward to grab Danae by the hair. Danae lets out a loud yelp.

"Let go of me! Ah!"

All I could see was red, profound fury heating my body. So tired of these bullies. I'm tired of our useless teacher letting these idiots get away with their hateful actions and no justice for me and the others.

I stare at Walter and Robert, wishing terrible things to happen to them. The voice is back in my head, reminding me.

"*Are you sure you want to do this?*"

"Yes! Yes, I do!"

I let my typically light blue aura turn red. Wishing with all my might, I envision my red, angry aura weaving its way around Walter's hands. It warms up with steam and burns his hands.

"OW!"

Walter lets go of Danae's hair.

She jerks away from him and gets behind me. Robert lunges for me, but my aura is already ahead, pushing him away. The force of my aura is too great. He stumbles backward and crashes into the other students, which breaks the student chain surrounding us.

A couple of kids catch his fall as he lands on them; they all land sharply on the ground right at Mrs. Young's feet.

"What in the world is going on here?"

Mrs. Young's face is beet red; her aura is a reddish brown.

She stares right at me. I'm still standing, shocked by what took place.

Danae, looking angry, steps in front of me, answering Mrs. Young's question in my defense.

"She didn't do anything! That jerk Robert smashed her milk carton into her chest. And Walter pulled my hair!"

"That's enough! All four of you report to the principal's office!" Danae's face turns beet red.

"That's not fair! Gina and I didn't do anything. Robert was bullying us!"

Richard, a shy, chubby boy with brown hair neatly combed back and piercing blue eyes, steps in and defends Danae.

"It's true! I saw what took place. Robert was bugging them."

Mrs. Young looks frustrated as she stares intently at Robert. He gets up from the ground and doesn't help the other two students.

They are both skinny little girls, one named Cindy with straight, brown, bowl-cut hair hugging her chin. Her light-blue framed eyeglasses are knocked off her face, so she crawls around on the ground looking for her glasses.

The other girl, Patches, has long, curly, red hair and gets on her knees to help Cindy. Strangely enough, Patches finds the eyeglasses nearby, right by Robert's feet.

He is too busy wiping his teary face with the back of his sleeves. He takes a step to the right and "crunch" go the glasses. His heavy step is enough to completely smash both lenses and crack the frames at the nose bridge.

Even though Cindy is nearsighted, she is too familiar with the smashing sounds of a foot stepping on her glasses. She gets up from crouching down.

"My glasses!" She looks around for Robert and stands in front of Mrs. Young by mistake.

"You stupid jerk! Why can't you leave us alone!"

I couldn't help but snicker under my breath while the other children giggle.

Mrs. Young puts a hand on Cindy's shoulder.

"Cindy, you're talking to me." Cindy's face turns red with embarrassment, and she gently steps back.

"So sorry, Mrs. Young, that was meant for Robert."

Mrs. Young's face softens as her aura turns a bright peach. She looks towards Patches.

"It's all right. Can you take Cindy to the nurse's office to call her parents?"

"Yes, ma'am! Here, take my hand, Cindy."

The two girls hold hands, and Patches bends down to pick up the broken glasses. They both walk back into the auditorium.

Mrs. Young turns her attention to us.

"Robert, Walter, Danae, and Gina, report to Principal White's office now."

My brain is screaming at me, and my heart is racing.

No! If you get into trouble, Stepdad will kill you!

I froze in place and glared into Mrs. Young's eyes.

"I didn't do anything to Robert! Why don't you believe me for once? He's been bullying me for the whole school year! I've complained so many times, and yet you won't do anything about it!"

Spit flies out of my mouth as I desperately form the words. She walks up and stares at me; I refuse to back away. Her behavior is to intimidate me as she breathes on me with her foul, stale coffee breath.

"One more word out of you, and I will make sure you are suspended from this school!"

My anger boiling inside me spills into my aura, turning it to a bright red. I stand defiantly in her face, close my eyes, and envision my aura. It obeys my request, wrapping around Mrs. Young's neck.

It tightens slowly; red marks appear around her neck. Her tongue sticks out; her eyes pop out in sheer surprise as she gasps for breath. I back away, horrified by what I'm witnessing.

Danae grabs my hand, and she notices, too. Our classmates watch in horror as Mrs. Young grabs her shirt collar as if it is too tight, causing her to gasp for air.

The voice in my head nags me.

"Any second now, Gi ... are ya trying to kill her?"

I back away again, then close my eyes. The aura obeys me and loosens its grip around Mrs. Young's neck. Her face is already blue, and the blood vessels in her eyes rupture, staining the white portions with cracked red lines. She takes a deep breath, then coughs uncontrollably.

Another teacher steps out of the auditorium. It's Miss Travis, new to the school and in her first year of teaching. Her tall stature and lanky physique remind me of a basketball player. Her short, pixie-cut blonde hair gives her a youthful, athletic look. She takes charge of this strange situation.

"Okay, children, please line up with your respective class now! I will send Mrs. Young to the nurse." She gently grabs Mrs. Young's left arm.

"Are you gonna be ok?" Mrs. Young nods: she tries to form words but coughs instead. Miss Travis raises a hand to gently stop her.

"It's okay, it will be difficult to talk for now."

The rest of us students stand watching. Miss Travis repeats her command but with a louder voice.

"I said go now, children."

We all reluctantly walk back into the auditorium. Mrs. Young struggles to talk but can't stop coughing. I grab Danae by the hand and move her to follow me back inside.

As soon as we go back into the auditorium, we line up with our respective homeroom classes. Mrs. Young is not there to walk us back to our homeroom. I don't bother to go to the principal's office, and neither does Danae.

CHAPTER FOUR

MEETING IRRA

The final bell rings, signaling the end of the school day. Mrs. Young goes home after she sees the school nurse, so we have a substitute. She's a sweet, tiny, older lady who's barely five feet tall with short legs and arms. Her snowy white hair is cut to a short, wavy bob and covered with so much hair spray it looks fake, like a wig. It's teased so rigidly and held in place so high that it reminds me of a cotton helmet.

Her sight isn't good, so she relies on her thick lenses with lines through the middle with black frames. I remember Grandma May telling me about bifocals and how much she hated wearing them.

Mrs. Chancellor, the substitute, must be wearing bifocals too. She gets up from the desk with a kind smile.

"Have a good evening, class. Don't forget your homework for tomorrow."

My classmates don't waste any time running out of the room, knocking the neatly lined desks out of place as they carelessly bump into them.

Danae gets up from her desk and follows me out the door.

We walk into the hallway, and our tennis shoes squeak on the shiny floor as we take each step.

Danae turns to me with a puzzled look. "You notice how forgetful the sub is?"

I shrug my shoulder, wondering why she would mention it.

"Why is that?" She gives me a mischievous smile.

"Well … I saw the pink slip that Mrs. Young left. It said that you, me, Robert, and Walter were to report to the principal's office."

I give her a puzzled look.

"And?"

She keeps smiling and then giggles.

"I waited for Mrs. Chancellor to look in the other direction when I asked her for the bathroom hall pass and yoink! I took the slip!"

She pulls the pink slip from her pocket and hands it to me. I look at it and then give it back to her.

"Are you crazy? Why did you do that?"

Danae jams the slip back in her jeans pocket, looking around and then at me with the same devilish grin.

"Because, silly! She didn't even see the slip. If she did, I doubt she could remember!"

I give Danae a concerned look.

"You know we're not getting out of seeing the principal, right?" Danae's smile drops, and she ponders for a few seconds.

"I'll talk to my aunt this evening and tell her everything. You know it isn't fair, right?"

"I know that. I'm more concerned about what my stepdad will do to …"

I stop myself, feeling nervous. Danae looks confused.

"You okay?"

I wouldn't say anymore, looking straight ahead. We reach the end of the hallway and enter the central foyer before going to the other side, where we can see the school buses lined up against the sidewalk outside.

"I'm all right."

The silence between us is deafening. We walk towards our school bus with the cardboard sign for "Western Estate." I let Danae get in front of me as we board the bus. She picks an empty middle-row seat so we can sit together.

She doesn't waste any time asking me the most compelling question.

"So … was I dreaming, or did Mrs. Young look like she was choking?"

I shrug and look out my window. Danae sits aisle side.

Just then, Richard jumps in the seat behind us and chimes in with Danae like a gossipy laundry woman.

"I was gonna ask you girls the same thing! I couldn't believe my eyes. It's almost as if some invisible person was choking her."

Danae turns around to join the conversation.

"That's what I was thinking! It's just so weird!"

They both turn to see my reaction. I'm not in the mood to talk, but I have no choice. So, I choose to be a little more practical.

"Or she could have underlying health problems we don't know about! Come on, guys! Really?"

Richard ignores me and continues with his conversation with Danae.

"What if …"

Danae leans closer since Richard's voice lowers to almost a whisper, and her eyes grow more prominent.

"Yes?"

Richard's face is only a few inches away from Danae's.

"What if some ghost haunts Mrs. Young? I mean, it only makes sense."

Danae's voice lowers to a whisper, which makes Richard lean in closer with lively interest.

"My mom is from the Shawnee tribe and told me about people being haunted by spirits because of bad deeds. I wouldn't be surprised if Mrs. Young is ..."

I see these two leaning into the aisle to speculate about our teacher. Their heads are close together, and their conversations become private.

I could only imagine the wild tales Danae is harping about. Losing interest, I lean my head against the windowpane.

I'm more interested in watching the birds flutter around each other as some land on nearby tree branches. Wishing I had wings right now. I'd give anything to fly away from this horrible place.

Still, I can't stop thinking about my aura, Mrs. Young's neck turning red, her face bloating, eyes popping out of her sockets as she struggled to breathe.

Did I do that?

It's almost like having magical powers. Smiling to myself. How great would it be if I had witchy powers like Samantha on *Bewitched*? I love that TV show so much and it's funny too.

My eyes continue to wander around, taking in all the beautiful springtime views of trees budding out with pretty blossoms, butterflies fluttering and landing on the nearby honeysuckle bushes ripe with bright red flowers.

The bus driver closes the door after the last student has boarded. The engine starts, the horn blasts, and the driver puts the bus into gear.

My eyes slowly close while scanning outside; today was a long one.

Something catches my eye, and then I blink for better focus. It is a crow sitting quietly on a thick branch. I pretend it can hear me when I whisper to it.

"Hello, little black crow! Are you magical too?"

The crow stares right at me, or so I imagine. His head tilts to one side, then he shakes his head.

"Yes."

I sit straight up in my seat; this is too weird. I whisper again.

"Nod, if you understand."

The crow nods its head up and down. I'm sure I'm only imagining the bird responding to me.

It lets out a "Caw! Caw!"

The voice in my head replies.

"*Yes, Gina, I can hear you. You have the power.*"

So maybe something else is going on, or I'm officially going out of my mind. The crow flies away.

A hand on my left shoulder pulls me away from my tired imagination. Danae's face comes into complete focus. Her hazel eyes bore into mine.

"Hey, you okay?"

I am sitting up and shaking off my lethargy.

"Yeah, it's been a long day... just a little tired."

She gives me an apologetic smile and throws her right arm around me.

"So ... I was going to ask if you're free to hang out and maybe do our homework together this afternoon."

Tears are welling in my eyes, and I am fighting hard not to cry in front of my newfound friend. My stupid nose becomes runny, so I take a deep breath to keep my nose from going full-on runny faucet.

"Wow, this is the first time anybody has ever asked me to come to their house." Danae's face pinches in confusion, and her eyebrows furrow.

"Really?"

"Yep ... ever since we moved here when I was nine."

I look in Richard's direction. He can't keep his eyes off Danae. His aura has been a cotton-candy pink ever since he laid eyes on Danae.

Interesting! He's got a crush on her!

Danae calls my name. "Gina! Hello, Gi! You there?" She snaps her fingers in my face.

Breaking out into a loud, boisterous laugh, I can't help but be entertained about Richard crushing on Danae. Her gaze is focused on my reactions.

"Care to let me in on the joke?"

I lean closer to Danae and cup my mouth with my right hand to whisper in her ear.

"Richard has a crush on you!"

She pulls away and rolls her eyes. "I know! It's really weirding me out!"

We laugh out loud for a few seconds. Richard looks at us with intense confusion but doesn't say anything.

We arrive at our Western Estate mobile home park. There was another bus behind us containing the lower elementary kids. Our bus stop is in the park's playground area. It isn't well kept, so it's normal to see broken swing seats or missing chains to hold the seats. There are missing steps to a few slides, and the monkey bars are rusted.

The only thing the mobile home park people do is trim the grass around the playground. This whole place should be condemned.

I never take my little sister here because of how dangerous and unsanitary it could be for her and others. Nevertheless, it doesn't stop the kids from coming off our bus to take out their football or baseballs to play catch before they go home.

Danae and I rush out of the bus. I walk a few feet away to stop and take a deep breath. Danae catches up with me, stops, and watches me.

"Are you okay? You've been pretty quiet on the bus ride."

My brain scramble to find something to say, but I just stutter.

"I-I got a-a-lot on my mind and worried a-about my mom, that's all."

She studies my face for a few seconds, but it might as well be an eternity.

"Well ... if you ever need someone to talk to, I'm right next door, you know."

Richard sneaks up behind Danae; his blue eyes become even more intense. He has a pleasant face but is shy and smiles a lot. His aura is a pink and peach hue. He's a nice guy, and I get the feeling this is the first time in his life to be attracted to someone. He's slightly plump around the waist, but he keeps getting taller and a bit less plump, especially after summer vacations.

He might become a good-looking guy someday. But for now, he's a clean-cut, all-around nice guy with a slight weight problem. He taps Danae on the shoulder.

"May I walk you home?"

Danae's face turns beet red, and now she's stuttering, too.

"I-I appreciate it, but I-I don't want to put you out of your way."

I chime in before Richard can say anything.

"I think I'm gonna walk home alone. Gotta lot on my mind."

That wasn't a lie; it would be nice to ponder what happened today and last night.

Too many things have changed for me, and I'm so confused. Maybe this is what it's like to be officially going through puberty. I'm twelve years old, and I'm starting to see myself go through physical changes, and now I'm going through some psychological ones.

Danae gives me a look as if I betrayed her. Glaring at me, her lips tighten.

"Whoa, wait a minute, Gi! I thought we were gonna do our homework at my place."

"I don't think I'll be able to. My stepdad is supposed to bring me to get my mother at the hospital, remember? Maybe tomorrow since it's a Friday. I still gotta ask my parents if I could even visit you."

Danae looked sad. Her aura was a pale yellow, and now it's more of a greenish blue.

"Oh … okay, I guess."

Richard's face lights up like a light bulb, lips breaking into a big smile.

"So, can I walk you home?"

I couldn't help but smile at these two. Richard, the blushing guy with eyes for Danae while she stands there looking sad.

"Hey Rich, I'm going to talk to Gina for a few seconds, then I'll take you up on your offer, ' kay?"

Like an anxious puppy, Richard's smile widens from ear to ear.

"Cool! Hey, Gina, I hope your mom is okay!"

Danae quickly grabs my arm and shoves me a few feet away from Richard.

"Yo, you gonna be okay? I mean, I'm here for ya. I think we could be best friends."

"I'll be fine! And yes, I want us to be best friends. It's probably good to have friends in our classroom, too."

Danae rolls her eyes at me and lets out a big sigh.

"You'll never know if you need help with your math homework or an ally in the playground. Since we're basically on our own with these racist bullies." Danae's voice sounds resigned and exasperated.

"Yeah. I guess. I'm gonna take one for the team by walking with Richard, BUT he's not my knight in shining armor! This is the '70s, man! I'm a liberated woman!"

"Well, tell me all about it. Give me a call, okay?" She smiles sheepishly after I give her a gentle pat on her back.

"And besides, I think you're safe with Richard. He's polite with the girls."

I wink at her discomfort, snorting out a smile and giggle. Richard steps up after waiting patiently from a distance. He offers his left arm for Danae. She looks revolted by his old-fashioned manners.

"Umm … this isn't a date, okay? Nor are you here to slay dragons for me. So, we're just gonna walk and talk like regular people."

Richard's hands go up in the air, surrendering to Danae's demands.

"Okay, okay! I'm just a gentleman. My parents made sure I was brought up to have good manners, that's all."

"Have a nice evening, Richard. See you in class tomorrow, and Danae ... call me, okay?" She tightens her lips, brows furrowing.

"Hell yeah, I'm gonna call you!"

I couldn't help but smile again as Richard gives me a thumbs-up. Danae only glares at me as she starts to walk with Richard. He doesn't waste any time asking her a bunch of questions.

"Ahh ... love birds!"

I begin taking my steps toward home. Walking by some well-loved gardens and lawns on a lovely spring afternoon with the sun shining on my face is exactly what I need.

My nose catches a beautiful rose aroma dancing around me. Then I hear a "Caw! Caw!" to my right, so I look in that direction. It is another crow perched on an old oak tree branch. I hear that same voice from earlier.

"I'm the same one, sweetheart."

I look around to see if anyone is outside or nearby. Most homes on this street are empty. I look at my wristwatch. Yep, it's only 3:45 p.m., so people are probably still at work.

I am looking back at the crow who is gazing right at me.

"Nah ... it can't be that bird! I'm going crazy from lack of sleep."

The lingering smell of roses swarms me as I keep walking toward home and away from the bird. Trying my best to ignore the nosy crow; it caws again and something else.

"Caw! Caw! Gina! Caw!" I look at the bird again to see if it called my name, but it keeps its steely gaze on me. I walk up to it; maybe it will fly away. One step, then another, walking faster to try to intimidate it. Nothing. It doesn't even move. I'm standing right in front of the tree and looking up.

It keeps its unwavering gaze as it looks down at me. I can't believe what I'm about to do.

"Hey, crow! Did you call my name?" The crow nods its head up and down several times.

"Can you talk, or am I imagining it?" The crow pauses for a few seconds, then looks away.

That's what I thought. It's all in my head.

My neck starts to hurt from looking up for a good five minutes. I look around to see if anyone is watching. I turn away from the tree and head home again. Looking at my watch, it's almost four. I better get going. The crow catches up, flying overhead.

"Gina, you need to follow me!"

I stop, my jaw dropping onto my chest. The crow nods its head up and down again. I can't stop staring at it.

"Follow me, Gina. There's someone you need to meet."

I feel dumb with my mouth wide open, rubbing my eyes to ensure I'm not seeing things.

"Yes, I'm talking to you! Irra wants to meet you."

It flaps its wings harder and flies in another direction, turning its head.

"Follow me, Gina Trabeck! Now!"

The crow doesn't give me any time to react; it takes off, flying towards the direction of my home.

"Can't believe I'm doing this. Here goes!"

Walking towards the bird's direction—it is flying too fast—I start to run.

The bird flies ahead of me. I'm breaking out in a sweat trying to keep up.

"Hold on! Bird!"

It stops at the yard with the silver bullet trailer and white metal swing set. A few oak trees provide shade, and a row of fragrant, pink roses is lined up in front of the trailer entrance.

The blonde lady I noticed earlier this morning comes out of the trailer. She has a genuine smile that reaches her light gray eyes. Instead of wearing the almost see-through flowing white nightgown, she's in a black dress with long sleeves.

One would think that wearing black in the middle of a sunny afternoon isn't very practical, but again, this lady is something else. Her long silver-blonde hair flowing down to her waist is now tied in a loose ponytail, revealing her long, pointed ears. She walks toward me as if her feet aren't touching the ground.

"Hello, Gina … I'm glad you're here."

Her aura is a soft, cloudy white with a touch of sky blue and a strip of gray. Even her fragrance smells of roses and a hint of herbs like fresh-cut basil. Her smile radiates warmth, and her eyes glaze with light gray pools.

The hairs on the back of my neck are standing on end; my pulse is racing in my head. I need to keep my wits about me.

"So you're Irra? I presume?"

Her smile widens, showing off pearly white, fang-like teeth.

"Aye."

"So, do you always summon people by crow?"

Irra breaks out with boisterous laughter, then she stops abruptly, her head turning in the crow's direction.

"Hey, Rav, you need to change back."

Now I'm confused by Irra's comment. The crow flies out to us and lands on the ground. It mutates from a sizable crow to a full-grown woman. Major transformations take place, from wings to arms, scaly, bird-like legs, and paws to human legs and hands, and from a beaky bird face to a human-like face.

She's just as tall as Irra but not skinny, with long, fiery red, wavy hair and emerald, green eyes. I can see little points poking out from the sides of her head; she has pointed ears like Irra. She gives me a huge smile showing fang-like teeth.

Even though she's smiling with her mouth, it doesn't reach her eyes. Her pupils change from round to thin black slits. It frightens me; she doesn't seem as warm or even remotely friendly.

"Hello, Miss Georgina, I'm Irra's twin sister, Ravanna, but you can call me Rav."

She takes a low bow for a few seconds, then stands up again.

"H-Hello, Miss Ravanna or Rav ... pleased to meet your acquaintance."

Giving her a slight curtsy as my mother taught me. I don't know why I didn't react to Rav's changes. I guess I'm too dumbfounded, or maybe I'm too tired, and I've had such a long day.

Ravanna smiles politely, but there's still some mystery there. Her aura is almost a rainbow of colors and has a gray streak. They can't be human. My grumbly stomach distracts my thoughts; Rav hears it too.

"I see someone needs some sustenance."

She looks squarely at me; her smile is frozen. My face burns with embarrassment.

"Excuse me ... must be getting close to dinner time. That reminds me, my parents must wonder why I haven't come home! I ..."

"Nonsense, my dear! Come! Join us for some tea and crumpets with some honey. You'll love it."

Irra sits at a round table draped with a yellow lace table-cloth and three chairs. The table is beautifully decorated with fancy, fine-bone china plates, teacups, and pots. Each item has lovely roses painted on it and is rimmed with gold lines on the edge. Each plate has some warm, steaming crumpets and is covered with honey. My eyes grow big as saucers; I couldn't help but sit at the table. Rav joins me. Irra pours some piping hot tea from the teapot into our dainty cups.

"Thank you!"

I take a giant bite of my tasty, warm crumpet. It's so delicious. It reminds me of eating a sponge cake covered with melted honey. Before I know it, my crumpet disappears—I practically devoured it.

The two ladies sit quietly, sipping their tea. My face burns with embarrassment again.

Why am I such a pig?

Remembering my manners again, I gently pick up my teacup with my right pinky sticking out. I gingerly sip my tea. The warm liquid flows down my throat. I drink some more until it is empty.

Irra has her hands gently resting on her chin. She is leaning forward, focused on me. It makes me feel uncomfortable, but I keep myself in check.

Don't let them see you squirm.

Rav lets out a soft giggle.

"It's perfectly fine, young lady. You were hungry and thirsty. I'm so glad you can refuel, so to speak."

"Why am I here?"

That was an abrupt and yet crucial question.

Irra smiles, shifts her weight in her chair, and gently relaxes.

"I've been looking for you, and here you are."

"Why? Am I supposed to know you? Should I be scared?"

Irra gives me a gentle smile, her voice light and airy.

"I'm not here, or we're not here to kidnap you, if that's what you're wondering. I've sworn to keep watch over you."

"Really? So, who did you swear to? Do I know this person?"

Irra squirms in her seat again.

"I've sworn to my late mother's grave I would look out for my sister or sisters. I think we could be related."

Ravanna gives Irra a surprised look.

What's this? There's a secret Irra is keeping from Rav? Interesting ...

"What? Are you kidding me? You realize I don't look anything like either one of you. And by the way, what are you guys? Neither of you is human, that I'm guessing."

The words fall out of my mouth. I'm irritated and a little

scared, and my anxieties are growing.

Getting up from my chair, I excuse myself.

"Okay, I've had enough. I do want to thank you for the delicious crumpets and tea. I must go now. M-my parents are gonna be mad. I-I can't take anymore ..."

Rav cuts me off; she rests her back against the chair.

"Beatings from your stepfather? Am I right?"

"We know about your horrible situation, my dear. I want to help you out."

Irra stands up from her chair. Rav gives Irra a squinty-eyed look, but it's hard to tell what she means.

I step away from the table slowly. Rav's eyes turn into slits again—predatory. She makes me feel like a trembling rabbit caught by an owl. All I want to do right now is run away, far away.

"Look, it's getting late. If you've been watching me, then you know Stepdad, don't mess around. He will beat me until I can't walk. H-he's done it before."

Irra's eyes go from steel gray to a soft bluish-gray, and her aura turns bluish. She has a lot of sympathy for me. She steps closer to me and takes my right hand. Her hand feels warm and soft to the touch.

"It's okay, child. We have powers like you, but different. You can use your aura to anticipate people's actions. It will become stronger as you age. Strong enough to stop people from hurting you. I can stop or slow down time and have some telepathic abilities."

She lets go of my hand and walks past me to sit on one of the swings.

"I'm a shapeshifter, a changeling to be exact."

Rav joins Irra on the swing set. They commence pumping their legs so they can swing higher.

"Join us! You know you want to!"

Irra swings faster, smiling at me.

"You've been admiring this swing set since you were ten.

This is your chance."

Rav lets out a quick laugh, then squeals in a high-pitched tone.

Now I'm irritated; I don't have time for this.

"Look, this is getting ridiculous! Have a nice evening. See you in the next lifetime."

I turn around to run home.

Irra flows out of the swing with wings expanding from her back. She lands in front of me, pleading, and puts up a hand.

"You'll be fine. I'll get you home."

Before I can say anything, she gives me a big hug. I feel her slip something into my hand. She whispers in my ear during her hug.

"Look at it when you get home, not here."

I don't know why I should do what Irra tells me. I barely know her. My right hand grips the cloth pouch tightly as I slip it into my front jeans pocket. Nodding my head, I let go of her hug. She steps back and shakes her head.

She waves me off.

"Bye, Miss Gina, I will see you soon!"

She becomes blurry as Rav stands beside her with her wings spread out. They both fade out of my sight. Overwhelming nausea takes over me. Feeling like I'm going to faint, I'm trying to maintain my balance. The world spins around; it's vertigo, all right.

Twilight zone, here I come.

My eyes become heavy, and I want to go to sleep. It takes over me, and I give in.

CHAPTER FIVE

TALISMAN

"That was one crazy dream."

I look at my alarm clock; it says 4:15. While I'm still ly-ing-in bed, my gaze goes toward my bedroom window. It's still light but barely.

So, is it the crack of dawn or sunset?

I hear a knock on my door, and Mom walks in.

"Gi-Gi, you awake?"

"Yeah, Ma, I'm awake."

Propping myself up from the pillows and pulling the cov-ers down, I watch Mom sit gingerly by me. Her face is swollen around her nose and covered with six individual stitches on her nose bridge. The skin under her eyes is black and blue. She's in her oversized, blue duster house dress; it's the only thing that fits her giant pregnant belly. She tries to smile, but I can tell it's too painful. She reaches over to hug me. It feels good to hug her back.

It's been so long! When was the last time she hugged me? I think right when I turned nine years old; it was a quick one. That was when she quickly pushed me away to face me and said, *"You gettin' too old for hugs, Gi! And no more toys!"* It *hurt to hear them, and it hasn't gone away.*

Shoving that sad memory to the back of my head, I turn my attention to Mom. She looks sad, maybe remorseful. Trying to balance her heavy front body while sitting on my bed proved challenging. She's still a pretty, petite Filipina with shoulder-length black hair, dark eyes, and small, pouty lips.

I get out of my covers so I can sit next to her, which helps her stability as she leans against me. I put my right arm around my mother, and this time she doesn't push me away. I notice I'm in my nightgown, and my day clothes are piled on the floor by my bed.

"Are you gonna be okay, Ma?"

Her aura is not the typical purple or black and blue. It's back to a warm peachy hue. She gives me a sad smile; a tear leaks from her left eye. Trying hard not to cry, she takes a deep breath and wipes away the tear.

"Where's Stepdad and Chrissy?"

Hopefully, that gives her enough time to get out of her sadness and focus on answering the question. Her voice is low and sad. It's difficult for others to understand her broken English when she's depressed.

"He goes to Missus Jinkins next door. He want me to stay here."

Of course, he would! Otherwise, he would have much explaining to do with Mrs. Jenkins. She already knows by the way she acts around Mom and me. I'm sure she hears the screaming, crying, and noise daily.

My concern for Chrissy grows; she gets anxious around her father.

"Do you think Chrissy will let him near her? She's scared of him, you know."

My mother's swollen face contorts as she tries to laugh off my accusation.

"She loves her Da-di, Gi! Why you ask stupid questions?"

Her aura, tinged with a streak of red, gives me an annoyed stare.

Taking my arm off my mother's shoulder, I fight off the feelings of disappointment about my mother's denial of our situation.

"I'm getting tired of this, this, this denial! Do you avoid the fact that Chrissy wets her pants every time her father comes near her?"

Mom pulls away from me; she gets back on her feet. Her arms cross her chest.

"You don't know what you talk 'bout, Gi! The doctor already told us that your sister has bladder problems."

I stand up to look down at my mom. It feels so good to have power for once in my life.

"Let's not talk about doctors, nurses, paramedics, or the police. It makes me sick to my stomach with how much we all must lie or cover up your ...your ... our abuse!"

She pinches the skin of my left arm and hisses into my face.

"You keep your mouth shut! They will take us away if you say any ting! You understand?"

Her aura is purple again. Tears run down my cheeks.

I can feel my aura burn with anger, and my skin around the area where my mother is pinching me turns red hot. She flinches away as if she had stuck her fingers on a hot iron. She looks at them to see if there is any damage. Stepping away from her is all I can do, so my aura doesn't hurt my mother.

Her eyes grow with fear, and her aura turns into a sharp reddish- blue more like magenta. She crosses herself, like how she was taught in any Filipino Catholic Church, then prays to herself.

"*Aye, Santa Maria, Sa ngalan ng Ama, at ng Anak, at ng Espiritu Santo!*"

She clasps her hands together and kneels on the floor.

Here I go again, rolling my eyes at Mom's theater performance.

"Are you serious? C'mon, Ma! I'm not an evil spirit, nor am I possessed."

She struggles to get on her feet and backs away from me in slow, deliberate steps. Her voice cracks as she points her finger at me.

"Y-you have his powers! You Evil!"

She turns around, leaves my room, then slams the door hard.

Defeated, deflated, and grossly misunderstood, there's nothing I can do but sit back on my bed and give myself a good cry. That voice in my head is back.

"*So, are you gonna sit there and feel sorry for yourself, or are you gonna get your sister?*"

"Rav? Irra? Anyone here?"

I am waiting for any response. Nothing. Trying to calm myself down, I get up from my bed. I see my jeans on the floor, so I pick them up to wear them again. I'm only going next door, anyway.

Feeling the pouch in my right front pocket rubbing against me, I take it out. It fits perfectly in my hand, so I pull the drawstring to see what is inside. The soft beige material reminds me of fake suede cloth, but it doesn't smell like suede or leather.

It has more of an earthy scent. It isn't unpleasant, but it is certainly not the designer fragrance samples my mom picks out at the department stores.

My finger rummages around in the tiny pouch, and I pull out a piece of parchment paper wrapped with something else. As I unfold the paper, something falls out and bounces on my carpet-covered floor.

Catching the object mid-air, I grasp it quickly. It's round, the size of a quarter, and smooth with a gold, round frame. The center is white glass, so I hold it to the light. A burst of colors emanates from it and shines on my face. The gold frame has a hook on one end, and it contains a gold chain looped through the hook.

"Beautiful necklace."

I put it around my neck. I look around for the parchment lying on the floor. There's writing on it, but I can't decipher what it says. It's in some old-world writing.

The gold frame pendant lights up on my chest and illuminates the letters. Strangely enough, the words were rearranged from old-world language into modern English.

"For I am Fae born, and this is my time of Forthing. With this talisman, I bear the responsibility of my new powers, never to use them for revenge."

Now I'm confused; what does this have to do with me? There are too many questions, and Irra is nowhere to be found. Looking at the clock, it shows 5:00. There are noises outside my bedroom door.

Feeling panicky, I try to take off the necklace. My guilt grips me. Why can't I take it off? This thing doesn't belong to me.

Hearing Stepdad's thundering footsteps stopping at my door distracts me. I shove the necklace under my nightgown and quickly shove the parchment into the pouch. Right when I throw the pouch under my bed, he storms in.

A swollen-faced and teary-eyed Chrissy is right behind him. Her pretty little dress is soaking wet like she has been playing in the sprinklers, but I know better. She's sucking her thumb while fidgeting with her damp dress. Her brown hair is messy and matted on her face while snot dries from her nostrils. Her aura is a deep magenta, just like Mom's—it's pure fear through and through.

My heart aches to see her so full of fear; I can't help but rush toward her. Stepdad pushes me back with one finger with so much force that it feels like a sharp object is jabbing my throat. An acute, intense pain radiates from my throat as I fall back hard, landing butt-first on the floor. His aura is a deep maroon-red, and his light blue eyes look glazed. He's been drinking again. His voice is cold, monotone.

"Take care of your sister."

He turns around, and Chrissy runs away from him and towards me. She buries her face in my chest as I hang on to her for dear life.

"I swear if you say anything to anyone, including the next-door neighbor, it won't be you I'll be throwing out the window."

Stepdad glances at Chrissy. She knows whom he is talking about; her little body shakes violently. She lets out a scream into my chest.

Doing my best to comfort her isn't enough. My anger turns into rage. I can't pry off Chrissy's leg wrapped around my waist, so I get back on my feet and carry her in my arms. I can feel my fiery red aura swaying from me and towards him.

"So you like hurting little girls, don't you? I'll never know what my mother ever saw in you! You-you coward!"

He rushes back into my room while pulling his dark blue, web, military belt he wears with his fatigues. The heavy metal buckle glints. Before he can free the rest of his belt from his belt loops, my aura wraps around his neck, joining with the black cloud aura.

"Argh!"

He clutches at his throat and bends forward on his knees. He raises his left arm in the air, pleading. My aura lets go of his neck as he stumbles on his rear end. The red marks around his neck are deep, then disappear. He gets back on his feet. He glares at me for a few seconds, then leaves. I can hear his footsteps fumbling towards the main bedroom.

Chrissy lifts her head, looks at me, and gives me a solemn smile. It hurts my heart to always see such sadness in her eyes. Taking her finger out of her mouth, she hugs me. Her body starts shaking because her pee-stained dress has saturated her skin, leaving her freezing.

"We need to change you into your jammies, Cookie Monster."

She giggles and wiggles out of my arms.

"Can I have a bubble bath?"

"Of course. Wanna sleep here in my bed tonight?"

She nods and follows me to the bathroom. Whenever horrible situations happen to both of us, Chrissy becomes silent. I've always wondered what she is thinking about.

Turning on the bathtub faucet, I let the water run until it is warm. Then I squeeze some bubble solution over the warm, running water. Chrissy is already out of her wet clothes and steps in. Her smile radiates happiness, and her aura turns from a light magenta to a melon color.

She reaches across the bathtub to play with some rubber toys. It's not unusual for her to go into a dream state where she loses herself in her toys. It's the only time she's at peace. I sit on the floor next to the bathtub while I listen to her talk to her toys.

"You can play for a few minutes, and then I need to wash your hair and your face."

"Okay, Gi-Gi."

There are a few seconds of silence as she plays with her toys again. Then, out of the blue, she asks a strange question.

"Gi-Gi ... do you have magic powers? Like Cinderella's fairy godmother?"

Giving her a puzzled look, I squirm uncomfortably.

"Why would you ask that?"

She splashes some water with one of her toys.

"Cuz Daddy choked. You stared at him, and he choked!"

Her eyes shine with anticipation as she stares at me, waiting for an answer.

I try my best not to lie to her, especially when she stares at me with those big, brown eyes.

"Your father might be sick, sweetie. His anger can cause him to choke."

Her little lips frown, and her voice trembles and squeaks.

"I don't like it when he gets mad. It scares me, Gi-Gi! He hurts me!"

Holding a washcloth in my hand, I rub her back with soapy

water, trying to calm her.

"It'll be okay, Chrissy. You have your big sis to protect you. I promise nobody will ever hurt you."

"With your magic, right, Gi-Gi?"

Chrissy smiles at me with those sad, liquid brown eyes.

"You have been watching too many Disney shows, girlie!"

I want to lighten the mood, so I pretend I am the fairy godmother as I stand up to sing.

"Bibbidi Bobbidi Boo!" And I dance around in circles.

Chrissy squeals with delight and claps her hands.

"More! More!"

I keep dancing and singing until I laugh so hard that I sit down to catch my breath.

The bathroom door opens slowly; Mom walks in with a pair of flannel footsie pajamas and underwear with training pants meant for Chrissy. Her swollen face still looks bruised, and her frown doesn't improve her image. Wearing her black sleeveless nightgown and black slippers reminds me of a witch's costume for Halloween.

Her movements are slow and sluggish as she throws the clothes down beside me.

"Here are her clothes. Make sure you wash her hair."

She leaves again without saying anything to Chrissy.

I take one of the plastic cups sitting by the faucet and the bottle of baby shampoo.

"Give me washcloth, Gi-Gi!"

"Sure, hold on."

I grab a clean, dry washcloth from the nearby towel closet. She stands up to grab the towel from me to cover her eyes.

"Sit down, please. It'll be easier for me to wash and rinse your hair."

Chrissy does what she is told. It doesn't take long to finish washing and rinse the rest of her. She takes pride in dressing, but I help her brush her teeth and comb her hair.

Chrissy follows me to the bedroom, as soon as I finish tidying up the bathroom. She quietly lies down on the left side of my bed. The alarm clock shows 7:45 p.m. I guess it is later in the evening. Chrissy rolls over and falls fast asleep. I guess we're not eating dinner tonight.

I'm too distracted to do any homework, maybe later. It's been a long day, and the muscles in my legs ache. Going back to bed looks too attractive, but my brain is too active for sleep.

I do the next best thing: sneak into the kitchen to raid the fridge. While I slip into the hallway's darkness, the floorboards creak a bit too loud while I'm trying to tiptoe on the linoleum floor. Some stirring noises come from the main bedroom, so I stop moving. Waiting for my parents to calm down is agonizing, considering my stomach is practically roaring at me.

"Come on!"

Then everything is quiet again after one last cough from my mom. Making a bunny-rabbit dash to the kitchen and then grabbing the fridge door open, I grab a couple of hard-boiled eggs, some grapes, and potato salad stored in a plastic container. I remember the tote bag in the shoe closet by the front door, so I quickly dash over to the cabinet and then back to the fridge. Feeling like a bandit stealing from my own family's food stash, I shove everything in the tote bag, plus a can of soda.

Opening the front door and silently closing it behind me, I breathe a sigh of relief.

Where in the world are you going?

"Good question!"

Sitting on the stairs, I'm thinking about my next move. I sit quietly, then I tear through the tote bag. I can't stand it any longer; I am ravenous. I crack open an egg, shove that in my mouth, grab a handful of grapes, swallow that, and pop open the soda. After I take a massive gulp of soda, my stomach stops grumbling.

Getting up from the metal stairs to the front door is a relief. It wasn't the most comfortable seat. Looking around to find a soft grassy area, I choose the location closest to Danae's house. Their lights are still on, but I don't want to bother her or Mrs. Jenkins. Stepdad probably told them I wasn't allowed to go over there since I was grounded.

Yada! Yada! Sigh!

Lying down on the soft grass and looking at the stars soothe me. Even though I want to sleep, I can't help thinking about my meeting with Irra and Rav.

It still feels like a dream! It doesn't make any sense! Especially with the paper and the necklace that won't come off.

Some lightning bugs flutter around me; they are so close to me that it is not very pleasant. Swatting them away only makes it worst—they are too attracted to my glowing pendant that blasts a beautiful array of colors through my nightgown.

"Go away, you stupid bugs!"

I'm hoping my parents didn't hear me. I sit still, listening for any other movement in the darkness. I sense something is there near me.

"Anyone there?"

Feeling something coming closer makes the hairs on my arms and neck stand on end. A soft, white glow appears before me; she is in her long, flowing, transparent gown. Irra materializes right beside me.

"You scared the daylight out of me!"

Irra's light gray eyes glow in the dark, but her smile is disarming.

"Hello, again. What do you think of the talisman?"

"So that's what you call it."

I sit up with my back straight.

"I only have one question."

"What's that?"

Irra's smile is steady, and she sits beside me on the grass.

"Why can't I remove this-this talisman?"

"Well ... for one thing, you are the rightful heir of our family's talisman."

Her gaze bore into me.

"Say again? OUR family? What?"

I'm still having trouble believing this. She must be crazy.

Irra let out a soft laugh, keeping her voice low.

"I had to find out if you're our half-sister. It took me a while, and my intuition was correct."

I was staring at her shimmery skin, light gray eyes, and calmness to see if she was joking. I can't tell the difference since I don't know her well enough.

"We're half-sisters, Georgina! You are half Fairy-Sidhe, to be exact."

She lay on her back to relax. Her head turns over in my direction.

I can't lie down. I just sit there and stare at her.

"The only way we could be related is that ... we share the same father."

That's just crazy! I have so many questions to ask Mom. Doubt she'll answer, though.

"Yes, your mother should've told you the identity of your father. I suspect she wanted to forget her encounter with our father."

As if she read my mind, which only makes me uncomfortable and awkward. My brain is squirming for more information.

"She said I was just like him! Evil! I have no clue what she meant by that."

Irra seems pensive, which only makes me anxious. She seems like she is choosing her words heavily.

"I'm not sure either. Look, you should talk to your mom before I say anything. For now, I must tell you something about your talisman."

She takes a long pause; maybe she's trying to find the right words.

"Okay, so far, I just found out I have a half sister who is a Sidhe Fairy. Am I also related to Ravanna? Because you two look nothing alike!"

"The answer is yes. Rav is your half-sister. Sidhe Fairies have many human qualities like height, similar physiology, emotions, and all that, except we tend to live longer lives beyond one hundred years or more and have unique abilities, as you may already know. All Fae goes through a coming of age where each child goes through a rite of passage called a Forthing, for which you must swear to only use your gifts to benefit others or for self-defense. If you use your gifts for revenge or vengeance, your powers will cause dire consequences for your friends and family. And it doesn't necessarily mean right away, it could happen before you are born, after you die, or even in the most unusual, unexpected way to someone you genuinely care for. Either way, there will be consequences. As for Rav being my twin, but only in age and nothing more. When you read the paper, did it adapt to your language, and did you read it aloud?"

I hesitate for a few seconds.

"Yes, I did."

"Then you have been officially indoctrinated. The talisman is your shavtal; it belongs to you and only you. But! There have been situations where other Fae can take it from you to steal your power either through deception, like a loved one can trick you into giving it up or deceive you into bestowing it to them in a will while on your deathbed."

"Is that what happened to you and Rav?"

Irra's smile drops from her face, and she sits up.

"Why would you ask such a question?"

"Well, when I saw you again this evening, your aura was a soft white, like something was missing from you. It reminds me of a battery that's not fully charged. Instead of 100 percent capacity, it's more like 75 percent."

I can't help but give her a pitiful look.

She looks away; her aura turns to a softer blue, telling me she's disappointed in someone. Somebody she knew and trusted deceived her. Her head turns in my direction.

"You're correct. I see the shavtal's gift has already present-ed itself to you. Your powers have enhanced considerably. You will be a lot more powerful than Rav and me. That's good, because we'll need you more than ever."

I am shrugging my shoulder because I don't understand what she meant by that comment. Her light gray eyes turn steely like polished metal; she reaches over to touch my hand.

"You're still so young, so much to learn, and Stepdad will not be the only monster in your life. You must be careful not to use your talisman for acts of revenge. It will be tempting, and the talisman will do your bidding, but you will pay for it dearly."

There are too many questions to ask; it's so overwhelming.

"Was it our father who deceived you when he took your talisman?"

Wait! How did I know that? I could feel the talisman press-ing against my chest like a heavy, lead weight.

Her sad eyes tell me all I need to know, but she wants to explain more.

"Our father's name is Rennick. He's smart, devious, hand-some, and vengeful. He took some of my power and Rav's by taking our talismans. Our talismans are heirlooms passed from our grandmother to my mother and her daughters. Ren-nick's thirst for power is insurmountable. He overthrew the King of the Fae from the Other World and took his powers, too. Now that I know you're half Fae, he's running loose in the human world."

"Did you love him? Were you close to him?"

Tears, the colors of glittery white liquid, run down her face; I hold her hand tighter.

"Yes ... since Mother died giving birth to Rav and me, he's the only family we have."

"Well, now you have me as your family!"

Hoping that would cheer her up.

"Shadow," a huge, black Maine Coon, who lives in our

neighborhood, comes slinking between Irra and me. His eyes are the brightest emerald green, blinking at me.

That's funny. I don't remember his eyes being that green; I thought they were more amber.

Raising my hand to stroke his fur between his shoulder usually makes him purr. Shadow flinches and growls. That's when I know this creature is not our friendly neighborhood cat down the road.

"Rav, is that you? Just change back to you. You're not fooling anyone!"

I put my hand down by my side. Shadow morphs from a cat back to a Rav, the Sidhe Fae. Her tall stature is wearing a beautiful, shimmery green gown that clings to all her curves. I must admit, she's a beautiful woman. Fae woman? Whatever, I'm sure any male species would find her attractive.

Her long, wavy, fiery red hair reaches down to her shoulder and spreads its waves across her chest, accentuating her smile. She quietly sits on the other side of Irra on the soft grass.

"How did you know?"

Irra cuts her off before Rav can ask any more questions.

"Why are you here?"

Rav's blank expression is hard to read right now. One thing is for sure, her aura is telling me she's hiding something. My shavtal quivers under my nightgown, but I will it not to glow. Somehow, I feel it isn't safe for Rav to know I have it. Her aura turns from hunter green to a matted gray, matching the subtle gray streak.

"Nothing else going on, so I decided to see what you're up to."

She flashes an innocent smile toward Irra and me.

"I see you're here with our human subject."

Rav's comment offends me.

"You make it sound like I'm some experiment. So, tell me am I the new plaything now?"

I flash an angry look at both Rav and Irra.

Irra raises both hands in the air, pleading.

"Now, wait a minute, we were having a heart-to-heart, and now you're accusing me of deceiving you?"

"If the shoe fits! I've only just met you both. I don't know whom to trust! So, which one of us is the deceiver like our father?"

I make quotation marks with my fingers. Rav's eyes widen, and her mouth drops.

"Our father? Irra, what is she talking about?"

Irra sits up and gives Rav a guilty look.

"She's the one, Rav! She's our half-sister!"

Rav's emerald, green eyes brighten so much they are glowing; her aura has a tinge of red streaks running through the matted gray. She gets up; her wings expand from her side.

"No! No, No, No! This can't be, Irra! Tell me you're joking!"

Irra looks at me.

"Gina, show her the talisman."

Rav flashes her angry eyes right at me. I will the talisman to glow through my nightgown. I imagine rainbow color lights bursting through; sure enough, it works.

Rav lets out a bloodcurdling scream.

"ARG! Irra, what in Favra have you done?"

She flies right into Irra's face so fast that it reminds me of an angry, giant bumblebee.

Irra's wings expand and lift her. She pushes back into Rav.

"I took it, okay? She's the rightful owner of that talisman, and there's nothing anybody can do about it!"

Human arguments are no comparison to Fae arguments. The sisters keep flashing back and forth in the night air. There were flashes of light zapping at each other. One was a soft white and blue, and the other was a deep red and gray. They collide with a lot of energy for a good while.

Surprisingly enough, it was fascinating and scary at the same time. I could no longer see the actual Fae bodies, just their aura zapping and zinging. I look around to see if the neighbors are disturbed, not to mention my parents waking up to this spectacle. Fortunately, the homes surrounding my home are all dark. Maybe I'm the only one who can see all this light show.

The flashing light display stops and both sisters fall to the ground next to me. They were both breathing heavily; liquid glitter covers their bodies— I'm assuming that's a Fae's version of sweat.

"Are you guys done? 'Cause I'm asking what to do now that this is out in the open."

They struggle to get up from their exhaustion, sitting up.

Rav gets up and dusts herself off. She looks directly at me while pointing at me.

"You don't know this, but YOU are forbidden to have that talisman, and it's illegal for you to be in the Other World! Do you hear me? No humans!"

Rav directs her gaze to Irra, who gets up and leans on her left elbow.

"And YOU! There will be consequences for your actions! King Finvarra will have your head, Irra! I will see to it!"

Her words frighten me. Irra senses my anxieties and reaches over to wrap her arms around me.

"It'll be all right! I know what I need to do."

Rav's eyes widen, and her wings expand and flap out. She ascends in the air until Irra slaps her hands together and nods. A flash of light emanates from the impact of her slap, then reaches out and grabs Rav.

Horror spreads across Rav's face as lights wrap around her arms and legs, binding her. The light lines wrap around her, engulfing her until they burst out and disappear.

Irra catches me with my mouth wide open as I witness what happened.

"What ...just ... happened, Irra?"

"Solving our problems for now," Irra says with confidence,

then lets out a big sigh.

"Okay … I sent her to a different point in time so she could cool off."

Standing up, dusting myself off, I pick up my food trash.

"So what's stopping her from going after us, especially me? Will she hurt me?"

That's when I stop what I am doing and look directly at Irra.

"She might. She's as dubious and opportunistic as our father."

I want to ask more questions, but Irra puts up a hand to quiet me.

"It's getting late, and you still have much growing to do, little sis. Go to sleep …."

She takes her right hand, holds up her index finger, and makes a circular motion.

"But I'm not ti …"

The world around me blurs, Irra's image blurs, and my eyelids snap shut.

CHAPTER SIX

TROUBLE AND MORE TROUBLE

Back in my bed again. This time my alarm clock rattles, clanks, and dances on my bedside table. It's my six o'clock alarm, time to get ready for school.

No! Oh my gosh! I still have a lot of homework to do!

So much to do and so little time. Now I'm racing against time to get schoolwork done. I roll out of bed and grab my book bag to sit at my desk.

One of these days, I'm gonna be a lot more organized about my notebook—everything is a mess!

So, first things first. The dreaded math homework, then some history worksheets, and put together a proposal sheet for the science fair.

"Science fair!? Shoot! What am I gonna do for a project?"

Talking to myself as I read through the instructions on my worksheet, right now seems like an impossible task. My brain is not into this, but I can't give up, and I don't have a choice. Scanning the sheet for the due date while my eyes are trying to focus. Fortunately, I don't have to submit this worksheet until next week. Whew! Got some time to think about it. Regarding math problems, it's all pre-algebra equations, not word problems. Easy peasy!

A soft knock on my door diverts my attention.

"Come in. "

A smiling Danae walks in. She's wearing an interesting outfit. Her short sleeve dress is powder blue with some attractive trim at the bottom of the skirt and on the bodice. Her long, brown hair is parted into braids with matching ribbons between her braided strands, with white feathers hanging from each braided end.

Her sunny, yellow aura is always a welcome sight since I'm so used to seeing red, magenta, purple, brown, and olive green.

She hands me a paper napkin-covered item.

"Here, it's piping hot. Figured you'd need it."

"Thanks! I'm starving!"

The warm swirling aroma coming off the napkin is just too tempting. I open it to reveal a freshly baked cinnamon-and-apple muffin. Smiling at Danae, I don't hesitate to take a big gulp of this delicious muffin. Danae laughs and plops herself on the edge of my bed. I swallow the last bit without wasting any time letting the muffin cool off.

"That was delicious!"

I automatically throw the wadded napkin in a wastebasket next to my desk.

"Are you doing homework right now?"

Danae gives me a surprised look. I nod while finishing the last question on my history worksheet.

I get up from the desk and put all my finished assignments in my book bag.

"Don't ask. It's been a long night!"

Danae gives me a frown.

"So, do you know what you're going to do for the science fair? It's only eight weeks away."

"Not a clue. Oh, by the way, you look nice. What's going on?"

Danae rolls her eyes, then rips off a loose thread from the bottom of her dress; I guess it drove her crazy just sticking out.

"Yeah ... since I'm the new girl and all, Mrs. Young wants me to introduce myself. So, what better way to talk about my Shawnee tribal culture? My mom made this dress."

"It's a beautiful dress. I love all the embroidered symbols on the trim. What does it mean? Or does it mean anything?"

I can't help but admire the complicated beadwork sewn into the trim. Danae runs her fingers across the beaded border and looks up. Her hazel eyes well up, lips in a downward frown. She sniffles hard to keep her nose in check and quickly wipes away any would-be tears. Her yellow aura turns more into a bluish mixture. There's no denying her sadness.

"I'm so sorry. I didn't mean to upset you."

She flashes a sympathetic smile.

"It's okay. I miss my mom, that's all. She's the one who made this dress. It was supposed to be worn for my thirteenth birthday."

She looks away to prevent any more tearful events.

"Is, is she alive?"

What a stupid question, Gi!

I'm already regretting asking. I can feel my cheeks burning.

"It's okay. She's in a coma at a hospital in Columbus. I lived there with my mom and dad until the accident. Some drunk driver hit them on their way home from a Christmas party last year. By the time the ambulance arrived at the hospital, my dad was dead on arrival, and my mother never woke up. She wasn't conscious."

"So that explains why you're here, then. I'm so sorry about your dad's death. I do hope your mom wakes up from the coma. We can talk about the symbols later."

I am giving her a reassuring smile. I wipe my tears with the sleeves of my nightgown.

"Shouldn't you be getting ready for school?"

She points at my alarm clock.

"It's already 8 a.m., and we gotta catch the bus in half an hour."

I didn't have time to answer and went into full action mode.

"Could you wait in the living room? I'll only be a few minutes."

Danae nods, then gets up, walks towards the door, then stops.

"Want me to grab your book bag?"

"That would be nice, thank you."

Danae picks up my book bag and heads for the door again.

"I'll ask your mom about your lunch box, okay?"

Running out my bedroom door, I pass Danae on my way to the bathroom.

"Sure! Be right out."

Several minutes later, I enter the living room. Danae is sitting with Chrissy on the floor at the coffee table. They're both watching one of Chrissy's favorite kids' shows, *Captain Kangaroo*.

Chrissy is busy handing some dried cereal to Danae, who doesn't mind eating some. They both giggle as Danae growls over her cereal. Right beside them is my red plaid-colored metal lunch box.

"Hey, you ready? I put together your lunch for ya."

Not wasting any more time, I put on my tennis shoes by the front door.

"Thanks again! I'm ready! The bus will be here soon."

Danae grabs my lunch box while I strap on my book bag. My mother is nowhere to be found. I observe the empty kitchen, then to Chrissy. She notices my concern.

"Momma is sleeping."

Worried about Chrissy being alone all morning, I'm agitated about Mom's absence.

"Can you wake up Mom, Chrissy? I'm not gonna leave until she comes out."

"Hey, Gina, it's okay. I'll call my aunt to come over to watch Chrissy. Your mom is about to give birth and probably needs to rest."

Chrissy jumps up from the floor and yells. "Mrs. Jenkins! Mrs. Jenkins!"

Danae runs to the kitchen and grabs the phone handle from the wall receiver. She dials, waits, and starts talking.

"Shhhhh! Momma is sleeping! Can you be quiet for now?"

Chrissy cooperates and sits back down. She picks up her little spoon and digs into her bowl of cereal with milk. Danae must've poured the cereal and milk for Chrissy.

There's a gentle knock on the front door; Mrs. Jenkins is already here. She comes in wearing a soft lilac-colored bathrobe with curlers in her hair. She flashes Chrissy and me a big smile.

"Good morning! There she is! I heard we're gonna have some fun together."

Chrissy runs right into Mrs. Jenkins' arms, squeals, and giggles.

Danae and I both signal to Chrissy to be quiet. Mrs. Jenkins puts a finger to her lips while looking at Chrissy in her arms.

"Okay, girls, you better go. Have a good day at school!"

Danae grabs the front door, and I'm right behind her.

The cool spring air hitting my face is refreshing; the sun is already warming us as we walk towards the mobile home park-playground area. We pick up our pace, especially after Danae looks at her wristwatch.

"The bus is gonna be here any minute."

She starts running off.

"Wait! I know a shortcut!"

Danae slows down so I can catch up. We make a quick right turn instead of taking the long way to the playground. We run a couple of blocks and pass the house of the woman that Stepdad visited the other day. I catch a familiar sight coming out of the woman's front door. He doesn't see us, but Danae and I instantly recognize him.

It's Robert O'Malley, all right—there's no mistaking his messy, red hair, tattered corduroy jeans, and gray sweatshirt. He has a slingshot in his hand and is too busy picking up rocks from the ground to shoot at any birds flying by.

"What a jerk!" Danae says, a bit too loud for my comfort.

I grab her by the arm and pull her behind some nearby hedges.

"I can't believe that's where he lives! He-he lives at that woman's house!"

Danae looks confused as I keep an eye on Robert walking around in his yard, still shooting rocks with his slingshot. We hear a cat screech nearby. His mother comes out yelling at him.

"Bobby! Stop that! Get yer ass to the bus stop! Now!"

He flips her off with his middle finger.

"Okay, Phyllis!"

He makes his way toward the sidewalk and puts his slingshot in his back pocket.

"He flipped off his mother! Who does that? What a piece of sh ..."

We hear Robert's mother yelling in our direction.

"Hello? Anybody there?"

Not wasting any more time, we both take off running again.

Robert must've noticed us leaving our hiding spot behind the hedges, hearing him scream.

"Hey, you! Come back!"

Danae picks up her pace. I try to keep up, but she is too fast for me. Robert's footsteps keep getting louder and louder, closer and closer. Sweating profusely through my clean T-shirt and jeans, my book bag feels like a lead weight slowing me down as it bounces off my right side. The straps keep digging into my left shoulder.

Danae arrives at the bus stop in the playground area well before me. I can see her stopping, bending over to catch her breath. My legs can't stop moving; even my muscles burn with red, hot pain.

A hand grabs my shirt from behind. My right hand is too sweaty to maintain a grip on my lunch box, so it flies from me. I can hear it crash-land from a nearby distance.

Robert pulls me closer as he spits his words in my face.

"You stupid nosy chink!"

I twist and pull away quickly, breathing heavily. Pure adrenaline floods my body when he lifts his right hand to form a fist. Before he can even punch me, I kick him in his crotch.

"Argh!"

Robert releases me, screams, and hunches over.

Danae and a bunch of other kids rush toward me.

"Hey, you all right? That was right on, man!"

I am trying my best to catch my breath, giving her a thumbs-up. Danae smiles at me.

"So proud of you! Woman power!"

She raises her fist in the air while the other kids watch.

Robert continues to whimper while some of the other kids gather around him. The big orange-yellow school bus pulls into the playground parking lot just a few feet away.

Danae hands me a tissue she pulled out of her book bag.

"Here, dry yourself off."

My breathing slows down, and I graciously take the tissue from her. There are a couple of water fountains nearby, so I walk over to one of them. I am pushing the button to release the upward, squirting water from its faucet and feeling the cool liquid wash over my face. The bus driver honks his horn while the other kids line up.

"I guess that means us!"

I swipe off some water from my face with the tissue. I locate my lunch box, and of course, all my wrapped food is scattered all over the place. Letting out a big sigh before picking up my items, I see a tattered, dingy white pair of tennis shoes intentionally step on my wrapped sandwich. The foot belongs to rat-faced Walter, looking down on me with an ugly smirk.

"Hey, chink! Heard you were nosing around Robert's yard. I should report you for stealin'."

He steps on my orange; it splatters under the pressure of his foot. He lets out a nervous laugh. Trying to get up from being on the ground, Robert doesn't waste any time and kicks me in the chest. The remaining kids that weren't on the bus come running toward us yelling.

"Fight! Fight! Fight!"

They surround the three of us with eager faces.

Tears are running down my face, and anger is seething from my aura.

Get a hold of yourself! This isn't the time to fight back!

Fortunately, the bus driver comes running towards us; he's a short guy with a balding head, wire-frame glasses, and is super thin. His grayish-blue uniform looks humongous on him, so while he runs towards us, his clothes look like they're swallowing him. He stops right before us, giving all of us an accusing look.

"What's going on? Why are you stepping on her lunch? Pick it up now!"

He looks right at Walter. The bus driver doesn't sway from his demands and stares down Walter, who eventually gives in. He reluctantly picks up my lunch items: a bag of chips, a bagged cookie, and my thermos container.

He hands it all back to me; I quickly shove all of it into my metal lunch box. I try to pull myself together by brushing off the dust from my clothes.

"Pick up all the trash you made too!"

The bus driver stands with his hands on his hips, giving Walter an intense, grim look. An annoyed Walter reluctantly picks up my smashed sandwich, which was still in its plastic wrap, and my squashed orange, bleeding out pulp on its sides.

Fortunately for him, there is an empty trash can near the water fountains. The bus driver turns to the other kids, his voice deep and commanding.

"All right, kids, get back to the bus now!"

Like sheep, they do as they are told.

Then he turns to Robert.

"And you! Does anyone tell you that you don't ever hit girls? What the hell is wrong with you?"

The bus driver pulls Walter and Robert aside; he's scolding them. Robert looks at the bus driver indignantly as he glares at me hatefully. The bus driver notices Robert's distraction and raises his voice.

"I said, look at me when I'm talking to you! Didn't your parents teach you any manners?"

I do not realize Danae is standing next to me all this time, which startles me.

"Apparently not, piece of trash!"

"Shhh, keep it down, Danae! Wanna get chewed out too?"

I give her a quick nudge with my right arm. Tired of the lookie-loos still crowding around us, I have to say something.

"C'mon guys! Nothing to see here!"

Without notice, I start walking toward the bus, and Danae follows me.

Everyone else takes our cue to board the bus, so we quietly file in line. Many kids keep their eyes on the bus driver and the two boys. Danae grabs the first row, so I plop down next to her. She can't take her gaze away. I'm just too tired to do any more gawking. I do the next best thing I can, break out my latest read, *The Hobbit* by JRR Tolkien. A highly recommended read by our school librarian, Miss Embers.

After a few minutes, Danae shakes me from my reading.

"Hey! Look! Robert and Walter were sent home! Yes!"

She keeps shaking me until I tear my eyes out of my book. Looking through the front windshield of the bus gives me a broad view outside; I see the bus driver walking toward us.

I also see Robert flipping us off too. Danae bursts out into a healthy laugh.

The bus driver boards the bus, takes a few seconds to clear his throat, then faces us. Danae stops laughing and sinks back into her seat. He scans the crowd of students sitting and waiting patiently.

"Bullying will not be tolerated. If caught doing so, you will be banned from riding this bus. Is that clear?"

Even though he's short for an adult guy, his voice is deep and full of authority. The little elementary kids accompanying us middle school students sit with their eyes and mouths gaping open. The older kids like me nod their heads to acknowledge him. He scans our faces again until he sees me sitting with Danae.

"You all right? Any damage?"

I shake my head with a "no." He stares at me for a while. His aura is the same as the paramedic I met the other day, a soft, powder blue.

"I need you to check with the school nurse as soon as we arrive. I will have to report this incident to the principal."

"Yes, sir."

He gives me a quick smile, then takes his seat, straps in, and starts the engine.

Danae, smiling at me, puts her arm around my shoulder.

"Finally! Somebody that cares."

Shrugging at her comment, I go back to reading my book. Danae takes her arm off my shoulder and sits quietly next to me.

God! I want this day to be over already!

We arrive at school but fifteen minutes later than usual. Everyone rushes out of the bus. Danae stops to give me a quick word.

"Hey! I'll see you in class."

"Yeah, I shouldn't be long with the nurse."

We go our separate ways. Many kids are scurrying to their

classrooms since all the other school buses had already arrived before us. The empty foyer feels eerily quiet.

It doesn't take long to sit through a laundry list of questions from our friendly but almost senile school nurse, Mrs. Wagner. Her thick, tortoiseshell eyeglasses can barely hold such thick, pop-bottle glass lenses. She keeps the clipboard six inches away to read the questionnaire.

It's also entertaining to see a little old lady wearing a traditional nurse's uniform of a long-sleeve, shapeless dress layered over with a white smock with a big red cross stitched in the center. Her all-white hair is in a bun and pinned with a traditional nurse's cap puts the finishing touch to her vintage look. Her voice quivers and rattles as she reads out loud the last question.

"Do you have continued pain in the area where you were hit?"

I shake my head from left to right a few times. She puts down the clipboard on the examining table to scribble some words. I roll my eyes while she is busy writing.

It's incredible how this little old lady is still working. She can barely write without shaking or losing some of her motor functions. She clicks her pen closed and then looks over at me.

"You're excused. Head back to class, please."

She hands me a pink excuse slip, explaining the reason for my tardiness.

"Aren't you gonna check me out? Or at least check my heart rate?"

"You said you weren't feeling any pain. What's the point?"

Surprised by her nonchalant behavior, I jump off the exam table. I leave her office feeling put off for some reason. I can't quite explain it.

I hand my excuse slip to Mrs. Young, who's sporting a bright red line across her pale, smooth neck. Her eyes are bloodshot and swollen, but I can still see a haunted look. Her aura turns from a soft blue-black to her muddy brown standing in front of her desk. She grabs the excuse slip and hands me back my vocabulary test.

It shows 100 percent for my grade. I can't help but smile. She glares at me and, as usual, doesn't congratulate me; instead, her voice takes on an accusatory tone.

"We need to talk about your grade on this test. And Principal White wants to see you after lunch period today."

My smile drops as I look up from the paper and back at her.

"I worked hard for this test! I practiced at home memorizing these words. As you can tell, my writing assignments have also improved tremendously! I didn't cheat, if that's what you're implying!"

Not waiting for her response, I turn around and walk toward my desk. It feels so good to tell her off. I read a lot and have a good grasp of my language usage.

Thank you very much.

Danae gives me a quick wink and mouths the words, "Right on!"

I continue to walk towards my desk, giving her a quick smile. The other students look amazed at my boldness in standing up for myself.

Or maybe they thought I was too stupid to make so much trouble for myself. Who knows ...

Of course, Mrs. Young won't let this drop. As soon as I sit at my desk, she stands up, glaring at me.

"You just earned yourself a visit to the principal's office! Leave!"

The whole class lets out a chorus of "Oooooh!"

Some whisper, "You're in TROUBLE!"

Even the mousey girl, Cindy, now wearing pink-framed glasses, doesn't say anything but looks at me with fear laced with admiration. She gives me a Mona Lisa smile. Danae stands up and raises her right hand with a fist.

"Fight the power! Fight the power! We want justice!"

The class gets louder, and some kids are booing while others are making noise. Mrs. Young gets her heavy bottom out from behind her desk. She stares angrily at Danae.

"Sit down! I said SIT DOWN NOW!" Danae gets out of her seat and joins me, walking towards the door.

"C'mon Gina, let's stroll to Principal White's office and explain Mrs. Young's prejudice to him."

Her brave smile weakens with every step. This is the first time she has been disruptive in a classroom. Her aura emanates a combination of red, blue, and white stripes dancing around each other.

We can hear the kids making a lot of vocal sounds while Mrs. Young tries to bring her classroom back to order.

"That's enough. You have exactly three seconds to quiet down! One, Two, Three ..."

Relief washes over me as I close the door behind us and step out into the quiet hallway. I let out a long breath, waiting for my heartbeats to slow. The blood vessels in my head are pounding so loud that it drowns out Danae's words. I didn't realize she was talking to me. We walk at a slow pace.

"Hey, you listenin' to me?"

"Hmmm ... what?"

She gives me an exasperated look.

"Geez! Earth to Gina! Come In!"

"Yeah ... sorry ... whaddya say?"

She slows down her pace and keeps her voice low.

"You notice there are no black kids at this school. Heck, there's no other kind of kids in our neighborhood but white kids."

Her aura turns back to a bright yellow again.

"Yeah, it's been obvious since I was nine when I first moved here. I felt like the latest zoo animal on display, and it was obvious when kids would dance around me, pulling back their eyes like slits and calling me a chink monkey or dead Jap baby. I've been pushed down the stairs and cornered in the bathroom. Yada, yada, yada. Nobody cares."

Shrugging my shoulder, my burden has been weighing me

down since I arrived in this horrible town. Danae's eyebrows furrow, her face darkens with anger.

"Jinkies! What do your parents think about all this prejudice?"

Do I really wanna talk about this? Sigh.

"They don't say anything but make me try to be more white to 'assimilate,' a word I learned from Miss Embers."

I make quotation signals with my fingers while rolling my eyes. Danae stops and looks at me.

"What do you mean?"

Rolling my eyes, I quickly retort.

"I was forced to go to speech therapy for three years to get rid of my Filipino accent, and they didn't want my mom talking to me in Tagalog and Spanish. That is what I mean."

Danae's face goes from confusion to twisted disgust and anger.

"NO WAY!! That's just insane! You're told that you're not good enough?" Shaking my head left then right, my lips tighten to a thin line.

"Yep, that's why I don't have an accent, but I do speak, read, and write quite well, I might add. And yet here's Mrs. Young accusing me of cheating on my vocabulary test. There's no way I'm capable of learning! No Way! I'm too brown to be smart."

It feels good to raise my voice in a sarcastic tone.

Danae puts a finger to her lips, then looks around.

"Yo ... We're almost at the attendance office. Gotta keep it down."

Sure enough, Mrs. Snodgrass is at the counter. She gives us both a frown. Her pinched nose and the loose skin under her chin flapping around while she talks reminds me of an arrogant turkey with white, puffy hair worn like a bike helmet. Her voice is high-pitched and full of accusations.

"What is it this time, ladies?"

Danae gives her an astonished look, feeling disrespected.

"EXCUSE ME?"

I touch her arm lightly, then placed my arm in front of her to signal a "calm down" gesture. As soon as she looks at me, I shake my head quickly. She gets the message.

"We're here to talk to Principal White about Mrs. Young's prejudice towards students like Danae and me. And, of course, about the bullying issues of this school. Frankly, we're getting tired of being the victims."

"How dare you! You, you!"

Mrs. Snodgrass's eyebrows raised, mouth gaping open, looks surprised. Danae aggravates the situation by cupping her right hand around her right ear.

"What was that, Mrs. Snodgrass?"

The door to Principal White's office, which happens to be adjacent to the front counter, opens. Out comes Robert O'Malley and his mother. Principal White follows them out. Mrs. Snodgrass is strangely quiet. He studies us quietly, then glances at Robert's mother.

"We'll talk to you in a couple of weeks, Mrs. O'Malley." She gives him a weak smile.

"Oh, please call me Phyllis, Phyllis Brooks. I'm no longer married to Robert's father!"

She straightens herself by pulling down her tight, low-cut, red blouse with the puffy sleeves. Her gray-streaked auburn hair is neatly combed back into a bun, which doesn't complement the rest of her clothing. It is frumpy compared to her short, black mini-skirt, tights, and high-heel pumps. She is dressed as a cocktail waitress or something like that. The dark circles under her eyes only accentuate the crow's feet, and wrinkles and deep curves around the outer edge of her lips stay there after she stops smiling.

The pearl necklace she's proudly wearing looks very expensive and too familiar. I remember my mother wearing a teardrop pearl hanging from an 18-carat gold chain like what this woman is wearing. The perfectly round, off-white pearl was carefully grown underwater in shallow riverbeds, where the divers put tiny grains of sand in each clam. It was the most precious piece of jewelry my mother had ever owned and had sentimental value.

It was a present from my biological father given to her on her birthday a year before I was born. She told me it was specially made for her by local pearl divers near Okinawa, Japan. She kept that necklace locked away in a metal box under her bed.

Wait ... no, it can't be! Did Stepdad give her my mother's necklace? Was the necklace hidden in that pouch he gave her?

My hands shake nervously, so I stick them under my lap as soon as Danae and I sit down. I clench my teeth as my heartbeat quickly in my chest. My talisman heats up under my shirt. Danae turns her attention toward me.

"Hey, you okay? You look upset."

My legs start swinging back and forth under my chair. I start to fidget around. Danae places a hand on my left shoulder.

"Seriously! Calm down!" I whisper a few words, but they aren't intended for Danae to hear.

"She's wearing my mother's necklace!"

There! It just fell out of my mouth. Danae's eyes grow big as saucers.

"What did you say?"

"It's nothing ... hopefully, I'm wrong."

The principal's booming voice startles us back to him. He is talking to Robert in his usual authoritative tone. Robert looks tiny, frail, and powerless with his hands in his jeans pocket.

His shoulders are hunched, his head hanging down, and his dirty tennis shoes pointing inward. Principal White looks annoyed while Robert casts his glance down at his shoes.

"Look at me, young man!"

Robert raises his chin and meets the big man's eyes.

"I will see you in two weeks. Don't come back until then,

you hear me?"

Robert sadly nods in agreement, his mother looking away with shame.

Phyllis directs her glance at her son. Even her aura is deep violet with hints of magenta. She grabs her son's arm, pushing him towards the exit doors.

"C'mon, you need to stay with your dad. I don't want to be late for work!" Robert pulls back and away from his mother's grasp.

"Okay! Okay! I'm not a baby!"

He follows her towards the glass door entrance outside the attendance office.

He catches sight of Danae and me sitting by the front counter. His aura is a muddy brown, then turns red as he stares at us. He makes a fist with his right hand with his index finger sticking out, running it across his neck and making a slicing gesture. I just want to laugh at his stupid threat. Instead, I smile at him.

Principal White sees us sitting and heads in our direction.

"Are you ladies together?"

"Yes, sir, we are."

Danae stands up proud, pulling her dress straight to keep it from wrinkling. He gives us a peculiar look.

"Okay ... this will be interesting."

I get up from my seat and step into his office with Danae. He closes the door as soon as we enter.

CHAPTER SEVEN

THE BUS RIDE

The school day has finally come to an end. Danae and I didn't get into trouble by complaining about the bullying and teacher prejudices. If anything, Principal White is on some tirade to end the racial bullying that's been a chronic problem in this community. He made us aware that's the reason why there are no kids of another ethnicity, because this town tends to run them out.

Lucky me, the principal chose us to set up an anti-bully campaign for the school. Since Danae and I are the only "minorities" in the whole school, this feels like we're being used as tokens. I'm sure he means well, but I doubt this is how to do it.

My homeroom class had to spend time at the library to do some research for the science fair. While I did do some research, it was to find more books by *JRR Tolkien*.

Oh, my goodness, I found the first book of the *Lord of the Rings* sitting on a shelf. Luck be my lady, as my mother used to phrase in Tagalog. *Fellowship of the Ring* was the only book I checked out today.

Miss Embers, one of my favorite people, chuckles to herself.

If a librarian must have a uniform look, she is the poster child for such a look. Her long tapering fingers, dark brown hair in a bun, black-frame glasses, and her nose in a book should be a cover model look for *Librarians Monthly* magazine. Of course, I made that up. She's also a wealth of information; if she doesn't have first-hand knowledge, she will go out of her way to research it for me.

She's one of the few adults who listen. That's why she's your favorite person.

She finishes exchanging the cards she had slipped into the pocket in the back of the book with a stamped due date.

She hands the book back to me.

"Enjoy your book, Miss Trabeck. Good pick, by the way!"

Her smile is genuine, friendly, and honest, just like her beautiful, soft yellow aura. She does enjoy her job.

Danae startles me when she creeps up from behind me.

"Hey, you ready for the bus?"

Slipping the book into my book bag and turning to face her, I snap at her.

"Don't do that! I almost jumped out of my skin!"

Danae and Miss Embers break out in laughter. Not understanding the humor, I stand there waiting for their laughter to end.

"The look on your face is priceless!" Danae stops laughing.

"Sorry, Gi! Sneaking up from behind was just too tempting."

Painting on a smile, I play along. "Yeah. Ha! Ha! I owe you one now."

Miss Embers' chuckle convinces me to smile. Danae pats me on the back.

"Come now, Kemosabe! We've got a bus to catch. And talk about our science fair project."

"What sci ..." Danae grabs my arm.

"C'mon! We'll talk about it!" She pulls me towards the library doors. Miss Embers waves us off.

"Good luck, ladies! Can't wait to find out more! Oh, and by the way, love your dress, Danae!"

Danae beams back a big, toothy smile. "Thanks, Miss Embers!"

Getting in line for the bus today is done in an orderly manner. It was mainly because Robert and his rat-fink friend Walter were banned from riding the bus. What a beautiful end to a long school day. Danae grabs a seat for us in the second row just behind the door.

"Hey, how did your show-'n-tell about your dress go this afternoon? I wish I had been there."

She gives me a weak smile.

"It was fine. Nobody asked questions about my heritage, so I did all the talkin' and finished quickly."

She looks uncomfortable and started fidgeting. Her yellow aura turns dark blue.

"I'm sorry to hear, Di. You know, I would've asked a ton of questions, especially about the beaded symbols on the trim."

I pointed at one of the symbols on the bottom of her skirt trim.

"This cross-arrow symbol reminds me of anti-war. Is that right?"

Danae's face relaxes. She replies with a calm voice. "Close, means friendship."

My eye catches the cross-stitches in random areas. "This doesn't have the same religious meaning, right?"

She shakes her head "no."

"In fact, it's about one's journey in life."

She continues to stare at me and my fascination with the symbols on her trim.

"Basically, your dress was designed to wish you happiness, friendship, and good luck in your life's journey. Right? It only makes sense."

Danae raises her hand, expecting me to give her a high five. "You figured it out! I knew I had picked someone as intelligent as me for a friend."

I return her high five with a proud smile.

I couldn't help but burst out into wild laughter. Danae gives me a confused look, then joins me.

We're almost halfway home, so I didn't want to waste any more time.

"Hey, you mentioned our science fair project earlier. Did you want to partner up?"

Danae's hazel eyes light with interest. "Oh yeah, almost forgot. I was gonna ask, but you beat me to it."

"Oh, my gosh! That would be so cool! I have yet to submit my proposal sheet, so this couldn't have come at a better time."

"Cool! I was thinking about studying the native plants and fauna of Ohio's wetlands. I want to look into protecting natural resources, like what's that word? It's about saving ..."

Danae snaps her fingers, asking for assistance.

"You mean conservation? Like preserving our natural biomes for ecological balance?"

"Bingo! You hit the jackpot! There's no way you cheated on any of your vocabulary tests! Mrs. Young is such a jerk!" Danae responds indignantly.

"Yeah, It doesn't fit her agenda from what she claimed at the beginning of the school year on how minorities don't do so well in school. I think it has everything to do with racial bias in our system. Minorities will always be at a disadvantage."

I gotta thank Miss Embers for her recommendation for To Kill A Mockingbird That was so intense and eye-opening.

"Figures!"

Danae rolls her eyes and then changes the subject. "So! Are we partners?"

"Sure thing! Wanna work on our proposal sheet tonight?" I ask Danae, knowing she will say "yes."

"Heck ya! We're gonna make a great team. I can see it now."

Danae's excitement wanes, and her face darkens.

"Are you still grounded?"

Darn it! I completely forgot about still being grounded. My enthusiasm fades.

"Oh yeah, I'm going to have to beg and plead that this is for school, and it's required. Yada, Yada ... I'll think of something."

The bus pulls to its usual spot at the mobile home park playground. It grinds to a halt and lets out a huge burp. At least, that is what it sounds like to me.

Before we get off the bus, Danae asks me a quick question.

"By the way, where were you after lunch, you know, during show-'n-tell?"

"Had to talk to the principal about my vocabulary tests, swore up and down I didn't cheat. I brought my binder, showing him all my other test results and graded writing assignments. I'm tired of being accused of something I didn't do."

"So he believes you, right?" Danae asks with nosy interest.

"I think so. He didn't say anything but looked through my binder."

I shrug my shoulders while Danae's face looks expressionless.

The bus is almost empty except for a handful of us waiting to get off. The rule is to let the kids up front get off row by row. Danae and I wait, talking for a little while. We are too focused on our conversation to realize that Richard has been sitting behind us all this time.

He taps Danae on the shoulder.

"Hi, Danae! What's up?" Danae, annoyed by Richard's voice, halfway turns around to face Richard.

"Hey."

She turns back to me, rolling her eyes, and I'm trying my best not to laugh at her reaction so I can avoid being rude to Richard.

Richard's aura turns pink whenever he sees her, while Danae's aura turns yellow to mustard. I guess she doesn't like him as much as he likes her.

He gets up at the same time we do. We are the last three kids departing down the stairs of the bus.

The bus doesn't waste any time driving away as soon as we get off. Richard starts following us but stays right behind us.

"Did you need something, Richard?" Danae seems rude toward Richard, who looks hurt by her harsh words.

"I-I was gonna ask if I can walk with you girls! That's all. My home is on the way."

Not allowing Danae to reject him, I automatically respond. "Of course, you can join us."

His blue eyes widen, and his chubby cheeks turn red.

Richard suddenly wipes his overgrown, mousy brown hair away from his eyes in an unconscious way and lets out a deep breath.

"You look nice today, Danae. Your presentation about your dress was fascinating."

Danae's cheeks turn a darker shade of pink. She avoids looking at him. She keeps her gaze on me.

"Thanks, Richard. That was nice of you."

"My grandma said we're like a quarter Cherokee, I think." Richard's voice is shaky, desperately trying to buy Danae's interest.

Unswayed by his comments, Danae continues with a monotone voice. "Yeah ... I ... uhh ... don't know anything about Cherokee, just my mother's Shawnee heritage."

We've been walking for a good couple of minutes now; Danae picks up her pace. I can tell she likes to run. It's such a workout keeping up with her. Things get uncomfortably silent as Danae is practically sprinting away from us. Richard is not outdoorsy since he carries weight around his belly. His short, chunky legs can't keep up with Danae's long strides. She seems much more athletic with her tan skin and lean physique since she's not even breaking a sweat.

Richard, on the other hand, is sweating profusely through

his long-sleeve, plaid Oxford shirt and his brown slacks. I must admit he's one of the more nicely dressed students at school; he even shines his patent leather loafers.

Richard struggles to keep up as his shiny loafers get dustier and dustier. Danae is too far ahead of us. I think she's running away. I see her pass a set of large oak trees with wide trunks.

That's when something or someone strikes her. I can't tell who or what. Her book bag strapped across her chest swings back, dragging her down to the ground. Her back slams on the ground with a huge thud!

Panic rises in me, and I pick up my pace.

"DANAE!"

Richard rushes to her too. When we get close enough but still a good five feet away, five boys come out from behind the trees. Two of them are Robert and Walter. I'm not familiar with the other three. Danae is lying on her back, groaning; red liquid runs from her nostrils. I notice Robert nursing his right fist as Walter is laughing at Danae's injuries. She's looking around, frowning, eyebrows furrowed.

Pure rage surges throughout my body, willing my aura to act.

Oh, it's payback time, all right! Robert, you dirty piece of trash! Aura, do your thing!

Running out of breath from my vigorous but desperate run, there's no time to stop and think. The other two unknown boys run up to Richard since he arrived earlier than I did and surround him.

Walter steps in between the two unknown boys surrounding Richard.

"You come to rescue your little Injun friend? How sweet!"

Richard stands up to Walter to face him, and that's when Walter punches him in the stomach. The other two boys grab Richard's arms while he is still moaning from the pain in his stomach. Walter kicks him in the gut this time. Richard lets out an "Oof!"

"Leave him alone, you idiot!" I yell at Walter, catching my breath. The neighbors in the nearby mobile homes start to come out to see what is happening, but don't say anything. Walter directs his attention to me, then his face lights with glee. Feeling pressure against my back, the pain explodes in my spine.

I can't stop leaning forward; there isn't anything to hold onto. The best I can do is put my arms in front of me to brace for my fall before I hit solid concrete. All my weight pushes down hard on my chest as my hands slide above my head. I hear a "pop" in my left shoulder, then burning pain surges through my body.

All I can see is red and too many things happening around me. Before my chin hits the concrete, someone grabs my shirt from behind. I'm hanging up in the air as the neckline of my T-shirt is tugged so high, it chokes me. I'm gagging and wiggling from the discomfort.

"This is how a chink should be treated. Hanging by her neck." Robert's voice proudly yells to his band of cronies. Danae gets up to try to help, and rage is written all over her face.

"Put her down, you piece of trash!" Danae yells as she leans on her knees to get up. That's when Walter kicks her in the chest. Danae cries in pain as she curls up into a ball, gasping for air.

They're going to kill us! Do something!

I thought I was yelling for Danae, but the only sound coming from my mouth was me gagging for air. Feeling so light-headed, helpless, and fearful for my life, all I can do is try to wriggle out of Robert's grasp of my shirt. I see myself floating above my physical body when I thought I would pass out.

I can see my aura rippling like a ribbon in the air. The maroon-red ribbon is split into five separate strips. The first one wraps itself around Robert's neck, quickly tightening.

He drops my body on the ground, so I land like a rag doll with no bones. The other strips are already wrapped around

Walter and his three other bullies. They are all writhing from wrapped-in-aura ribbons with their mouths gagged.

Feeling my body again, opening my eyes, and smelling the concrete under my nose, I slowly rise from my hands to my knees and let out a cough.

God! My throat is so dry! You don't have time for that! See Danae!

It hurts to put all my weight on my feet while coughing uncontrollably. I look around while my throat grows raw and sore from this persistent cough. More people are coming out of their homes.

Are they just watching us?

My coughing slows down enough for me to focus on Danae. She's still lying down, silent, and I can't tell if she's breathing.

Please, Mother Mary, let her be okay!

Crouching down to Danae's side, I put my left ear next to her nose and mouth. There's a slight breath seeping through her mouth. Trying to check her pulse on the side of her neck gives me the creeps.

Her neck is cool to the touch and shiny with sweat, but not injured; I check for her pulse. There's a faint beat, but it's steady. Her beautiful dress has Walter's grubby footprint on the bodice, and part of the handmade trim on the bottom of the skirt is ripped off.

She looks like a beautiful doll that an undeserving child recklessly threw around. I try to brush away her disheveled hair from her face with my hand. Tears run down my cheeks.

I am distracted by moaning not too far away; I glance over to Richard lying on the ground, face up.

"Hey, Richard! You okay?" As I'm yelling at him, he slowly gets up. "Take it easy. We'll get help!"

From a distance, I see a figure running toward us. Meanwhile, Robert and his gang struggle with my aura wrapped around their bodies. As the figure gets closer, I realize it's Mrs. Jenkins.

"Oh, my God! Gina, You Okay?" A frantic Mrs. Jenkins is crouching down between Danae and me.

"I'm okay. It's Danae! I'm worried about her!"

She tries shaking Danae on her shoulder. "Dannie! Baby! Wake up!"

Mrs. Jenkins says with moist eyes and a nervous voice. Danae doesn't respond; she is unconscious.

"Somebody called me about a fight. They called an ambulance. I didn't catch her name."

Mrs. Jenkins frowns; her voice cracks while tears run down her cheeks.

"She's breathing, but it's shallow. It's scary that she's not responding." My voice trails off. I'm trying to avoid coming off as hysterical.

"You should check on your friend, and what's up with those boys? They're acting strange." Mrs. Jenkins cocks her head towards Robert and the other boys.

Getting up and dusting myself off, I explain to Mrs. Jenkins calmly. "Richard is okay, I think. Those boys there were the ones who ambushed us while Danae, Richard, and I were walking home. Their leader is that redhead guy named Robert. I think he's the one who punched Danae in the face."

Richard has been watching us for a while; he gets up and walks over to us. "Are you Danae's mom?"

"No, sweetheart, I'm Danae's aunt on her Dad's side. Are you okay?"

"I-I'm all right, and I wished I could've done more."

Richard crouches down to an unconscious Danae lying on the ground.

"That's okay, and you're here like Gina. By the way, what's your name?"

Richard dusts his hands off the side of his dusty slacks and offers his right hand to Mrs. Jenkins.

"I'm Richard Kline. Pleased to make your acquaintance."

"Nice to meet you too, Richard. Did you see what happened?" Mrs. Jenkins looks curiously at Richard, who's frowning.

"We just got off the bus, walking home. Danae was ahead of us, and that's when Robert, Walter, and three other boys pretty much ambushed us from behind those trees. Robert was the first to punch Danae."

Richard's gloomy expression drifts downward, avoiding Mrs. Jenkins' gaze. She was about to ask more questions when the whirring sound of the ambulance approaching us drowns out Mrs. Jenkins' words. She stops talking to us and stands up. Richard turns in the ambulance's direction.

Feeling safer that the appropriate adults are here to help my friend, I will my aura to let the bullies go. They all drop like flies and collapse on the ground. Robert regains his senses and bends down to shake Walter, who is still out.

Three paramedics come running out of the vehicle. The first tends to Danae, while the other runs over to Robert and Walter. Fortunately for the bullies, they are all conscious, coughing, and looking confused, including Walter.

Choosing to stay close to Mrs. Jenkins and Richard, we watch the paramedic check Danae's vital signs. The other two paramedics talk to Robert, Walter, and the three other boys.

One of the boys looks panicked, breaks through the crowd surrounding us, and runs off. The third paramedic shouts after him, then shrugs his shoulders. The other two unknown boys are looking anxiously at Robert. He doesn't bother to say anything and keeps his gaze on me.

The police arrive in a black-and-white car with "Waitborne Police" marked in black letters on the white doors and pull up next to the ambulance. The red and blue lights rotating on top of the car flash blindingly bright against the early evening skies.

Since Robert and Walter are already checked out by the second paramedic, he immediately assists the other two.

All three paramedics gently lift Danae onto a stretcher. Her face is covered with an oxygen mask, while her left arm has an IV line connected to a fluid bag.

It's hard to believe that she was sprinting away from us only a few minutes ago, full of life and energy. Now she's lying on this stretcher unconscious, totally fragile. As they are getting ready to load her into the ambulance, Mrs. Jenkins finishes giving the police her statement. She approaches me.

"Gina, I'm gonna ride with Danae to the hospital. Are you sure you're okay?"

"I'll be fine. Do they need my statement?"

She quickly shakes her head left and right.

"I told them what happened. I'm a retired police officer for Columbus PD, so they took my word for it."

She holds me tightly, and I give her a weak smile and a quick hug.

"Well, I better get home. It's gotta be late by now."

"Hey, I can have the Waitborne officer drive you home. It's safer that way." I let go of her tight hug. She reluctantly let go, her lips frowning.

Panic rises in my chest; I quickly take a few steps away from her.

"T-That's okay. I'll explain what happened to my parents. I-I'll be all right. Send Danae my love, I'm really worried about her!"

"Hey, hey, hey! You'll be fine! I'll have Officer Banedridge drive you home. I don't like the way that Robert keeps lookin' at ya! Okay?" Mrs. Jenkins says in a reassuring voice.

"I'll be fine. I gotta go." I quickly pick up my book bag, lunch box, and whatever items fell out and landed in various areas.

Mrs. Jenkins sighs long and bends down to pick up Danae's items. She finishes picking up the items and walks towards the ambulance.

I turn around to run away from this scene. The lookie-loos

still hanging around are too busy watching the police car and ambulance. That is my opportunity to take off without being noticed, especially by Officer Banedridge.

The sun is already setting on the horizon, making the mobile home park look creepy.

Okay, feet, do your thing!

"C'mon! Faster!"

My heart races. I'm picking up my pace, running as if my life depended on it. With just a few more steps, I finally see my home.

The lights are on; I can hear yelling.

"What else is new?"

I keep my voice low; I wish I could appear in my bedroom with the door closed and pretend I've been home all this time. No such luck.

As I walk up to the front door, it swings open. Stepdad is standing there looking at me with bloodshot eyes. He's gripping his belt with his right hand while holding the doorknob, and I knew he had no intention of listening to whatever I had to say.

"Get in before the neighbors see you!" he yells, slurring, his aura is a maroon-red, and I also see the angry black cloud wrapped around his neck. It's always there, like some invisible morbid necklace. All I can see behind him is darkness. I can't hear Chrissy or Mom; now that worries me. Standing my ground, I choose to remain outside.

"Where's Mom and Chrissy?" I ask suspiciously; I can feel my aura stirring. My knees are wobbling, and my body shaking, so I clasp my hands into fists to calm myself.

"I'm giving you three seconds before I come out, grab you by your hair, and drag you in the house!" he hisses while staring through me.

"If you do, I will scream at the top of my lungs so people will come out and see. I also know that you took Mom's pearl necklace and gave it to that lady down the road. I saw her wearing it today at school," I say, smiling with all the courage I could muster.

He drops his belt and punches at the door, which slams against the inside wall of the mobile home. His aura is a mixture of black and maroon, and the black cloud around his neck is thicker, covering his whole neck.

I can see him shaking with so much anger that he staggers away from the door and leaves. I wait for a good ten seconds, just staring at the open door.

I'm not a victim anymore! He's not gonna hurt me anymore! I'm not that little child with nobody to turn to!

Mom appears, looking haggard, and leans against the doorway.

"C'mon, Gi! You come in now!"

Her aura is a dark blue; I can tell she has been arguing with Stepdad since both of her eyes are puffy from crying. Not saying a word, I drag myself to the front door. Pure exhaustion blankets me as I manage to walk up the stairs and into the mobile home. My legs feel like lead weights; my book bag is still strapped across me and now feels like a hundred pounds. She stands there staring at me.

"Oh, by the way, Danae, myself, and another classmate were attacked by five school bullies. An ambulance picked up Danae. She was unconscious, and Mrs. Jenkins rode with her. Just in case you were curious, the other classmate and I are okay," I say in a snarky tone. Mom's jaw drops, and I walk past her.

"Gotta do my homework, shower, and then go to bed."

Too tired to wait for her reaction, I continue towards the living room and into the hallway.

I hear the front door locking, and then she walks into the kitchen.

"Your plate is in fridge, Gi, okay?"

"Okay," I mumble back to her; I finally arrive at my bedroom door. I can't even look at her right now, so I close the door.

CHAPTER EIGHT

THE THREE LADIES IN THE KITCHEN

So glad it's Saturday morning, and I didn't sleep much, considering my alarm clock is ticking at 8:00 a.m. Last night was rough, with my stomach grumbling all night. I could hear Stepdad watching television in the living room into the wee hours of this morning, destroying my plan of sneaking into the kitchen for some leftovers in the fridge. My suspicion of him intentionally hanging out in the living room so he can let me starve all night is nothing new. Too often I have gone to bed hungry; it's his way of playing God with me.

So, to curb my hunger pangs, I spent a good part of last night reading *Fellowship of the Ring*. I'm halfway through the book, so I'm daydreaming to slow down my reading pace. I hate moments like these because they give me too much time to think about the crazy things that have happened. There's too much to take in right now and not enough time to think.

For instance, what's up with Danae?

It hurts too much to think about my new best friend, my only friend.

With my stomach grumbling so loud, feeling shaky and light-headed, I can't think anymore. I can't take anymore.

NEED FOOD NOW! My poor stomach is killing me!

Grabbing my slippers from under the bed, I slip them on. I tiptoe to my bedroom door, open it quietly, and peek into the hallway. Everything is quiet until I hear whispers in the kitchen. Now my curiosity is too great to ignore. Do I have a choice at this point? Not really. Hunger—correction, starvation—will overpower anything right now. I take a deep breath, letting it out slowly as I cautiously take one step in front of the other.

My eyes light up to see Grandma May, Mom, and Mrs. Jenkins. Chrissy is in her usual highchair, eating her breakfast. Before I pick up my pace to join them sitting at the kitchen table, my eyes scan the living room area for Stepdad. He's not around. My mood lightens up, and my anxieties disappear.

"Good morning, everyone!"

I walk towards the kitchen and acknowledge their presence. Grandma May, whose lineage is from Warsaw, Poland, flashes me a big smile. She's a short lady, no taller than my mom, with a thick body and dyed auburn brown hair worn in a 1930s-style bob but with big waves. Her light blue eyes have weakened over time, so the lenses of her eyeglasses have gotten thicker, but she still doesn't miss anything.

She observes before reacting to anything, and there's quiet energy. She owned her own Polish bakery business in Buffalo, New York, but retired a few years ago. Aunt Kathy, Stepdad's youngest half-sister, now runs the business full time.

Grandma gets up from her chair to walk toward me; her tiny but full body frame reminds me of a Momma Bear. Even though she's wearing a feminine-like top with short ruffles on the front of her off-white, long-sleeve blouse paired with blue polyester slacks, she still comes across as a masculine woman. She's one thick, short, stocky woman who loves to give hugs.

"Come here, little *skarbie!*"

She says in a high-pitched voice, with her arms reaching

out to grab me. Even though she's lived in the United States for several decades, her thick Polish accent can make her sound like she's speaking another language.

"Hey, Grandma May! So good to see you!"

I return her hug with a long, tight squeeze; she smells soapy and clean. She lets go of me and stares at me intensely. She still holds her hands on my arms and studies me up and down.

"You look different, Gi-Gi! What's going on? You okay?"

Grandma's eyebrows furrow with concern; her sharp eyes don't miss a thing. She lets go and motions for me to sit down.

"You eat first! You're too skinny! "

She says to me while she walks over to the stove to scoop some scrambled eggs, bacon, and pan-fried potatoes on a clean plate.

No arguments there!

"Everything smells so good, Mi Ma! "

I smile at everyone around me and place a paper napkin on my lap. Mrs. Jenkins raises her coffee cup.

"Yep, Your Mi Ma makes a mean cup a Joe! Nice and strong."

She goes back to gulping her coffee down. My mother sits quietly with a painted smile. She moves her food around with her fork, takes a small sip of apple juice, and looks down.

"You okay, Ma?"

Mom doesn't answer; she keeps looking down at her plate. Grandma places the plate of food and a big glass of chocolate milk in front of me. She gives me a big wink as I pick up my fork. The smell of my food is just pure heaven and time for me to dig in.

While I'm making a pig of myself just chowing down, Mom gives me a disgusted look.

Time to turn on the aura alert senses! Something's up!

I am slowing down from my feeding session, feeling embarrassed about my pig-like table manners.

Geez! My last meal was lunch at school yesterday ... so

yeah, I'm gonna chow down!

I gently put my fork down, pick up my chocolate-milk glass, and take a long gulp.

Ahhhhh! Drink first, then contend with a moody mother. Sigh!

"Are you done, Gi? We have too many tings to talk 'bout!"

Mom snaps at me. She knows how to shame me; I can feel my cheeks turn three shades red—her aura changed from peachy orange to reddish melon.

"Yes, Mom, I'm done. "

I look directly at her, waiting for her to speak again.

Mrs. Jenkins places her right hand over my mother's trembling hands.

"Hey, Rose, it's gonna be all right, okay?"

"What's going on?"

I ask, keeping my gaze squarely on Mrs. Jenkins.

All three ladies sit there, just staring at me. Their auras are quite similar, with Grandma's being peachy with shades of yellow, Mom's peachy with shades of blue, and Mrs. Jenkins' being peachy with shades of light gray.

Yep! Mrs. Jenkins is a bit worried ... maybe about Danae?

This silence slowly kills me as my heart rate thumps loudly in my chest. Mrs. Jenkins couldn't take it anymore and decided to take the lead.

"Okay, here goes: First off, Danae is doing fine. She does have a serious concussion on the back of her skull due to her falling backward from Robert's forceful punch to her face. She also has a cracked rib. Fortunately, she's conscious and lucid. They have her on fluids and are keeping an eye on her, so she needs to stay at the hospital for a few more days to ensure her symptoms don't get worse. She's looking forward to seeing you later today. Your mom is allowing me to drive you and Chrissy to the hospital."

Mrs. Jenkins' eyes are baggy, with dark circles. She gives me a weak, tired smile.

"Thank you, Mrs. Jenkins. I would like that. I-I don't have any money to buy flowers or balloons, but I'm sure Chrissy and I can make Danae a get-well card for sure!"

I'm doing my best to cheer her up with an appreciative smile, but I can still feel the tension around me.

"That would be great! Danae will love that and, more importantly, she would rather see you and Chrissy instead of flowers, anyway."

Mrs. Jenkins said, trying her best to sound cheerful. Her aura tells me otherwise, and I sense she has more bad news.

"Is there something else, Mrs. Jenkins?"

I'm dreading what she's about to say.

"Well ... it looks like Robert will not face any kind of repercussions for his actions. None of the neighbors who were outside watching it all happen would give any witness testimony to what took place. They claimed they only came out when the ambulance arrived, since it was noisy. I was talking to Office Banedridge about it early this morning. He stopped to see if Danae could give him a statement. She was still asleep. He gave me a rundown from the statements he took from the boys, even though one of them took off. He and Richard couldn't find you for some reason. You will need to give Mr. Banedridge a statement. He changed his mind for some reason. "

Mrs. Jenkins studies me for a few seconds.

"So, do you mean that Robert won't be punished? I thought what he did was considered an assault, not just bullying. "

I'm trying to keep my anger in check, but not surprised to hear Robert won't be punished.

Don't tell Mrs. Jenkins why you ducked out on the police yesterday! Way to go!

"It looks like Robert and his family have a long, disturbing history in this town. The other police officers usually let Robert practically get away with murder, since his dad is also a police officer in this county.

There were rumors of Robert's dad being violent toward

his wife, Phyllis. That's why she divorced him a couple of years back. She's been a victim of his abuse since Robert was a baby and filed charges against his father. "

Mrs. Jenkins takes a sip of her coffee and lets out a long sigh.

It's peculiar how Robert's mom is as much a victim as Mom.

Mrs. Jenkins continues with additional news.

"His unit, as well as his commanding officer, covered for him. It's interesting that whatever formal charges she filed, none of it was presented in court. I can't imagine what she's gone through with that man. She was eventually labeled as a crazy woman or highly unstable, so she has no credibility in the community."

Mrs. Jenkins says solemnly; she quietly takes another sip of her coffee. Grandma May looks stone faced, grunts to herself, and gets up to make another pot of coffee. Mom squirms in her seat, especially when Mrs. Jenkins mentions Phyllis's abuse.

I observe all three ladies in this kitchen, realizing how each couldn't be any more different from the other. As much as I wanted to hate Robert's mother, I can't help but feel sorry for her. I am looking back at my mother sitting in front of me with sad eyes and fidgeting with her dress. She seems nervous, but why?

"Ummm, Mom, are you gonna ride in Mrs. Jenkins' car when we see Danae? Or do you have other plans?"

She clears her throat and swats her hair back.

"Your gurand modder will drive me to my duc-tor's appointment. I have check-up today and need to get blood pressure checked."

"It's all taken care of, Skarbie! Your momma has pre-eclampsia, so she has to rest as much as possible before giving birth. That's why I'm here to help her out. I will make sure she follows the doctor's orders."

Grandma finishes pouring another cup of coffee for herself and Mrs. Jenkins.

Trying not to sound worried, I ask calmly, "What's pre-e-clamp..?"

"It means her blood pressure is too high, and her urine test has too much protein. But it can be treated with lots of bed rest and decreased stress levels. She's scheduled for another C-section if her blood pressure rises."

Grandma May gives me a reassuring smile. It doesn't help.

I wonder if it has to do with the abuse. Maybe?

"Well, I'm glad you're here, Mi Ma! Momma can use some well-deserved rest, right, Ma?"

Mom won't look at me, but I reach over to hold my mother's hand. She pulls away and puts both of her hands under the table.

Now that hurts! She knows how to twist the knife in my heart. I don't know what I did wrong!

Grandma May takes notice; she reaches out to grab my left hand and looks me in the eyes.

"It's okay, *skarbie*, your momma is tired, and there's too much going on. When we return from the hospital, I will make sure she gets to take a nap."

Mom pushes her plate away, takes the napkin off her lap, and straightens her yellow sundress with short, puffy sleeves. Her belly has dropped and enlarged; there's no mistaking that she's ready to give birth. She steps out and pushes her chair against the table.

"I'm done! Too tired wit all dis talkin', I go lay down. Gi-Gi, I need for you take care of your sister. And tank you Lau-ra for takin' my dauters to visit Dannie. I pray for her!"

Mrs. Jenkins pats Mom on the back before Mom leaves the kitchen and heads back to the main bedroom.

"It's no problem, Rosie. Glad to see that you're getting some rest before you go to the doctor. Talk to you later."

Mrs. Jenkins gives Grandma and me a puzzled look.

We waited for Mom to go to her bedroom and close the door. Grandma pulls Chrissy out of her highchair; the tray is littered with bits of food.

"I'll clean up after Chrissy. Gi-Gi, why don't you get ready, and I will call ... ummm ... Laura, is it?"

Grandma snaps her fingers.

"Yes! That's right, Laura Jenkins or Laurie works too. The phone number is on the list there on the fridge door. Gi-Gi, I'll be waiting for you at my house. This will give me time to take a shower and freshen up before we head out."

Mrs. Jenkins gets up from her chair. She starts clearing the table with the dishes left by my mother, but Grandma shoos her away.

"Hey, don't worry about the dishes. I'll clean them when we're all done. Go ahead. Oh, by the way, are you married? I notice Gina calls you Mrs. Jenkins."

Grandma listens while she wipes down Chrissy's hands with a wet rag.

"Nah, never been, it's fine. I like living on my own. I only regret not having kids, but Danae fills that void, so I'm happy."

Mrs. Jenkins shrugs her shoulder and puts her empty coffee mug in the sink.

"It's just out of courtesy Mi Ma. Momma taught me to address ladies as 'Mrs.' or 'Miss,' that's all. I didn't know if she was married when we first met, and it's rude to ask adults, right?"

I reassured Grandma, who nodded and gave me a quick wink.

"You're a good kid, Gina! See you in a few minutes."

Mrs. Jenkins was already by the front door, grabbing the doorknob. I can tell she's ready for that shower. I turn to Grandma to see if she has Chrissy taken care of.

"Mi Ma, are you gonna be okay with Chrissy? I'm gonna get dressed and brush my teeth to be ready."

"I'll be fine with my *babu*! You go on ahead. Get yourself ready. I'll get Chrissy ready too. Before you go, I have a question for you."

"What is it, Gran?"

"Mrs. Jenkins said that the bully boys were acting like they were frozen in place, like something was binding them. Did you ...?"

Grandma's eyes bore into me; she had known about my aura-reading ability since I was five.

"I didn't do anything. Robert is twice as tall and much stronger than me. He has a reputation for picking on little kids like me at school. He's been suspended from school, you know!"

I can't believe Grandma's accusations. Why would she ask such a question?

"It's all right. I'm not here to blame you for anything. Mrs. Jenkins assured me you had nothing to do with those bullies being hurt."

"Then, what are you asking?"

"Your gift ... you still have, right?"

Grandma asked, almost whispering, standing close to me.

"I don't know what you mean, my gift. I thought I wasn't supposed to talk about it, right?"

My voice is cracking; my throat feels dry and tight.

"Don't worry, skarbie, you did good! You helped your friend. Hug *babula*, okay!"

Grandma said, smiling with her arms stretched out. Running into her arms and hugging her back is one of the greatest feelings in the world. I quickly let her go; she hangs on to me and studies me. She finally lets me go.

We didn't say anything more. She had a thousand questions and was in no hurry to ask either.

CHAPTER NINE

SATURDAY AT THE HOSPITAL

Keeping Chrissy safe in her seat with the seat belt on her has become a significant challenge. She's too little for these seat belts to keep her safe if something happens. I let her sit on my lap so she can stick her face out of the window while Mrs. Jenkins drives.

"Wee! Ahh!"

Chrissy squeals while sticking her tongue out to lick the air whipping through her face. Her knees dig painfully into my lap.

"Chrissy, please sit still! You can't keep pushing your body out of the window! You'll fall out!"

I'm desperately hanging onto her tiny waist, making sure I roll the window halfway to keep my little sister from falling out. Chrissy won't stop wiggling. Mrs. Jenkins giggles under her breath as she trades glances from focusing on the road and my struggle with a wiggly three-year-old.

"We're almost there, Chrissy. I want you to sit still, please!"

"Okay! I sit down," Chrissy says, with her tongue hanging out; she lowers herself and sat on my lap. She sticks her tongue back into her mouth.

"Wow! She listens to you!"

I wrap my arms around Chrissy and bury my face into her pretty chocolate-brown hair. She turns around, smiling at me.

"Eww, Gi-Gi! No kisses. It's yucky!" Chrissy yells in my face. The Bronco turns into the parking lot of Waitborne General Hospital.

"We're here!" Mrs. Jenkins says with an excited voice. She drives around to find a parking space. The big, gray building that's four stories high is just too familiar to me.

Especially the Emergency Room with the number of times Mom has had to go in for that "accidental fall or pregnant lady clumsiness" excuses she had to make up so that she could get the treatment she needed to recover from the physical abuse from Stepdad.

I'm sure I'll be back here for Mom's C-section in a few more days. So glad Grandma May is showing up; that means she will help take care of Chrissy and clean the house. That also means less opportunity for having to face Stepdad's abuse.

Stay focused, we're here for Danae! One step at a time!

"Okay, ladies, are we ready?" Mrs. Jenkins says with a giant painted smile, waking me from my thoughts.

"Ya! Ya! Ya!" Chrissy yelps, smiling and bobbing in my lap. She slams against my chest. It's getting annoying. Not waiting for permission, I quickly pull up the peg lock on the passenger side door and pull down the handle to open it.

Chrissy doesn't hesitate to jump off my lap, almost falling out of the car, but luckily, I still have my right arm wrapped around her waist.

Mrs. Jenkins doesn't hesitate to jump out of her driver's seat, run around to our passenger side, and pick up Chrissy in her arms.

"Thanks, Mrs. Jenkins! She is such a handful."

I can feel my right arm throbbing; it is such a relief to be able to let go.

"Not a problem, Gi. Let's get going."

Mrs. Jenkins bends down to let Chrissy walk. I quickly grab Chrissy's left hand before she takes off on us.

"Let's stop by the gift shop to pick up a small bouquet. Sound good?" Mrs. Jenkins says, smiling at us.

"Sure, that sounds good."

I give a big smile to Mrs. Jenkins while I stand outside of the car. She pushes down the peg lock before slamming the door on the passenger side.

We make our way toward the main entrance of the hospital. When we open the front glass doors, the pungent smell of chemical cleaners swarms me. This place is so depressing, aside from my family's frequent visits. I'm not a big fan of being at hospitals; it's just a reminder that we're all so fragile. It's so easy to get hurt, get sick, and so many ways to die.

Wow! Can I be any more depressing?

My tennis shoes squeak across the shiny floors of the front area filled with people waiting on couches and chairs that are not too far from a vast front counter, with nurses and clerks checking in.

The hospital's gray, almost gloomy outside appearance doesn't compare to the interior of this giant waiting area. The shiny, just-buffed floors of light blue to dark blue blended color and hints of gold glitter remind me too much of being someplace other than a hospital.

The couches and chairs contrast with the floor since they are all bright yellow with blue flower prints. Chrissy and I continue to follow Mrs. Jenkins' lead by passing the vast front counter with many people milling around it.

Mrs. Jenkins leads us towards a hallway; I could see the gift shop on our left. The fragrance of roses fills my nose as soon as we step in. Mrs. Jenkins walks up to the refrigerator section with the double glass doors. It's filled with a variety of floral bouquets. Some are huge and fancy, while others are small, simple arrangements. I admire a small blue glass vase filled with a handful of daisies. Mrs. Jenkins notices what I am looking at.

"Those daisies look just suitable for Danae, don't you think?"

I nod with a smile. She opens one of the fridge doors; it lets out a suction sound, and cold air whips at us. She grabs the blue vase.

"I think she'll love them!"

I continue to look around and realize Chrissy isn't holding my hand. Panic rise in my chest, and my eyes scan the gift shop. Mrs. Jenkins is already making her way toward the cashier's desk.

"Chrissy? Where are you?"

Keeping my panic in check, I look around. The shop is crammed with sections of greeting cards, candy boxes, and snacks. There's a rack with stuffed animals hanging off them, and there she is. Chrissy admires them with big, shiny brown eyes filled with desire and a big smile. She's eyeballing a cute tan-colored teddy bear with a big, red ribbon wrapped around its neck with a bow.

Her little sandaled feet stand on her tippy toes, her body leaning against the unstable turnstile rack, and her tiny arms reaching for it. Her little tongue sticks out from the left corner of her mouth as if it's going to give her the extra height, she needs to grab the teddy bear. She hasn't seen me yet since I'm just out of sight.

Another adult, a man in his mid-thirties, walks by after admiring the greeting cards section of the gift shop. Chrissy stops reaching and stops smiling. She looks up at the man with big, sad, almost puppy-dog eyes.

"Hey, there, little lady! Do you want that teddy bear?"

Chrissy nods her head shyly. "Hm-Um!"

He had no trouble plucking the teddy bear off the branch arm of the turnstile. His aura is a light blue, showing his compassion towards Chrissy. But there's something familiar about it; I've seen his aura before.

It reminds me too much of Irra's aura, particularly her signature. Her Fae aura has a strip of black on the edge. Sometimes I see it, and sometimes I don't. I've seen something like Rav's, but her signature is more grayish blue. I've never told either one that I can see their signatures. It's troubling because this guy's aura has a signature at the ends of his aura. One second it appears; another second, it disappears. *Could he be Fae?*

"Tank you!" Chrissy says with a sparkle in her eyes and a genuine smile. As soon as the man hands her the teddy bear, Chrissy grabs it greedily. She runs off in my direction and slams into me.

"Look, Gi! That man gave me this teddy bear!" Chrissy holds the bear up to my face. I push it down to look at her.

"That's nice, Chrissy, but we don't have any money to …"

"That's okay! I have the price tag and adding it to my bill," the man says, holding up the tag he pulled off.

That was nice of him, but how will I explain this to Mom or Grandma May?

"Thank you, but I can't pay you back, and we can't take this. My-my parents will be upset," I say in a frustrated voice as I walk up to this tall man with long legs and long arms dressed in a green plaid Oxford shirt and brown slacks. His long sleeves are rolled up just above his elbows. He takes his right hand and runs his fingers through his sandy brown hair, almost bumping his wire-frame glasses off his nose bridge.

He gives me a nervous smile. "It's fine. You can say Chrissy found it. I gotta go."

He quickly walks to the cashier counter, pulls his wallet out of his back pants pocket, and throws a $20 bill along with the tag and greeting card on the counter. The cashier takes the money, and the man is already by the exit.

"Wait! Sir! Don't you want your change?"

He was already out of the door; he turns his head, nods, and waves.

"Hey, keep the change or donate it in that can there!"

Before the cashier can object, he is already gone. This must be the first time she's ever experienced this, and she looks like she is barely out of high school, with long straight, golden blonde hair and green eyes. She shrugs her shoulders, rings up the sale, and puts the bill in the drawer. She takes the change out and put it in a collection tin for a heart disease fundraiser.

"Wow! That's rare! How generous of the guy!" Mrs. Jenkins says right behind me. I nearly jump up in the air, with her just sneaking up on me.

"Oh, my goodness! You made me jump! Danae did the same thing to me just yesterday." My voice trails off when I realize it was only yesterday. Danae was so full of energy. I look down.

"Sorry ' bout that Gi. I was watching what was going on with Chrissy and that guy. You never know about people these days! Hey, you okay?" Mrs. Jenkins says, looking confused by my reaction.

"I'm okay. I'm looking forward to seeing Danae, that's all."

Chrissy grabs my hand with her left hand while hugging her teddy bear tight with her right arm. She leans next to me, looking a little tired.

"Let me pay for the flowers. I have the picture Chrissy made in my purse. Why don't you girls wait out in the hallway? Is that all right?"

Nodding in agreement, I lead Chrissy out the door to wait in the hallway. Leaning against the cool concrete wall feels good, so I close my eyes a little. Trying to make sense of the weird but nice guy buying Chrissy a teddy bear was just too strange. He seemed okay, but there was something familiar about him. He even mentioned my sister by name. Feeling a tapping on my shoulder, I open my eyes.

"You ready?" Mrs. Jenkins says, holding onto the bouquet. Chrissy jumps up and down with delight. She continues to hold on tightly to the bear.

"Yep!"

We walk back to the main entrance area, and the crowd cleared around the front counters. There's an echo of voices of people still milling around as well as others sitting in the waiting area. Walking on the other side of the waiting room, I see a set of elevators in another short hallway. There are a handful of people waiting to get on the elevators. Among them is a familiar face.

Richard is holding a small bunch of flowers and, like usual, is dressed up in a light blue Oxford shirt, black slacks, and penny loafers. He's standing next to a lady, and I assume she is his mother.

She's petite, dumpy around the waist, and her pretty, dark blue dress isn't hiding her fat rolls. Her brown hair is cut at chin length, with big curls, and tamed down with her matching dark blue pillbox hat. She reminds me of June Cleaver, the mom from the TV show *Leave It to Beaver*.

The only difference is June Cleaver has a friendly face; Richard's mom is missing the pleasant part of her stone face. Her nose is long and turned up like someone used a clothespin to keep it from falling off. Her brown eyes look weathered at the corners, with deep lines stretching back towards her hairline. She's wearing a frown, almost a look of instant rejection. We approach them, and Richard recognizes me.

"Hey there, Gina! You here to see Danae, too?" Richard beams a bright smile at me.

"Hi, Richard! Yep, got my little sis here too. Her name is Chrissy," I say, holding Chrissy's hand and pulling her towards Richard. Chrissy hesitates, lets go of my hand and sticks a thumb in her mouth while clutching her bear tightly.

"Say 'hello,' Chrissy. This is my classmate, Richard," I say with a tightness in my voice. Chrissy continues to suck on her thumb and looks down. I'm not going to push her anymore; she's uncomfortable.

"Hello Gina and Chrissy! Is this your adopted mother? Mrs., Mrs. uh ..." Richard's mom interjects with a high-pitched voice.

"Oh! Uh ... I'm Danae's aunt, Laura Jenkins. I offered to take the girls to see her since Gina's mom is at another appointment. Nice to meet you," Mrs. Jenkins says with a boisterous smile while she offers her right hand to Richard's mother.

"Oh ... sorry ' bout that! So, you're Laura Jenkins. I'm Gloria Kline. We talked on the phone yesterday," Richard's mother said, giving a weak smile but shaking Mrs. Jenkins' hand anyway.

The elevator door dings and opens, and we all step in. Mrs. Jenkins hits the "number" button on the panel. The door closes and dings; we can feel the elevator cart lifting us and lights dinging as we pass each floor.

Chrissy hides her face in my shirt while sucking on her thumb. Mrs. Kline, Richard's mom, looks annoyed. She bends down to talk to Chrissy.

"You know you shouldn't suck on your thumb. It's terrible for you." Mrs. Kline's high-pitched, strained voice only makes Chrissy's eyebrows furrow, and she looks away. She buries her face in my shirt and groans. I hold her closer to me for protection, feeling her heart beating heavily against my waist.

Mrs. Kline stands back up, her face pinched as if she smells something rotten.

"Does she understand English? Why doesn't she answer me?" Mrs. Kline retorts rudely to Mrs. Jenkins.

"She understands English just fine. It's the rude strangers she's not used to, and I can't blame her," Mrs. Jenkins says with a calm voice and a smirk on her face. Chrissy looks at Mrs. Jenkins, who gives her a reassuring smile and a wink.

You're my Hero, Mrs. J!

I can't help but smile at Mrs. Jenkins, too. Chrissy takes her thumb out of her mouth and smiles. She continues to cling to her bear and buries her face in it.

The elevator dings to let us all know we've arrived on our floor. Mrs. Kline gives Chrissy and me a disapproving look while her aura emanates a nasty mustard color. Richard looks squeamish and fidgets with the tissue paper wrapped around the flowers. He keeps his eyes down, avoiding my glances.

"Let's go! Everyone!" Mrs. Jenkins says with an enthusiastic voice. Chrissy grabs her right hand, so they both step out first. Richard and his mother step out next, and I stay behind them. We all go a good twenty feet before we stop at the nurses' check-in station. There is a handful of them, and one of them takes notice of all of us approaching. Her round face seems kind, and her big, brown eyes alert. She keeps her eyes on us as Mrs. Jenkins approaches.

"Hello, I'm Danae Jenkins' next of kin, and we're all here to pay her a quick visit," Mrs. Jenkins says with a big smile and polite voice.

"Well, she's got lots of fans today! I'll need the adults to show their driver's licenses and sign this form for all attending children."

She hands out two clipboards with a couple of forms, one for Mrs. Jenkins and the other for Mrs. Kline. The two ladies start filling out the forms at the counter while Richard, Chrissy, and I wait patiently.

I decide to lean against a nearby wall; Mrs. Jenkins gave me the bouquet while she filled out the forms. Richard follows my lead and leans against the wall next to me. He looks a little nervous, his right hand gripping tightly to the flowers as if they are a burden.

"Hey, how ya doin'?" he asks, looking into my eyes. I can tell he doesn't seem sincere, but politely asked me anyway.

"Okay, I guess. Are you in any pain from yesterday?" I ask with genuine curiosity. His aura is a combination of a pale yellow with some blue stripes laced in. He takes a few seconds to figure out what he will say. His eyes dart between his mother, whose back is facing us, and me. He relaxes a little bit since his mother isn't watching him.

"Got some bruises on my chest. It's a bit tender. I had to see our family doctor earlier this morning, but he didn't find anything else. I'm fine," Richard says, trying to look brave, but I'm not convinced for some reason.

"Well, I'm glad to hear you're all right. I'm happy you're here. I'm sure Danae will appreciate you being here," I say, hoping my words will bring him some comfort. Richard nods, stiffens up quickly, and looks down at the floor. I look toward the counter to see how Mrs. Jenkins and Mrs. Kline are doing.

Mrs. Kline finishes and looks directly at Richard. Her gaze goes over to me; she gives me a stern look.

I really don't like this lady.

She walks towards Richard, who starts fidgeting with his shirt.

"Come, Richard, we'll go to the cafeteria for lunch while Mrs. Jenkins and ... the girls visit with Danae," she says authoritatively and grabs his sleeve to pull him away. He gives me an apologetic look and waves quickly.

Mrs. Jenkins slams the clipboard on the countertop and turns around to face Chrissy and me.

"Finally! Let's go, girls!"

Mrs. Jenkins lets out a breath and waves us to follow her. Chrissy grabs Mrs. Jenkins' hand again; she bends down to carry Chrissy instead. Mrs. Jenkins holds my little sister in her arms for a few seconds and gives her an index finger boop on the nose. Chrissy giggles and hugs her back.

"I'm so sorry Chrissy had to experience that horrible woman. I was trying to control myself because I didn't want to scare you kids with my loud mouth telling her where to go. The nerve of that woman!"

I didn't know what else to do but shrug.

"It's okay, Mrs. J. This may surprise you, but I'm used to people like Mrs. Kline. I can't do much about it, I suppose."

Mrs. Jenkins gives me a look of disbelief.

"Good grief! You poor thing! I-I didn't realize how much people discriminate." Chrissy squirms in her arms.

"Where's Di-Di?" she demands. Mrs. Jenkins smiles at her.

"You're right! Let's find Di-Di!"

Mrs. Jenkins picks up her pace; she almost leaves me behind.

"Wait up! You're walking too fast!"

A nurse, who just happens to be walking by, puts her index finger to her lips.

"Sorry!"

She gives me a thumbs-up to let me know it's all right and continues walking in the opposite direction. Mrs. Jenkins steps into a room on her left. I pick up my pace, trip on my feet, and almost drop the daisy bouquet I'm still holding.

Mrs. Jenkins and Chrissy give out screams of delight in the room. I finally catch up and walk in, smiling.

Danae is in bed with an IV tube in her left arm; she's resting in a half-reclined position wearing a light gray hospital gown. Her caramel brown hair is tied back into a low ponytail, and shadows under her eyes tell me she hasn't slept much. Mrs. Jenkins briefly hugs Danae while Chrissy jumps up and down.

Danae gives both a weak smile; she turns her head in my direction. I walk up to Danae's side and present the daisy bouquet.

"Hey there! Your aunt bought you these."

I give her a quick hug. Danae moans, so I let go immediately.

"So sorry! Did I hurt you?" Danae shakes her head and struggles to sit up from the bed.

"Just sore. I have bandages around my chest, got a cracked rib."

Danae props herself up to sit and grabs the daisies to admire them.

"Thanks for the flowers. Daisies are my favorite!"

Mrs. Jenkins pulls out Chrissy's drawings from her purse. "Almost forgot these! Our little artist drew this for ya!" Mrs. Jenkins remarks and hands the paper to Danae.

Danae smiles brightly at all of us and especially Chrissy. She looks at the drawing for a second, then puts it on the bedside table near her, along with the vase of daisies.

"You're so thoughtful, Cookie Monster! Thank you! Wait! Is that your bear?" Danae asks Chrissy, smiling with pride, holding the bear up.

"Ya! A nice guy buy dis for me! I call him Yogi Bear!"

She climbs up on Danae's left side of the bed. Danae's eyebrows raise, and she smiles back.

"Whoa! Chrissy, be careful!" I say, pulling Chrissy, who resists me, off the bed.

"Yo! I'm not broken, not much. Come here, Chrissy! Sit by me!"

Danae's arms reach out; Chrissy rushes back onto the bed and sits quietly by Danae's side. Mrs. Jenkins and I each grab a chair to sit closer to Danae.

"So, some random guy bought Chrissy a teddy bear? Weird!" Danae seems just as surprised. Chrissy offers Yogi to Danae. She inspects the bear with a smile and hands it back to Chrissy.

"Did you charm the guy with your big puppy-dog eyes and cute smile?"

"She's a little charmer. She took off on Gina here, so I kept an eye on her. It was nice of the guy," Mrs. Jenkins says in a matter-of-fact voice.

"Yeah, she gave me quite a scare. So ... how's the hospital food here? Anything good?"

My stomach was quietly rumbling just thinking about food.

"So typical, Gi! Always thinking of food. I was too drugged out to eat my breakfast. I managed to get a couple of bites of cold scrambled eggs and some O.J., but that's about it." Danae's voice is steady as she leans against Chrissy on the bed.

"I bet the nurses made you eat anyway. Right?" Mrs. Jenkins says accusingly, her smile frozen in place.

"Yeah! It was almost like you were there. You put them up to it?" Danae gives her aunt a cockeyed stare, smiling slowly.

"Didn't have to! They're just doing their job. Silly girl!" Mrs. Jenkins winks at Danae.

A figure shows up in the doorway, a police officer.

"Knock, knock. I'm Officer Banedridge. Can I come in?"

Mrs. Jenkins stands up from her chair, looking startled. She walks up to the cop and grabs him by the arm. She whispers words I can't hear and steps into the hallway with him.

"What's he doing here?" Danae looks annoyed. I shrug my shoulders with my palms up.

"So ... when do you get to leave the hospital?"

She gives me a blank stare, then shrugs her shoulders.

"I'm hoping I could leave tomorrow. They want to keep an eye on me 'cause of my concussion. I guess..."

Danae becomes quiet, and Chrissy curls up next to her. They both hold onto Yogi Bear. I look around this room, it's plain and empty. The window to the left of Danae's bed doesn't have a curtain, but blinds. Everything is all white or gray; it doesn't feel right. It's just too sterile and not comforting for someone who needs to heal.

I must be hungry, and my thoughts are running away with me.

Richard walks in, carrying his paper-wrapped flowers. His appearance startles all three of us. Chrissy gasps in surprise and buries her face in her teddy bear. Danae's face also looks surprised.

"Hi, Richard! Nice flowers!" Danae says with a pleasant voice. Richard's worried face changes to a small smile with raised eyebrows.

"Hi, Danae, I'm glad to see you're awake, and these flowers are for you, obviously."

He places them on the bedside table next to Danae and quietly sits in an empty chair.

"Thanks, that's very nice of you! I thought I saw you hurt, but so much of it was a blur." Danae casts her eyes on her hands resting on her lap.

"I'm sorry I couldn't help, but I couldn't believe what I saw with Robert and them." Richard's voice sounds strained; his cheeks turn a couple of shades red.

"A lot happened, you guys; we all were hurt. Our minds can get confused after what we've gone through."

I hope they don't ask questions as to how Robert and the rest stay suspended in the air

"Honestly, I thought I was dreaming like I was in some crazy Bugs Bunny cartoon. I thought that Robert and them were tied and gagged by some invisible rope. Sounds crazy, right?" Danae pleads with Richard and me, hoping we will both agree.

"You did say that you have a concussion and that the doctors want to keep you here another day. Is seeing things a symptom of concussions?" I ask Danae and Richard, knowing that's not a typical symptom. They both shrug their shoulders.

"Maybe it's something you can ask your doctor or a nurse." Richard's voice trails off, his eyes looking out the window.

"All I saw was Robert or someone coming out from behind a tree to stop you, Danae, and you went down. That's when Richard and I tried running towards you, but we were attacked too," I say, trying not to sound too nervous.

"That sounds about right! That's what I saw too!" Richard agrees with me, but Danae looks troubled and stares at me for a while. She reaches over to hold Chrissy's hand. Chrissy fell asleep while we were talking. We hear footsteps and louder conversations just outside the door.

Officer Banedridge and Mrs. Jenkins, along with Mrs. Kline, walk in.

"Georgina Trabeck, I want to ask you a few questions."

Officer Banedridge looks directly at me. Everyone casts their eyes in my direction. Sweat breaks out over my nose and back. My talisman feels warm against my chest. Mrs. Jenkins can read my uneasiness.

"It's okay, Gina, I got permission from your mother to allow the officer to ask you a few questions, and I can be present when he asks. Is that okay with you?" Mrs. Jenkins asks me, trying her best to smile.

"I guess so ..."

I stand up and look at Danae and Richard. They both give me a sad look. Luckily, Chrissy is fast asleep for now. Officer Banedridge and Mrs. Jenkins follow me out of the room. I am picking up my pace, searching for a private spot down the long hallway. There are three comfy chairs parked by a lab. I pick the one closest to the lab entrance. Mrs. Jenkins and the cop choose the other chairs. As soon as he sits down, he pulls out a small writing pad and a pen.

"Are you ready, Miss Trabeck?" The officer's voice has a business-like tone. I nod my head.

"Tell me what took place yesterday. Do your best to recall what you experienced." he says, looking into my eyes. I quickly look away; his stares bother me.

"Danae, Richard, and I just got off the school bus, and we all walked home together. Danae was walking ahead of us, then started running, leaving Richard and me behind. She was several feet ahead of the path we took. There are a lot of big oak trees in the area, so when Danae ran past a couple of them, someone either pushed her or punched her down. She fell backward and landed on her back. Richard and I screamed for her, tried to run toward her, and were both ambushed by Robert and Walter. There were three other boys there too. That's all I remember."

The officer studies me for a while. He seems guarded, hopefully not against me. He keeps his gaze on me. Refusing not to let him make me feel small, I stare back in defiance.

"Do you remember anything else? Doesn't matter how small the detail." He sits back in his chair, writing on his notepad.

"When I got close enough to try to help Danae, who was already passed out on her back, I recognized that it was Robert O'Malley who hurt Danae. Richard was outnumbered by Walter and two other boys beating him. I couldn't help him. Danae tried to help me, but I felt something strike me in the back, and that's all I remember until the ambulance came." I rest back in my chair; my stomach feels tight. He looks at Mrs. Jenkins and then back to me.

"So, you're saying you passed out? How did you manage to wake back up?" he asks skeptically, not taking his eyes off me. His thinning gray hair on top of his head reminds me of leftover cotton candy barely hanging onto its paper cone.

"I don't know. I only remember feeling pain in my back and falling on my face. I don't know when I woke up. I wanted to stay by Danae's side. I was afraid she was going to die. I was afraid both Richard and I were going to die. People were standing around watching what was happening but didn't do anything about it, "I snapped back, feeling my talisman burning hot against my skin. My aura is seeping out, rising from me and moving towards the officer. I can't help but stare in its direction.

Officer Banedridge turns his head to see what I am looking at. He doesn't see anything, then directs his gaze back to me. That breaks my concentration; my aura drops then disappears.

Wow! Just like that!

"Are we done?" I'm growing anxious and impatient. The officer reads over what he wrote and puts the pad back into his shirt pocket.

"I think we are," the officer says, looking somewhat disappointed. He gets up from the chair and motions for Mrs. Jenkins to talk to him privately. That is my cue to go back to Danae's room.

CHAPTER TEN

PEARL NECKLACE

The visit with Danae wore me out, mainly from the stress of talking to Officer Banedridge and putting up with Richard's witchy mother. Even though she's a real piece of work, Danae and I found out it was Mrs. Kline who called for an ambulance. She was concerned about Richard not coming home at his usual time. When she saw that Walter had ambushed him, she ran back into the house to call Mrs. Jenkins and 911 for an ambulance.

Hopefully, Richard doesn't get punished for hanging out with the likes of Danae and me. I'll find out soon enough.

"Hey, you all right? Penny for your thoughts?" Mrs. Jenkins says, sitting in the driver's seat, taking us back home. Chrissy is in the back seat, taking another nap. She's curled up with her teddy bear, and her right thumb is in her mouth. I wish I could easily tune out from this world like my little sis. I look back at Mrs. Jenkins who is keeping her eyes on the road.

"Hmmm? Yeah, I'm all right. Just got a lot on my mind. Thanks for lunch. I enjoyed my turkey-and-swiss-cheese sandwich."

"No problem! I can tell that the police officer's appearance bothers you. He's just doing his job by collecting information."

"Do you think the officer believed me? I felt he didn't believe anything I said. Did he even question Robert and them? Since they were the ones that started all this!"

I can feel my irritation seeping into my tone, but I continue to study her profile while she drives.

"I'm not sure if he believes you, but I did hear from Mrs. Kline about what she saw. She thought she saw things with Robert and his gang's strange behavior. I can't corroborate what she said, but Danae said the same thing," Mrs. Jenkins says, keeping her attention on the road in front of her.

"Did Richard say anything about that? 'Cause he didn't say anything about it to me." I ask her, curious to see if Richard mentioned anything.

"He didn't say much. It's weird whenever his mother is within earshot, he clams up and does not say anything."

She glances in my direction; I decide to rest my head against the glass window of my passenger front seat. My eyelids grow heavy and let the whole world zoom by while Mrs. Jenkins drives us home.

Feeling my shoulders shaking back and forth, I open my eyes to see Mrs. Jenkins standing in front of me. She opens the passenger side door with her right hand on my right shoulder.

"Hey, lady, we're here!"

Opening my eyes slowly, twisting around, I look in the back seat; it's empty.

"Is Chrissy in the house already?" I ask, rubbing my eyes with the back of my hand.

"She's inside. Your grandmother came and got her."

Mrs. Jenkins is patiently waiting for me to get out of her car. The bags under her eyes, slumped shoulders, and vacant look tell me she's had a long day.

"Thanks for taking Chrissy and me to visit Danae. And for being next to me when the officer took my statement."

I give Mrs. Jenkins a sympathetic smile. I jump out of the car and land on my feet. The Bronco is high off the ground compared to Stepdad's station wagon.

"You're welcome, young lady! Well, I'm going to hit the hay for a while before I go back to see Di this evening. Have a good afternoon."

Mrs. Jenkins closes my passenger door. She waves quickly and walks towards her mobile home. I wave back and walk a few feet away toward my home. Not having any fence between the yards is convenient so I can dash to the front door.

Stepping into my home, smelling a familiar aroma from the kitchen makes my stomach grumble. Pots and pans are filled with excellent food, with steam seeping from their lids. I look in the living room to see Grandma May on the couch, watching TV with Chrissy sitting quietly on the floor. She is stacking wooden blocks on top of each other and knocking them down with her new teddy bear. Grandma looks back at me with a small smile; she's wearing a light green duster with yellow flower prints. She's in the middle of her needlepoint project and barely paying attention to the television.

"Dinner will be ready in an hour, skarbie. Did you have a good visit?" Grandma asks with genuine interest, glancing toward me and focusing on her sewing.

"It was all right. Danae gets to go home tomorrow. Whatever is cooking smells perfect, Mi Ma! I can't wait! Do you need some help? Want me to make some biscuits?" I ask, offering to help with the cooking because she's Mi Ma. Grandma gives me a warm smile. Her aura is a lovely cotton-candy pink.

"There's some fruit salad in the fridge. It will hold you over till dinner."

I didn't waste any time taking three giant steps to the kitchen. Helping myself to some fresh fruit salad in a big glass bowl, I grab a clean bowl and a spoon and get to scooping out some fresh fruits. There are fresh-cut strawberries, cantaloupes, pineapples, and honeydew melon. I take my bowl with a fork and sit down next to Grandma.

"I'm glad to hear your friend will be coming home. I will pray for her recovery. Those bullies need to be punished! I tell you!" Grandma says with an air of righteousness, pointing her right index finger at nobody in front of her.

"I don't know what to think about those bullies. I get the feeling they won't get punished, and kids like me will always be looking over our shoulders," I say sadly. I stop eating. I've lost my appetite.

They're going to get away with it! You know that!

"Have faith, *skarbie*. The bad guys get theirs sooner or later," Grandma says with pride. She goes back to her sewing. Chrissy seems at peace, playing with her toys.

"So, is Mom and St-St-, I mean Dad, home?" I ask, wondering why the house seems so quiet. The television volume is so low that it becomes a low-level noise that lulls me to sleep. It is only Grandma's voice that brings me back from my drowsiness.

"Your father said he has to work at the base today, and I don't know where your mother went. She said she wanted to go for a walk."

Grandma puts her sewing down on her lap. She stares at me for a few good seconds. The concern is growing inside of me; something isn't right.

"How long has Mom been gone?" I ask Gran, my talisman feeling warm against my chest.

"I haven't been keeping track. I've been too busy making dinner until I got Chrissy. I know she left right before you ladies came back," Grandma says, her aura turning from pink to light green. I can tell her curiosity is growing. I get up from the couch and hold onto my fruit bowl. I'm standing over her and Chrissy.

"Do you mind if I go look for Mom? It seems strange she wants to go out for a walk. Did she seem okay?" I ask, trying my best not to sound too worried.

"She seemed all right. Maybe anxious, she said she couldn't rest. Even when we returned from her appointment, she just wanted to go outside. I thought some fresh air would do her some good." Grandma's eyebrows furrow; she puts her sewing project next to her and starts to wring her hands.

"Why don't you leave your bowl on the coffee table and look for your mom? If it makes you feel better." Smiling at Mi Ma, I reach over to hug her. Grandma waves me off, picks up her round, wooden frame with cloth strapped in, and goes back to her needlepoint.

"I won't be long. See you guys in a few," I say, opening the door and stepping out. I can tell the sun is about to set, but there is still enough daylight to walk in the neighborhood.

What troubles me is that Mom couldn't have gone too far with her big belly, but she's been gone for a good thirty minutes, at least.

Where could she have gone?

Stepping into the front yard, I look to my right towards the Jenkins' home. The Bronco is still parked in the driveway, so Mrs. Jenkins is home.

Maybe Mom's over there? No, it can't be. I would've seen her earlier. So, where is she? She doesn't know anybody else in this mobile home park!

My heart picks up a few more beats, so walking might calm me. The air is calm; plenty of kids riding their bikes, ladies out in the yard tending to their gardens, or just enjoying a day out on the patio with their little ones running around. The smell of fresh-cut grass lingering in the air and hearing a lawn mower cutting grass from a distance tells me that summer is just around the corner. My feet seem to be on autopilot, just turning around one corner, then crossing the street to another corner. Some people see me and give me a wary look, while others don't see me at all.

Why do I have to be so different? Why can't I be like every-one else? Why do they treat me as if I'm less of a human being than them?

I look around, trying to focus on where my mother could be, and now I may have a clue. I'm back by the oak trees, the same area where Danae, Richard, and I were attacked. My heart drops. Sweat is running down my back as I look to my right and see Robert's home.

The run-down mobile home with the rusted sidings, peeled paint, and broken windows covered with wood or cardboard sits quietly, staring at me. Walking closer to it, I try to keep myself out of sight by hiding behind their shaggy bushes. The yard is sparse, with tons of weeds, bare spots of dirt, and some grass growing in random patches.

I am sneaking into the yard, curious to see if anyone is home. Walking towards the front right side of the mobile home that doesn't have any windows, I can hear voices inside. It sounds much like an argument between two women. I rest my right ear against the side of the mobile home- my curiosity was getting the best of me.

"Get out of my house! Or I'll punch you in your pregnant stomach!" A woman's raspy voice sounds like that of Robert's mother, Phyllis.

The other woman shouts back with pure anger. "You gimme back my pearl necklaz, you putang!"

The mobile home shakes and shimmies side by side, some-thing physical is going on. And that was my mother's voice on the other side. Then I hear: Crash! Bang! And more struggling.

Worried about my pregnant mother, I must do something. I close my eyes and concentrate on her name, whispering.

"Irra! Please Irra! I need you!" My right hand clutches my talisman under my T-shirt; I feel its warmth in my palm.

I open my eyes and look around and see the leaves of the bushes and the oak tree leaves rustling.

Irra! Please hear me!

Feeling hopeless and too impatient to wait for Irra any longer, I do the next best thing. Distraction! I walk towards the front door and knock loudly.

"Hello! Hello! Is everyone all right?" I shout between banging on the front door. There's a doorbell, so I push it constantly but don't hear any sound of a bell ringing or buzzing.

It must be broken! Darn it! Back to banging on this door!

"Open up! Mom! I know you're in there! It's me, Gina!" I shout again; in fact, I am so loud a couple of the nearby neighbors come into the yard. And, of course, it's just a nosy middle-aged lady and her husband just standing and watching.

What's with these people?

Meanwhile, there's still a lot of yelling and thrashing inside Phyllis's mobile home. I look back at the nosy neighbors, and I am about to ask for their help.

A quick flash of wind rushes by, rustling the trees and bushes. The wind becomes more robust, a lot more forceful. I can feel my body swaying away from the door.

The neighbors look around, trying to figure out if it's going to rain. The nosy lady screams in her husband's face. "It's gonna rain, Hal! C'mon!"

Her zombie-like husband shrugs his shoulders and follows his wife back home. The wind picks up to almost hurricane strength; dust blows around me. I wipe the tears from my eyes, I see a blurry figure. Blinking a few more times, my vision becomes a little transparent. It's Irra standing before me.

"Aye, What do you need?" she asks, showing concern on her face. Her long, silver hair flows around her body as she lifts an index finger, rotates it, and the strong winds die. She puts her finger down and turns her attention to me.

"Please help me, Irra. I think my mother might be in danger! I know she's in there arguing with Phyllis! Nobody answered the door!" I plead with Irra. She gives me a sad look.

"Why would your mother be here? I don't understand."

Irra's eyebrows furrow, her lips pull downward.

"This Phyllis woman is the same woman that's having an affair with my stepdad. I saw him give Phyllis my mother's pearl necklace. I think that's the reason why my mom's here! She wants it back. It's the only thing my dad—our dad—gave her!"

Tears are running down my face, and I'm feeling desperate. The mobile home's shaking and swaying have become stronger. Then, Bang! Something or someone has crashed against the front door. Then there's a thud!

Irra takes her index finger and rotates it a couple of times. She whispers some words that don't sound familiar to me.

"Isha na, ra na!"

Visible wisps of cool air flow out of her lips. The front door flies open, and my mother's limp body falls out. She's covered with blood, clutching onto her pearl necklace in her right hand and holding a bloody knife in her left. Her eyes are closed, and she is breathing in a ragged rhythm.

I am picking up Mom in my arms, trying my best to be brave. She doesn't appear to have any open wounds on her.

So, where is the blood coming from?

Mom jerks up, lets go of the knife, and doubles over.

"Ah! The bebe is coming! Gi! Help me!"

Mom cries in pain, and water bursts out between her legs. She's squirming violently as the pain becomes intense.

"She's going to have the baby! Hold on!" Irra shouts, with worry in her voice. Her shimmery, white wings expand from her back, flapping slowly to lift her. She crosses her arms and quickly expands them outward to create another windy condition, but with waves of white, soft, glitter light thinning out into a long ribbon. It gently wraps around my mother's body, lulling her to fall asleep. My mother levitates while curled up in a ball.

"I will send your mother back home to her bedroom, but I can't guarantee that she might not give birth there," Irra says in a calm voice.

Phyllis bursts out from the front door. "Help me! She cut me! Please help me!" Phyllis yelps, crawling on her hands and knees. Blood is gushing out from the side of her neck; her tattered gray bathrobe is soaking with so much blood.

That's where the blood is coming from! Oh, God! Mom stabbed her!

I can only stand there and watch her beg so pathetically. Phyllis reaches out with her right hand, expecting me to grab it; the horror on her face, along with her thin brown aura barely visible, tells me she is losing too much blood.

I don't know why I'm so frightened! I can't help her ... she's the enemy!

"Isha na, a- ran na!" Irra's voice is louder but silky smooth. A storm of windy rain comes down on Phyllis and me.

"Irra! What's going on?" I yell, confused and getting drenched by the second while the storm becomes stronger, louder, and scarier. My wet clothes weigh me down, robbing me of all body heat. My skin is numb with the cold; I can feel my fingers and toes getting stiff. My lips tremble, and I can no longer talk.

"Close your eyes, Gina! Concentrate on a place that brings you happiness and stay there. This will all be over soon."

Irra is floating in the air with her arms, controlling this storm. Not having any other choice, I do what she tells me.

Closing my eyes, I let the talisman warm me, dry me. I think about being in bed, curled up with a favorite book. There's a cup of hot chocolate on my bedside table. All is quiet and so peaceful I can feel myself drifting off to sleep. My eyes are like lead weights, slammed shut as I drift off. It's not raining on me anymore. I'm warm and dreaming about sleeping peacefully.

"Ah!" Mom is screaming at the top of her lungs.

My heart is beating violently in my chest, and I bolt straight up in my bed. Scrambling from my bedroom to her bedroom, I see Grandma May sitting behind my mother on the bed.

Mom's back is resting against Mi Ma's chest with her legs spread out. Chrissy is crying at the foot of Mom's bed. She's clutching onto her teddy bear for dear life.

"Ahh! NO! I don't wanna have my bebe here! No!" Mom screams in sheer terror, her legs thrashing around, almost kicking Chrissy, who shrieks louder and buries her face in her teddy bear.

I have had enough of this. I reach over to Chrissy and pick her up in my arms. She wraps her little arms around my neck.

"Skarbie, can you take your sister to your bedroom? The ambulance will be here any minute now. Okay?" Grandma says to me, looking shaken while rubbing Mom's shoulder. I nod and turn around to head back to my bedroom.

"Sh! It's okay now, Cookie Monster," I whisper into Chrissy's ear to calm her down. I lay her down on my bed, she didn't hesitate to pull the covers over her and her bear. I can hear her sucking on her thumb.

Still tired and extremely confused, I lie next to Chrissy. She rolls away from me and falls asleep. It's comforting to listen to her quietly snore. Trying to make sense of what's happening, I'm immediately distracted by the ambulance siren going off in front of my home.

The red and blue lights flash on and off through my window. Chrissy stirs from the loudness, so I rub her back to calm her again. I can hear her stick her thumb back into her mouth. I roll over to my right side, waiting for what feels like forever for my sister to go to sleep.

I hear Grandma's footsteps moving to the front door to let the paramedics in. There is so much commotion from Mom's bedroom that it is hard to ignore her screaming and moaning. Thankfully, Grandma can calm her down so Mom can cooperate with the paramedics.

Looking over at my alarm clock, I see it's 7:00 p.m. I guess Irra fixed the timeline, and I'm grateful she did. I have a ton of questions for her. Then I sit back up on my side of the bed. There's one thing missing from what took place.

"Wait! What happened to Mom's pearl necklace? I almost forgot about it."

Hoping I didn't wake Chrissy, I look over at her. She's out, snoring.

Still, I hope Mom's necklace hasn't been left behind.

"Irra! Yo, Irra- can you hear me?" I hiss while grabbing my talisman over my nightgown; I close my eyes to concentrate.

Even though my bedroom window is closed, her translucent gown, matching her dragon fly wings flows in the air. A shadow in the corner of my room appears.

"Irra? Is that you?" I can feel the hairs on the back of my neck stand up.

"Aye! It's me!"

Irra steps out from the shadow. She looks grim and wears a pearl necklace. It glows on her the same way my talisman shines on me. My eyes target the pearl necklace as I quickly sit up in my bed.

Irra grips the pearl pendant with her right hand; it's still shimmering between the cracks of her fingers.

"Are you gonna take that off? It belongs to my mom!" My voice is hostile, throat tight. Irra's gaze is intense; her gray eyes lighten to a glowing silver. Her lips tighten to a thin line, and her eyebrows furrow.

"I can't ... I believe this is my talisman. My powers are at full strength now, so I could erase the memory of the events around this talisman. I'm sorry your mother will not have her necklace, but at least she won't have any memory of ever receiving it," Irra explains in an apologetic tone. Her eyes go back to her normal gray, and her face relaxes. She takes a few steps to sit next to me on my bed.

"I can't and won't give the necklace back to your mother."

Irra's words sound final. She reaches over to hold my hand, but I flinch away.

"I think this is a good time for us to talk about your talisman too. You'll be turning thirteen and typically go through a forthing ceremony. It's a coming-of-age ritual like human celebrations for when a girl transforms from a child to a woman. You should've received your talisman then, but we're in an unusual circumstance." Irra gives me a sad look, then looks away.

"So ... what's gonna happen now? Do I go through a forthing thingy too? Or is that even possible since I'm a human?"

"I don't think so. I took the talisman from the queen's grand corridor before she knew it existed. Every time a Fae child is born, a new talisman appears on our family's crest or an heirloom table. Sure enough, I found it. I felt you're half Fae. I saw your signature from my visions. I had to find out if it was true."

"What if that wasn't true, and you still gave me the talisman? What would've happened?"

"You-you probably would've perished excruciatingly, my child."

"And yet you gave it to me anyways? What the heck!" I say, feeling the pulse in my neck pounding. My talisman lights up under my nightgown.

"That's another thing we need to discuss: controlling your emotions because your talisman will react to it. I noticed you have almost no control. You allow your aural powers to hurt others." Irra's words sound harsh and judgmental.

"Well, it's not like I was using it to be evil towards others! Oh my God! I only live with a violent stepfather and put up with bloodthirsty bullies who want to hurt me for my skin color! You know what? I would've thrown this stupid talisman away if I could. I don't want it!" I shout back at Irra. She puts her index finger to her lips to remind me there's a sleeping child next to us. Trying to calm down, I sit quietly, not saying a word. She puts her finger down by her side. I still can't help but feel slighted by her.

I don't know if she can be trusted.

Crossing my arms in front of my chest only makes her frown.

"Regardless, your talisman belongs to you and only you! It picked up your signature and connected to your aura. And if you're wondering why your mother didn't experience a similar fate with my talisman, it's because she's human, not another Fae." Irra scolds me under her breath, so she doesn't raise her voice. We stare at each other for a few good seconds.

"I don't see the point of having this talisman. It's only added to my confusion. If I already have aura powers that react toward protecting me, why do I even need this?"

"You're only twelve years old, half human and half Fae. I don't know what my Father was thinking to procreate with a human. It's beyond me, and it's undoubtedly overwhelmed Rav. It's strictly forbidden for anyone from the Other World to have any intimate relations with humans! I sent Rav away to another portal of time, but it won't take long before she figures out how to return here. She will not be as cooperative as me, and I'm sure she will send her changelings on you for a bounty! Do you understand? I know you didn't choose this life, but here we are. You deal with it! You will use your talisman to gain control of your powers, or you will be no different from our father! I mean it! If you succumb to revenge, it will hurt you or someone you care about." Irra's voice is steady and stern. Her eyes search me. She leans closer, but I move away.

"This is too much! I-I don't understand, and I don't want to! I didn't ask for any of this! I want to be a normal girl with friends, make good grades, and have a loving family. Is that too much to ask?" I say in a desperate tone. Irra reaches over to grab my right hand; I pull away. I'm not in any mood to be touched. I'm angry and frustrated at everything and everyone. She hangs onto my hand anyway and gazes into my eyes.

Those gray eyes almost seem to glow like a soft flashlight.

"You've also been dealt a cruel hand in life, an abusive stepfather, an insecure mother who comes from poverty, racist bullies at school, and an apathetic neighborhood. I don't understand how humans can be cruel to each other. You judge each other so superficially! Who cares about your skin color or different languages and cultures? You're all still humans. Try dealing with bridge trolls, changelings, wood elves, and pixies, not to mention the variety of water and air creatures! Yet we manage to live in cohesion in the Other World. War was unheard of until humans existed," Irra says sadly. She lets go of my hand. Her aura that's been a misty white has gotten thicker, with tinges of red on the outer edge.

"I still don't see what this has to do with me! I'm not here to cause a war. I want to be a normal human kid who will grow up as an average human adult. Right now, all I can do is protect myself. If my aura powers do that, so be it! Otherwise, your presence is more of a danger to me. So, if there is a bounty for me because I'm some abomination, I blame you for bringing it!" I hiss with uncontrolled fury. Irra's eyes flash from a muted gray to a silver shimmer. She levitates as her wings expand over me. Her aura is a smoky red cloud expanding and filling up the ceiling. For the first time, her fury scares me. I cower back against my headboard.

"Hear this human child. You're lucky we're related! This is my last warning before I leave! I've already told you that Stepdad is not the only monster in your life, but he will break you. He will push you in your weakest moment until you can't take anymore and strike back with revenge. If you let your aural powers cross over to kill someone in retribution, there will be repercussions. I will not come back to clean up your mess!" Irra's wings flap frantically, then she takes an index finger to make a circular motion. Her body emits a massive flash of light and then disappears.

Not sure how to feel about Irra flashing out on me, I'm

relieved this conversation is over. Now I'm so tired, I wonder if anyone could die from complete exhaustion. I certainly feel that way.

Rolling off the bed since I've been sitting on top of my bed covers all this time, I crawl under to hide from the world. I can't think anymore; I want some sleep. It will be all right; I'm not one for revenge anyway. She's blowing it all out of proportion.

You think? What are the repercussions she mentions? Hmmm?

CHAPTER ELEVEN

TO BE NORMAL

It's been three weeks of living like I'm an ordinary girl again or ever. Danae is recovering from her hospital visit. Even though she can't go outside for recess or attend physical activity class, we still hang out at each other's homes.

Between working on our science fair project, math homework, and studying for exams, we hang out for sleepovers on Friday nights, went to the Spring Festival last weekend, and ride our bikes with Richard on a Sunday afternoon. So, this is what it's like to live like an average American kid.

Even Mrs. Young backed off from harassing me, and I continued to do well at school. I'm having the time of my life. Grandma is still with us to take care of the house and Chrissy. Mom is taking a while to recover from her C-section but doing well.

Grandma enjoys her time with her newborn granddaughter, Natalie, while Mom takes catnaps to reserve her energy for the late-night feedings. I'm not being used as a built-in babysitter for the first time.

Stepdad is a different story because many demands have

been put on him at work; he comes home later than usual. He must answer Grandma not my mother. This is the first time I've ever witnessed his behavior with his mother, and it's not pretty. She is the one who oversees their relationship.

Today after I come home from studying at Danae's house, we have dinner later than usual. It is only 7:30 p.m.; we had just finished dinner, so I help Grandma with the dishes. Chrissy sits with Mom in the living room. Mom is sitting on the couch, giving little Natalie her bottle of formula.

Stepdad steps in, looking wary and exhausted. His green air force fatigues are covered with a lot of motor oil; his face is red and sweaty. He looks at Mi Ma and me but doesn't say anything. He walks over to the fridge to grab a beer. Rummaging around looking for his fix, he comes up empty.

"Is there any more beer, Ma?"

Stepdad, looking annoyed, keeps his gaze only on Grandma. This is fine by me; I can focus on drying the dishes and then go to my room.

"You ran out! It's time you dry out too! You have another daughter, and it's high time for you to be a father!" Grandma says, her eyes squinting with anger. Her aura is a purple-bluish tint; it's typical whenever she's around him. I guess her disappointment in him angers her every day. He slams the fridge door hard and stares down at me.

I could see the black cloud hanging around his neck become thicker, darker, and more constricting. He clutches at his neck but can't seem to loosen the grip that tightens daily.

Grandma gives him a look of confusion, watching his odd behavior, but doesn't mention it.

"Why don't you grab your plate wrapped in foil in the fridge? There's also some lemonade too." Grandma says in her best cheerful voice. She gives me a quick wink.

"I'm out of here!"

Stepdad steps away from the fridge. Grandma steps in front of him, blocking him from returning to the front door.

"Where do you think you're going, Ofiara? You come home late every night! You don't spend time with your family and your newborn daughter! I oughta slap you upside your head! Get out now! Jestes rozczarowagiem!" Grandma screams right in Stepdad's face.

He forces his gaze into Grandma's eyes and spits his words right into her face.

"I'll tell you who's the loser and disappointment, dear mother, it's that whore who married me so that she can bring her illegitimate child to the US! I'm done here!" he says with all the vile venom he can conjure. He gives me a wicked smile and laughs at Grandma and me.

"You! Get out! *Talunan!*"

Mom's voice trembles, breathing heavily and labored. She puts her hands on my shoulder; it's sweaty and hot. Feeling her fear near me, tears well up in my eyes, choking back the hate and hurt I feel right now.

Mom walks past me to stand with Grandma. Stepdad moves back; he has a look of defeat on his face. He points his right finger at Mom's face, but she doesn't back off.

She gives him a defiant look with her hands on her side. Grandma helps her stand up to him, and that's cool.

"You're lucky my mother's here. Otherwise, I'll deport you and your stupid freak of a daughter!"

Stepdad's voice is deep and menacing, as he keeps his hateful gaze on my mother. He takes a few more steps backward as if my tiny mother and grandma would ever have the strength to overpower him.

His words cut me deep.

This isn't the alcohol talking this time. It's him.

Not saying another word, he turns around and grabs the car keys from the key hooks next to the front door. He swings the door open and slams it shut. Unfortunately, it wakes up a once peacefully sleeping Natalie in her nearby bassinet; she screams out loud. Mom rushes to an angry Natalie, picks her up, and sways her side to side. Natalie calms down at Mom's rhythmic movements and soothing humming.

Putting the last dry dish away in the cupboards, I hang the kitchen towel on its usual hook by the sink.

"Mi Ma, I'm done. May I be excused? Have a lotta homework to do before I go to bed."

I ask Grandma politely. Sitting with Chrissy on the couch, she nods her head in approval. Before leaving the living room area, I look closely at everyone. Mom looks exhausted, with dark circles around her eyes, gently cradling Natalie in her arms.

She quickly lost much of her pregnancy weight, so she's much more active. I hardly see her eat much, nor does she take any particular interest in Chrissy or me. She can only focus on Natalie.

When Grandma takes over, Mom is usually found napping on the couch. Looking over at Chrissy, she's never seen without her teddy bear. Strangely enough, none of the adults even mention the teddy bear. And I'm not going to say anything either.

Little Sis is happy, and that's all that matters to me. I can't appreciate Grandma any more than I do; she's the adult who's her son's boss. Sadly, I also realize how much she may have limited him as a man who can honor and appreciate women as human beings—trying not to let this evening get to me, especially with Stepdad's hurtful words.

Let the words roll off your back! Words don't matter, remember?

Who am I kidding? I will never forgive or forget those words.

Remember Irra's words! Revenge will cost you, or worse, your loved ones!

Irra's words ring in my head daily. It's hard not to hear them. Speaking of which, it's been wonderful not to feel anger and not feel my talisman heat up under my clothes. I need this break.

I'm making an oath to forget about this talisman and live like an all-human girl who doesn't have any aural powers. Now that Irra left off in a huff, I've accepted that life is back to normal. I am going to bed tonight with a clear mind and at peace with myself.

"Tick, tick, tick," is the sound I hear in my dreams.

"Tick, tick, tick." There it is again! Annoyed by the sound, I open my eyes and look at my alarm clock. The glow-in-the-dark numbers say it's 3:15 a.m.

"Of course, on a school night! I wouldn't want it any other way!"

I whisper to myself, roll out of bed, and walk toward my window. I look out to see if there's a stray dog or cat.

The neighborhood seems so peaceful, but so dark. Even streetlights cause more shadows than illumination. A movement across the street catches my eye.

My home faces a street that separates into a "Y" shape a good twenty feet down from the right side. There's just my mobile home and Mrs. Jenkins' next door. Our backyards face a wooded area that leads to a wetland area. All the other homes are farther down the street. So, there's just the yard across the road with a double-wide mobile home opposite the yard. A row of trimmed hedges borders the yard and the street.

My eyes continue to scan the area across the street and nearby hedges. That's when I spot another movement; it scats out from under the hedges. Then another and another. Several of these little creatures are bigger than rats, but smaller than the typical house cat.

Their eyes glow with a loud orange-red glow, searching for something. As they scan the area, one glances over at my home. My heart drops into my stomach when it locks eyes with me.

My talisman heats and lights up under my nightgown. I duck down and peek over the windowsill. It scurries over, crosses the street, and towards my yard.

Calm down; it probably didn't see you! Why did my Talisman light up now? It hasn't done that in weeks!

I move away from my window, making sure I don't move the curtains.

I let out a long sigh to calm my ragged breathing.

Why are you so scared? You're inside, they're outside. They're probably little swamp creatures hunting for food.

Howling sounds and scrambling footsteps circle my home. The hairs on my arms and the back of my neck stand on end. I bite my lips to keep from screaming. Are they after me? Are they looking for me? I just realized I'm covered in sweat and shaking uncontrollably.

Could these creatures be the changelings that Rav might've sent after me? I don't think Irra would come around this time. She's too upset with me! What am I gonna do?

Crawling back to my bed, hiding under my covers, I close my eyes and do my best to breathe slowly. My talisman isn't helping me since it's been glowing on my chest like crazy. Especially when I was under the window. I was afraid those creatures had already noticed.

The light coming from the pendant glows with so many colors and intensities that it vibrates with a low humming sound. I close my eyes; why, I don't know. It seems like the natural thing to do is relax and shut out everything.

As I focus on its intensity, the humming calms me. The next thing I know is being in a dream-like state surrounded by the colors. Lifting my hand to hold it in front of my face, I point to my nose with my index finger. I can feel the cold, clammy touch of my finger. I pat my shoulder, lift my leg, and then take a few steps forward.

Jinkies! I'm physically here! But where? Let's keep walking around.

Looking past the barrage of a rainbow of lights, I realize I'm floating outside above my home. The dark creatures have surrounded it; they're scratching at the door and the side of the house and trying to jump up to the windows.

They're trying to get in!

They cry in unison, a loud, bloodcurdling scream. One of them looks up at me and lets out a frantic scream. The others look up, growling at me. I see red-orange glowing eyes looking straight up at me in complete darkness. Their growling grows louder and more noticeable.

Lights coming on from the Jenkins' home capture my attention. Maybe I can lead them away from our homes. I take a few steps further left to lead them away, but they just stand there. Some are howling while others growl.

Anger and frustration make me sweat; it doesn't help to have my talisman heating up. The stronger the light it bears, the stronger the creatures below howl and scream at me. My aura is now a bright red, splitting into several strips of ribbons.

Remember what Irra said: You can't let your powers control you!

Then again, she's not here, and I have every reason to let my powers do their thing. I can't help but smile when my aura ribbons dance their way down to the creatures.

One by one, each ribbon approaches a creature. They try to grasp the ribbons with their sharp, glow-in-the-dark teeth. The ribbons yank away from their grasps, which only makes them furious.

While some creatures jump up to catch the ribbon, others are already wrapped in their ribbon noose. Within seconds, all the creatures are choking on a ribbon, and the more they struggle, the tighter the grip around their bodies.

Listening to them struggle and choking on my aura makes me cringe. There are snapping sounds, then screams of pain. Many are still growling, but eventually become pathetic cries. Their sounds of pain and anguish become less and less until they all stop.

The glow from their eyes and teeth becomes dim until there's no light. Now there's nothing but darkness. All is quiet again.

God, that was sickening! I'm so glad it's too dark to see what grossness has taken place!

Closing my eyes, I focus on my aura ribbons to collect and become one again. Each strip is dripping with glowing orange liquid. They shake altogether to sling off the orange fluid. There is a momentary glow in the air, then it disappears.

Looking down to scan the area, it's all back to normal. I close my eyes to focus on being back in my room.

It's such a relief to fight these nasty creatures from hell! And yet it's frightening to think about how much my powers can do without me asking them to work for me. Is this what Irra was talking about?

Opening my eyes again, I find myself lying in bed. Exhaustion settles in; I can barely keep my eyes open. Did I imagine it all? If so, I have one heck of an imagination.

You don't believe that, do you? Being that you're half fae?

So maybe the idea of changelings isn't an unrealistic notion?

Great, more crap to deal with!

Trying my best to find my routine again, I grab my latest read, *The Two Towers*. It's time I put myself in a productive mode. I know it will take me a while to fall back to sleep. After a few minutes of trying to focus on the book, I can't seem to lose myself in the story.

There are too many things dancing around my head. Like a bounty on me from some fairy world because I'm half human, and that's a big no-no or Stepdad showing his true colors in front of my mother and me. His apparent hate for having to care for me is blatant. It's bad enough that he has a wife and two other kids, but I'm the one he truly hates.

I want so much to tell him how I feel, too. How much he

brings misery to my life to say those terrible words in front of me, my mother, and my grandmother. What hurts the most is neither of the women defended me. I think my mother tried to do so, but I'm having difficulty seeing it.

So, what's the point in reading my book when all these thoughts and recalling what happened this evening keep me occupied?

You can't ignore it or bury your face in a book; you need to do something about Stepdad before he does something to you!

Frustration and rage surge through me so much that I throw my book against the opposite wall of my bed. Tears are already flooding my vision; my nose is leaking fiercely. I wipe my nose with the back of my right sleeve. The tears won't stop now, so I roll over to bury my face in my pillow. Letting loose all the tension, frustration, and pain through my bawling is all I can do for now. My body sinks into my bed as I continue to let out all this pain I've been burdened with for years. My pillow is soaking wet with tears. Lifting my head to look for the time on my alarm clock; it says 4:55 a.m.

Great, if I can get a couple of hours of sleep, maybe I can still go to school rested. All this crying is giving me a headache and heavy eyelids. Yielding to this irresistible yawn, I stop fighting it off and give in. That's when my eyes slowly shut; my body relaxes for now. I can't fight it off anymore.

Bang! Bang! Bang!

I keep hearing it, burying myself further down my covers and under my pillow, back to my dreams, back to peace, how I love the peaceful early mornings.

"Gi! Hey! You up? C'mon man! It's me, Danae!"

The voice from the other side of my bedroom door is yelling, and she's banging loudly.

"Georgina! *Skarbie*, wake up! Your friend is here!"

Grandma May's voice bellows from the other side. Somebody opens the door and a draft of air whips in. Footsteps march into my room. I finally peek out from under my pillow. Somebody pulls it off.

"Hey, Yo Gi! How 'bout you get your butt moving so we can start on our science fair project, remember?" an irritated Danae barks out at me. She pulls off my covers. My once sweaty body is drying off and shaking to the cool draft that sweeps over me. I can't stand it any longer and sit straight in my bed without warning anyone. Danae and Grandma look startled, with their mouths gaping open and eyebrows raised. I must look frightening to them; I can feel my eyes burning and dry. I need more sleep but have no choice.

"Okay, okay, I'm up! Please go now so I can dress and brush my teeth!" I growl at whoever is listening.

"Not in any mood to go to school today. Need more sleep!"

"Whoa, Gi, don't you remember? It's a school holiday, so the teachers have an in-service day. We planned on walking through the wetlands to take pictures," Danae says in her usual cheerful voice, which is irritating right now.

"We'll leave you alone to get dressed. I got *nalesniki* with blueberry sauce for breakfast, so get off your *tylka* and get moving, skarbie!"

Mi Ma says, with more patience than Danae.

"Thank you, Mi Ma! I miss your *nalesniki*! Be right there!" I say a little more enthusiastically.

"Wow, what's a Naleesh?"

Danae looks confused, asking her a question. Grandma gives her a big smile.

"It's Polish pancakes and homemade blueberry syrup. You'll love it! Have some while you wait," Grandma says while leading Danae out of my room.

"No arguments here, ma'am!" Danae says in her cheerful voice again.

Grandma closes the door behind them, but she gives me a

quick wink before she does. It's difficult not to smile at Mi Ma.

Rolling out of bed, I quickly grab an old but well-loved blue T-shirt and a ripped pair of faded blue jeans with a big hole in the left knee. Comfort clothes, that's what I'm all about.

Rushing into the bathroom to brush my teeth and comb the tangles out of my hair, I successfully put my wavy hair into a ponytail. I take one last look in the mirror; there are still bags under my eyes and a downward frown on my lips.

Maybe someday you will have a reason to be truly happy. For now, you've got work to do, and that's to stop him in his tracks!

Pushing those horrible thoughts out of my head, I distract myself by sniffing the lovely aroma of Mi Ma's pancakes in the kitchen.

Watching Danae dig into her pancakes, bathed in heavy blueberry syrup, makes me smile. Grandma hands her a bowl of homemade whipping cream, which Danae happily takes and dumps a massive tablespoonful on top of her pancakes.

My mouth waters because I'm next to dig into those fattening but flavorful pancakes. They both look up and smile at me. I notice we are the only three people here in the house.

"Where's Chrissy, Natalie, Mom, and them?"

I ask without mentioning Stepdad, and God forbid addressing him as "Dad" to make Mi Ma happy.

"Your parents took the girls for a drive and a picnic. They need to spend some time as a family," Grandma says absent-mindedly. She is busy serving my plate of pancakes as I pull out a chair to sit in. I can't believe she said that. It feels like a knife tearing into my heart. So, they're a family, and what does that make me?

You're the so-called redheaded stepchild, the oddball nobody wants.

"Wait! Shouldn't Gina ride with them? She's family too!" Danae is confused by Grandma's words. Grandma waves off Danae's response like she is waving off an annoying fly.

"Of course! That's not what I meant, skarbie!"

Grandma gives me an apologetic look. Disgusted by what she said, I drop my fork on my plate. It clanks loudly against the ceramic edge. I sit and stare, fighting like hell from crying like a baby in front of her.

"May I be excused, Grandma? Danae and I have a lot of work for our science fair project."

I ask politely, then glance over at Danae. She gives me a sad look and nods her head.

"You barely ate anything. I need you to take at least three bites. Then, you may be excused," Grandma says with a disapproving look. Knowing how stubborn she can be, I reluctantly pick up my fork, cut three tiny pieces from the top pancake, then dip them in blueberry sauce. I shove all three pieces in my mouth. Chewing for quite some time until there's nothing left to chew. I put my fork down.

"Now, may I be excused?" I ask defiantly, still angry at her. Grandma stares at me harshly for a few seconds. If she's trying to scare me, it's not working. Returning a harsher look, she looks away.

"You're excused. Be home by 5:00 p.m. so you can help me prepare dinner."

"Yes, ma'am," I say respectfully, then push my chair back under the table as quietly as possible.

"Thank you for the lovely breakfast, Mrs., Mr. ..." Danae says, stumbling on how to address Grandma.

"You can call me Mrs. May, little lady!"

Grandma says in a stern voice. She glances in my direction and gives me a disappointed look but says nothing.

Danae and I grab our book bags resting by the front door. I quickly run to the kitchen cupboards to grab a thermos to fill with tap water and put it in my book bag.

We step outside quietly. Taking a deep breath and letting it out all at once calms me. The sun is already bright and beaming in our faces.

"You ready?"

She gives me a thumbs-up and a big smile. We walk around the back of our homes to cross the yard and the wooded area.

CHAPTER TWELVE

SCIENCE FAIR PROJECT

The warm sun beams down on our backs. Danae is busy looking around, taking quick snapshots with her instant camera. It must be nice to afford new cameras; I hear they take excellent pictures in color. The Polaroid instant camera, which pushes out a picture right after clicking, only produces black-and-white shots.

Mom doesn't take many pictures of me, only when I'm sitting next to Chrissy and lately with me holding Natalie for a few seconds. As much as she encourages me to smile, I don't. I have control of my body and nobody else; she can't make me smile if I don't want to. I go out of my way not to smile in her pictures.

You remind her every day that life is ugly. Why lie about it in the photo albums she tries to put together, right?

I can't help but smile at my thoughts as we continue to walk. Not realizing that Danae has been watching me for a while, I don't hear any more camera clicking.

"Penny for your thoughts … you wanna talk?" Danae asks,

looking concerned while holding onto her thermos. She uncaps it to take a quick drink. Not a bad idea, so I stick my right hand into my book bag to take out my thermos too. She keeps her gaze on me until I stop fidgeting with my bag. She motions for us to sit on a couple of boulders nearby. The coldness of the stones is such a relief as soon as I plant my bottom down.

"Ah! Nice and cool!"

Smiling to myself, Danae lets out a quick giggle. We take a few moments to sit, enjoy the warm sunshine and the coolness of sitting on the boulders, and quenching our thirst. Danae takes one last sip from her thermos and then screws the cap back on. She places her thermos back in her book bag in exchange for her camera again.

"Hey, any film left over for the actual wetland creatures?" I ask out of concern. We have another fifteen minutes of walking to get past this heavily wooded forest area. Danae gives me a reassuring smile.

"Yeah, no sweat. Got two more rolls. That's another forty-eight more exposures. We can get a dozen good shots in a couple of days. Are you in any hurry?" Danae waits patiently for my response.

"No, not really. I wish we were already done with the science fair and making plans for summer vacation," I say sadly, not that my family goes anywhere during the summer. At least this summer, I have a friend to hang out with.

"Got any plans for the summer?" Danae asks curiously, sweat forming just above her lips and the tip of her nose. Her hair is in two separate braids and bound by a red bandana, the sun constantly beaming down on her, making her sweaty. She wipes some sweat off her forehead with the back of her hand.

"Nah ... it'll be another boring one where I get to watch my sisters while Mom starts her Avon thing again. She'll push me to drop off those little brochures at school and around the neighborhood. That's the only exciting thing for me, walking around in the hot sun, dropping off brochures, picking up orders," I say, rolling my eyes, trying my best not to get back into my bad mood. I rummage through my book bag until I pull out my spiral notebook and a pencil that doesn't have a broken lead tip.

"Wow! That sounds like a lotta work. Do you get paid for it?" Danae asks while she swats away the flies buzzing around us.

"Are you serious? Hello—slave labor here! Mom's been doing this for the past three years. She says it's her mad money. I guess I never asked for an allowance. Stupid, huh?" I say, feeling embarrassed, looking away to avoid any look of pity, or worse, judgment.

"Hey, it's okay. I didn't find out I could earn any allowance until I heard about it from other kids bragging about it at my old school."

Her shoulders slump and carry her gaze past me; she becomes quiet. Her face forms a frown as she daydreams about something in her past.

"Let's get going, take some pictures, and I'll take notes," I say, doing my best to cheer her up and get her out of her sad thoughts.

"You're right. Let's go. We're not gonna get anything done sitting here feelin' sorry for ourselves."

Danae jumps off the boulder and stretches herself. I do the same and take the first steps, with Danae joining me.

We walk silently for a few more minutes. The sun is no longer beating down on us as we go farther into the wooded area. There are some crickets chirping off and on, maybe a cry from some bird in the distance. The only sound is our footsteps crunching on dead leaves, broken branches, and loose pebbles. Danae doesn't bother to take pictures because it's too dark and, strangely enough, getting darker.

"Hey, I didn't ask if you have plans for summer vacation," I say but instantly regret it, considering her father has just passed away and her mom was in a coma.

"Yeah ... not sure, something Aunty and I haven't discussed. Hey! Why don't we hang out? I can help out with the Avon orders now and then," Danae says, her face smiling again. Her aura has been blue all this time, but back to its sunny yellow mist. We keep walking until more sunlight breaks through the trees ahead of us.

"I'd like that! We can ride bikes, turn on the sprinkler and run through it, and I'm sure Chrissy would have a ton of fun with that!" We chuckle. As we keep walking, there's an opening to more light.

"Hey, I think we're getting closer!" Danae says excitedly; she picks up her steps to get closer. I follow right behind her. Danae starts running gingerly, stepping over any rock or branch in the way.

For some reason, I don't feel like running. I pick up my pace a little. She reaches the open area where the sun is beaming over the tall grassy areas with cattail plants jutting out. Several dragonflies, flies, butterflies, and other insects are fluttering above the marshy areas.

Danae is clicking away with her instant camera while I continue to walk around and take notes.

"Hey, Gi, do you mind plucking some grass samples growing in different areas? I got some sandwich bags for you to put them in." Danae asked kindly. I nodded in agreement. She quickly sticks her camera in the front pocket of her overalls. She unslings her book bag and gives it to me. I pull a handful of clear sandwich bags from its container and stick them back in the book bag. She reaches out to retrieve her purse and slings it back on.

"I'll pick a sample in the marshy area and dry ground. Would you like me to pick grass samples over there too?" I ask Danae, pointing at a nearby pond. She nods as she crouches down to take a picture of some bug resting on a flower. I continue to walk towards the pond area up ahead. It's so peaceful here, and I can tell this pond is a reliable watering hole for nearby wildlife.

Walking around the pond's diameter, I can see tadpoles swimming around while a nearby frog sits quietly on a dead log resting near the pond's shore. Trying my best not to scare it away, I crouch down to watch it.

Some clouds move to block the sun's beaming light and instantly shade the area. My ear perks up and stretches back when I suddenly hear rustling among the grassy areas behind me. I turn in that direction and scan the pond and the tree line. There's no movement now. The crickets and birds stop chirping; the pond area is eerily silent. There's no breeze or leaves swaying to any air movement. As if the forest is holding its breath.

My heart is pounding; even my talisman lights up under my shirt.

Good God! What now? Some demon dog or rabid deer getting ready to attack me? Geesh!

My eyes scan back to where I left Danae; I don't see her. Checking back to the pond area, even the frog took off, and the school of tadpoles swimming around seem to have disappeared. I stand back on my feet, walking back toward Danae's last location.

"Danae? Danae? You there?" My voice cracks and my throat is dry and hot. My mouth is so pasty, and of course, my stomach starts to grumble violently. I stop walking to listen for any other footsteps. Nothing. Now I'm panicking. Where could she be?

"Danae! C'mon, man! If you're joking around to scare me, I'm not laughing!" I shout nervously, the hairs on my arms and the back of my neck standing on end. I hear a subtle growl just to my right by the tree line.

A ghostly woman who seems transparent is standing by the tree line. Her face has a smile so wide that it stretches from ear to ear. If she didn't have long, black, straight hair flowing past her shoulders and down to her waist, along with her long-sleeve, sheer gown with torn edges at the bottom, I would have mistaken her for a smiling alligator.

She points a long, bony finger at me and lets out a blood-curdling scream.

"Argh! Ssss! ...you!"

Right behind the ghostly woman is Danae, bound and gagged with green vines wrapped around her mouth and body. I can't take my eyes off her tear-stricken face. She keeps shaking her head left, then right, and back again.

What in the world is going on? Who is this ghostly woman thing? No! Not Danae!

My knees shake, my throat is dry, and I'm sweating through my clothes. I feel so helpless and frightened. Tears run down my face, and my hands are in tight fists as I grit my teeth.

Call Irra now! Call her now!

"I can't! I can't call her! She hates me ..." I whisper under my breath, trying my best not to run up and snatch Danae from that ghostly woman! Why? Why me? Why her? I don't get it!

"What do you want? Leave her alone!"

I shout at the ghost, and she lets out a loud, shrill laugh.

"You! You are an abomination! You half-breed Fae! Undeserving of such powers! She will pay for your mistakes!"

The ghost points backward in the direction of Danae, who's struggling to stand up while gagged. She lets out a muffled shriek as she sways to her left and lands sideways.

What in the world is this woman talking about? Danae hasn't done anything! Is she talking about me?

"Let her go! Now!" I shout in the most commanding way I can.

Something is hiding behind some bushes near my left side. The leaves rustle and move, and a tiny creature almost a foot tall emerges. His skinny body, long arms, and legs are brown, almost bark-like. His sandy brown hair sticks out in all directions. His eyes are big and golden and shine like honey in the sunlight. He's wearing a green tunic, no pants, and green pointed shoes. He gives me a big, toothy smile.

"Use it!"

"Use what?? What the heck are you?" I ask, annoyed by this tiny creature.

"Stay focused! Use your powers to defend your friend!"

The creature's voice is high-pitched and squeaky. Does he know about my powers?

Who else knows?

The anger grows inside me, fanning waves of red light into my aura. I watch the red light dance around my colorless aura until it gives in. Now my aura is different shades of red, shredding in several strips. The strips race toward the ghostly woman, and she glides back in horror. Her mouth drops open, and her eyes widen with giant black holes. She lets out a high-pitched scream.

"Ahh! You will pay for this, you abomination!"

She tries to avoid my aura strips targeting her limbs and her neck. The strips are too fast for her; within fractions of a second, every strip bounds and gags her. I focus on the strips so they can tighten and squeeze her all over.

She wiggles and struggles to move but can't; instead, I focus on her floating in the air. The creature talking to me is already on the other side and propping a bound Danae against a tree.

She doesn't look awake, fortunately for her. Her limp body lays quietly against the tree. The little guy turns his attention toward me.

"Hey, let the banshee go! Tell her to go away! You can command her!"

The creature runs towards me as the surprised look turns into a panicked expression on his face.

"Why should I? That ghost woman was about to kill Danae." I answer the creature in defiance. Anger and frustration occupy me, and I keep the constricting grip of this ghost woman with my aura strips. Maintaining my focus, the strips continue to tighten. The ghost woman or banshee cries in total pain.

"Please, please! I will go away! Please let me go!" she pleads pitifully. I let out a loud, roaring laugh. It feels good to laugh, not because of happiness, but for having total control of this situation. My aura is now a deeper maroon. Curiously, I focus on loosening the grip around her neck; my aura obeys my command. The banshee's head falls forward; she lets out a sigh of relief.

"Who sent you here? I want to know!"

She lifts her pale, greenish face to look at me. Her lips widen to an alligator smile.

"You have a bounty on your head, Half Fae. I'm here to gather you for my mistress," the banshee replies; she wiggles around in my aural bounds. I will my aura to tighten again. She screams in pain.

"Not today! Or EVER!" I shout, closing my eyes to focus on making my aura so tight she was gagging and struggling again.

The little creature is tugging at the bottom of my T-shirt, pleading with me.

"Please, Miss Georgina! This is NOT the way to handle this! Stop right now!" His golden eyes look watery; tears run out of the corners. He pleads again. "Let her go. I can summon my Pixie army and all the forces of nature to send her back to the portal! Just don't kill her!"

The creature shouts so loudly that the leaves shake on the nearby trees. The banshee looks pathetic, gagging, whimpering under my power.

There's a sleeping desire; it's been quiet for so long. It wakes up and takes over me. This desire has all my attention.

Kill her! Send a message to the Other World that you're not playing games! You have the power; use it! If you don't, she will capture you!

The aura strip used as a gag around her mouth loosens

and joins the other strip wrapped around her neck.

My eyes focus on those strips to see if she's a living, breathing being. She chokes as the strips tightened until I hear a *Crack! Snap! Crack!*

Her eyes bulge, popping out of their sockets. Her head falls back; her body is limp. I stop smiling. My aura releases the banshee's body; it pops into several rays of light and then disappears in the air.

The creature who was pleading with me shrinks down to his knees. He falls forward face first as he yells, then punches his tiny fist onto the ground out of frustration.

"Ah! Why? Why did you do that?" he cries, lifting his head to the sky. He looks over at me. He stops crying and gives me a dirty look. His eyebrows furrow in anger, and he points at me.

"You! You! How could you! Do you know what you've done?" He gets back on his feet and walks toward me. His face is angry while he stands with his hands on his hips.

"First of all, who and what are you?" I respond commandingly, walking past him to get to Danae. He runs back and stands in my way again.

"I'm Telly, commander of the Pixie Army, at your service!" He takes a low bow in front of me with his hat off. Wiping some tears from his face, he pulls himself together.

"Okay, Telly, how 'bout you help me with Danae? It's getting late, and we need to be heading back."

I'm busy trying to untangle or rip the vines wrapped around Danae. She's still out; her body is on the ground instead of leaning against the tree.

"Did you not hear what I just said?"

Telly stomps his feet, jumping up and down. I can tell he's frustrated with me. I look at him for a few seconds to check out his aura. It's a light misty white smoke with a small strip of light blue, reminding me of Irra's aura.

"Irra sent you, right?" His eyebrows are raised, and his mouth falls open.

"H-how did you know that? I was about to tell you!" Telly looks confused.

"Your aura looks a lot like Irra's. I can tell you care, too." I smile at Telly, and his face relaxes.

"So you also see Other World signatures. Irra didn't mention that." Telly's face relaxes, and his tone is curious.

I check for a pulse on the side of Danae's neck. Her skin is slick with sweat and cold to the touch. Her pulse is slow but steady. She's sleeping like a baby. I continue ripping off the vines that are wrapped around her body.

"Here, let me do that!"

Telly closes his eyes as he hovers over Danae. His arms raise by his sides; light emanates from him. The light shines brightly from him onto Danae's bound body. The vines loosen, sliding back, relaxing, and sliding back again. Telly's light guides the vines to let go inch by inch.

Within seconds, the vines retreat to a nearby plant. Danae is now sleeping peacefully on the ground lined with wildflowers.

"Thanks, Telly! Tell Irra I said 'hi.'"

I retrieve our book bags; Telly steps in front of me again with his hands on his hips.

"Not so fast! Irra sent me to look out for you! So, you owe me payment! I don't work for free!" Telly holds his right hand, palm up, ready to receive a payment.

I get back on my feet to look down on him, and intimidate him.

"I don't have any money. Hold on!"

I rummage through Danae's bag and find a plastic bag full of chocolate chip cookies. I am holding the bag in front of him as his eyes get big as saucers.

"Will this do? I don't have anything else. Sorry!" Telly quickly snatches the plastic bag of cookies; he gives me a satisfied smile.

"Those will do nicely! I was gonna say that human currency has no value to me or my kind. We Pixies love our sweet treats, especially human-made cakes and cookies." He gives me a low bow, then opens the bag to take out a cookie. He sniffs, inspects it, and throws it in his mouth. He lets out a big burp.

"Ahh ... that was good!"

Telly pats his full tummy. Ignoring him, I turn my attention to Danae.

What are you gonna tell her when she wakes up? Think of something.

So much has happened, and I'm racing against time or face some catastrophe. My body is feeling exhausted as well as hungry.

I sit next to Danae while she snores peacefully, not knowing what to do next, but taking a quick breather. The sun is already past the trees. I gently look at Danae's wristwatch; it's 4:15. Telly is resting against a tree, looking just as exhausted as me.

He can't be taking a nap now. He's got a lot of answers to some outstanding questions. Wake him!

Walking over and sitting next to him, I nudge his small shoulders. He jumps up in sheer surprise. Flinching back from his reactions, he realizes where he's at.

"Beg your pardon, Mistress Georgina!" He bows again, then sits next to me.

"Just call me Gina ... the Mistress Georgina thing is too weird for me. You mentioned that I would be in trouble because I killed that banshee. So, what are you talking about?"

"I'm positive that Rav summoned the banshee. Irra told me she expects her sister to return with a vengeance. She also told me you're a half sister to them both. I'm here to help you learn how to control your Fae powers, but alas, I've failed." Telly bows his head down.

"As far as I'm concerned, I just saved my best friend's life by destroying that banshee. I don't know you from a hole in the wall. Did you honestly think I would listen to you?" Telly shakes his head from left to right. He pulls out the plastic bag of cookies, opens it, and grabs another.

"Maybe if we had met just minutes before, things would be different, but I'm not gonna feel bad about stopping some creepy ghost lady doing any harm to my friend or me! Look, I have to go. It's almost dinner time. I have to get Danae home!"

I get back on my feet to dust myself off. Telly shoves his bag of cookies into his tunic and pops the half-eaten cookie in his mouth.

"Looks like you're hungry too. I'm gonna wake her up so we can walk back home! Okay?" I sling both our book bags and strap them onto my left shoulder. Telly still looks troubled, even angry.

"Don't you feel even the slightest guilt for killing another creature? You've opened the Portal from the Other World with more creatures coming after you! Rav will see to it." Telly points his index finger toward my face in a scolding manner.

Should I feel bad? I didn't kill another human being, so why should I care?

Feeling troubled by Telly's words, it all doesn't feel real to me. He's searching my face, and he grows more concerned.

"I will do you this one favor so you won't have to walk so far to get home. I will also make sure there are wards of protection around Danae. She's as much in danger as you, if not more." Telly grabs Danae's school bag to help lighten my load.

"What do you mean by that? She's not Fae, and they can't hurt her!" I give Telly an annoyed look at his cryptic statements.

"Look, you used your powers for revenge and also killed a creature from the Other World in your human world. There are consequences to your actions. Danae's family and Danae will pay dearly for your fatal mistake! Do you understand?"

Telly's eyes grow dark, and his aura changes from light blue to purple. He doesn't have to tell me he is disappointed, and his violet aura tells me all I needed to know.

He's telling the truth, and you know it. Danae doesn't deserve this. Bad things have already happened to her!

"I-I want to go home. I'll think about it, okay?"

"Irra already put a ward around your home before she left; it will at least stop any creature from getting into your home. Wards are spells for protection. I can do the same for Danae. It's the least I can do to keep her from being attacked."

Telly doesn't wait for me to answer; he stands over my sleeping friend and raises his arms from his side. The same white light emanates from him to Danae. The light forms an invisible bubble around her. I'm sure she won't detect it, but my aura powers help me see such things. This bubble of white light gives off a low vibration, buzzing smoothly like electricity from a light bulb.

"Thanks, Telly. Can you send us home now?" He shakes his head left and then right.

"I can't. I'm not as powerful as you. I'm limited to what nature can provide here in the human world, but you can go beyond that. Just focus. If you ever need me, I'm only a whisper away. Go on now! It's almost sundown. There will be others!"

He stands at attention and gives me a salute. Standing next to Danae, asleep on the ground, I close my eyes to focus on us reaching our backyard.

Opening my eyes again, we're in the grassy backyard area. I shake Danae awake.

CHAPTER THIRTEEN

STRANGER DAYS

Danae gets up, wipes the drool from her mouth, and looks around.

"What just happened?"

She gets up on her feet but falls again.

"Whoa! Take it easy, Di! I have your thermos, so drink some water."

I'm concerned she might be dehydrated. She sits up and moves next to me to grab the thermos that I've been holding up for her. She takes it from me and takes a few seconds gulping down the water.

"So, what do you remember?" I hope she doesn't remember much so I can develop a good story.

"Uhh ... I-I don't remember much. S-Something grabbed me while I was taking pictures of the water lilies nearby ... I guess." Danae rubs the area between her eyes with her right forefinger and thumb. She stops and looks at me for a while.

"Wait a minute, how did we get here? Did you carry me while I was out?" Danae's face is perplexed as she scratches her head.

"You don't remember walking a while before you passed out?" I ask casually, my voice slow and steady.

"I mean, you're still trying to recover from a concussion, remember?" Danae seems troubled; her aura is a greenish blue. She gets up slowly and checks the time on her wristwatch.

"Geez, it's already 5:20. Don't you have to make dinner with your Grandma?"

Not waiting for another second, I get back on my feet and sling my book bag over my shoulder.

"Yeah, I better get going. Mi Ma won't be happy I'm late. You wanna try again next Saturday to get more samples or put together our notes?"

"Yeah, let's do that. See you tomorrow at school, Gi!" Danae puts her right hand out. I slap her hand back in our usual friendly goodbye greeting. She hugs me for a few seconds.

"Seriously, tell your aunt to set up a doctor's appointment. I'm worried about you, Di." Danae's face darkens, and her lips turn down.

"Yeah, you're right. Have a good evening." I give her a reassuring smile as we turn in opposite directions, feeling somewhat relieved Danae didn't ask any more questions.

Walking back into the front door of my home, I see Grandma in front of the stove with pots and pans full of steaming food. Her hair is in curlers covered with a sheer scarf and she wears an orange house dress. Even though her dress is a bright, cheerful color, her facial expressions don't match when she turns around to see me walk in.

"Good! You're finally here! I've called Mrs. Jenkins, and she didn't know where you and her niece were. You had me worried!"

She's stirring a pot with a wooden spoon. She puts the spoon on the counter next to the stove and wipes her hand on a kitchen towel.

"I need you to peel potatoes. They're right over there."

Grandma points at a bowl of a dozen potatoes on the kitchen table; a peeler and another empty bowl are waiting for me.

Putting my book bag by the front door, I walk to the kitchen sink to wash my hands. I must do my chores, even if I'm tired or not. My stomach won't stop grumbling as I try my best to focus on peeling these potatoes.

"Make sure you dice them too! I'm making mashed potatoes with stuffed cabbage for dinner tonight."

Grandma opens the oven door to check out the stuffed cabbage pieces in a long glass pan. The aroma bursts out, tickling my nose, which only frustrates my stomach so much.

"Everything smells so good, Mi Ma. Can't wait for dinner."

I peeled the last potato and got up from the table to rinse them under running water. She doesn't say anything and smiles at my compliment. The front door crashes open, startling me so much that I drop one of the potatoes on the floor.

Little Chrissy runs into the kitchen clutching onto her teddy bear with tears streaming down her face and a nose full of snot. Her little pink sundress is dirty, covered with grass stains, and soaking wet with what I assume is urine. Her sandal is missing from her right foot. She runs straight for me and buries her face in my chest.

I pick up the dropped potato and put it back in with the other potatoes in the bowl. Bending down to hold her, I wipe her tears and snot with the kitchen towel I am holding. She swipes off my towel and lets out a bloodcurdling scream.

"Gi-Gi, he hurt me! He hurt me! Ah!"

She screams again, then buries her face into my dusty T-shirt. I wrap my arms around Chrissy, doing my best to comfort her.

Within a split second, Mom runs in with Natalie screaming in her arms. Tears are also running down Mom's face; her pretty, pink, matching sun dress is torn, and her left eye is swollen. She hands Natalie to Grandma and runs to lock the front door.

She turns to rest her back on the door and continues crying loudly. Grandma and I are both confused by this outburst while we try to console both Chrissy and Natalie.

Carrying Chrissy in my arms, I quickly run to the living room window to see if Stepdad is in the station wagon parked in the driveway. Nothing. He must've driven off. Feeling my talisman heating up under my T-shirt, I remember Telly's words about controlling my aural powers. I stand for a while to close my eyes and focus on calming myself down. My aura goes from red to transparent.

Chrissy tugs at me, sucking her thumb. Feeling too agitated to console her, I quickly place her on the couch. Chrissy revolts and clings to me even more. So, I sit with her on the sofa as she puts her head on my lap.

Mom wipes the tears from her eyes.

"That's it! I am done wit him! I'm too tired for dis!"

Mom's voice is desperate, shaky. Grandma puts an index finger to her lips to signal Mom to keep her voice down. Natalie is quietly sucking on a bottle as Grandma rocks her to sleep.

Grandma pulls out the bottle and places Natalie over her left shoulder to pat her on the back. Natalie lets out a loud, "Burp!" Then she lays her head on Grandma's shoulder. Grandma rocks the baby gently and walks toward the back of the mobile home.

Mom goes over to the refrigerator. She pulls out the ice tray to shake some ice cubes loose and puts some on a clean kitchen towel. Wrapping the ice cubes in the towel, Mom puts it over her swollen left eye.

"Mom, can you lie down on the couch next to us?"

She nods her head and walks over to Chrissy and me. Mom plops to my left and rests her head back to let the ice pack work on her swollen eye. Her right hand reaches over to Chrissy's feet and rests there.

"You okay, Ma?"

Mom's aura is a deep blue with some purple stripes. Her head is still resting on the back of the couch; she's deep in thought. Then she turns her head towards me.

"I'm okay, Gi, just really tired."

Grandma walks back into the living room without Natalie. She looks straight at my mom.

"Gi-Gi, can you take your sister to your room? Let her lay on your bed? I need to talk to your momma alone."

It must be something serious if I'm not allowed to listen. I nod my head to let Grandma know I've been listening. Chrissy has grown and put on some serious weight since Grandma has been living with us. I gently pick her up and carry her to my room. She stirs a bit, still clinging to her teddy bear.

"It's okay, Cookie Monster, putting you in my bed so you can sleep." I whisper in Chrissy's ear, laying her down gently; I notice her left shin is bruised badly and swollen. Her dress is soaking wet with urine. It sticks to her body, making her shiver.

I run out of my bedroom and into the main bedroom to rummage through Chrissy's dresser for some underwear and pajamas.

Quietly tiptoeing back to my room, I can hear whispering from the kitchen. Curiosity gets the best of me; I can't help but sneak a little closer down the hallway without being seen. Good thing it's getting dark so I can rest in a shadowy corner to be nosy. Looking over at the kitchen table, I see Mom and Grandma sitting together.

"He'll be back, Rosie; he needs to sleep it off, that's all."

Grandma places her hand over Mom's hand on the table. Mom flinches her hand back; she buries her face into a napkin to quiet her crying. She lifts her head.

"No ... no, not dis time! He almost killed Chrissy if I wasn't there ... I-I don't know. I don't know!"

Mom's face is twisted with worry and pain. Tears flow from her eyes; her left eye shows a new black-and-blue ring under it. Grandma shrugs off Mom's crying.

"Oh! You don't mean that! There's no way he'd kill his child."

Grandma is in pure denial. Anger grows inside me; my talisman is humming under my shirt. I take a breath and close my eyes to calm down.

"He punched me! You see it! He's been using me like a punch bag! Now he wants to hurt my daughter because she spilled her food on the picnic blanket? He's-he's a coward!"

"You need to keep it down. Now pull yourself together. You're lucky enough for my son to bring you to the States, and this is the gratitude? Stop being so dramatic."

Grandma looks at Mom with anger and disbelief. Mom leans back in her chair and gives Grandma a very long look. She gets up from her chair.

"You-you brought up a monster! You see my face! How many times will I have to go to hospital before he puts me in grave? No! No more!"

Mom slides the chair under the kitchen table. She makes her way toward the living room and hallway.

Don't let her catch you listening! Go! Go! Go!

It only takes a few steps to creep back to my bedroom quietly.

Footsteps stop at my bedroom door; Mom doesn't knock on my door. Then she walks away to the main bedroom. I'm already inside, changing my sister into some clean clothes.

Slipping into clean clothes and combing my hair, I go back to the door to put my ear against it. I don't hear anything else.

No longer ignoring my stomach, I open the door to step out into the hallway. Walking towards the kitchen, I see Grandma put away some food in containers and foil wrapping.

"Mi Ma, may I have some food? I'm sorry about dinner getting ruined."

She pulls out a clean plate and a fork from the cupboards.

"Sure, *skarbie*, let me put some stuffed cabbage on your plate."

She scoops four pieces onto my plate. I'm not usually a big fan of cabbage, but willing to overlook that so I can get to the meat and rice combination inside; now that's worth eating. Grandma watches me happily wolf down my food.

"Thank you, that was very good, Mi Ma. I better go to bed now since I have school tomorrow. Are you going to be all right? Would you like for me to wash my dishes?"

Even though I have a million questions, it feels like this isn't the right time to ask. She seems a million miles away.

"That's all right, you may go to bed. Chrissy and Natalie will be up early, so I'm going to bed too."

Grandma's exhaustion is all over her face. For the first time in my life, I'm looking at my grandmother differently. It bothers me that I'm not part of her blood family; she made it painfully obvious earlier today when she mentioned my family having a picnic without me.

She picks up the empty plate from me and starts to wash it in the sink. I hug her, but I catch her off guard. She wipes her hands on a towel and hugs me back. It isn't a tight hug like the ones I usually get. I feel some significant changes ahead and a horrible sense of something terrible happening soon.

I let go immediately and smile back. She doesn't say anything more and turns to wash more dishes in the sink.

Walking back to my room, I check out Grandma again. Her aura is a mustard color, which bothers me so much. She doesn't notice me as she continues to wash the dishes and clear the table. I still can't shake off that bad feeling. There's nothing more I can do but turn back to my bedroom and close the door.

Chrissy is under the covers of my bed, sleeping the night away. I try to distract myself by picking up my book to read, but no luck. Telly's words keep ringing as he screams about Danae getting into trouble because I killed the banshee. Sitting up in bed, I realize what Telly said. Irra had placed a ward on my house before she left. I wish I had known before then. That explains why they couldn't get into my home. I killed those changelings unnecessarily.

Killed—not a word I'd ever thought of using in my daily vocabulary.

Everything seems so strange, so different. Even Grandma appears like another person. Mom comes home with yet another swollen eye, and Chrissy is terrified. Stepdad is nowhere to be found. For the first time in my life, I've witnessed Grandma denying Mom's suffering. Now I can't sleep.

Getting out of bed, I rummage through my dresser drawers for some clean clothes and quickly dressed. I remember leaving my book bag by the front door; I sneak back into the hallway. All the lights are out in the living room and kitchen, so I'm taking some quiet steps toward the front door. I can hear Grandma stirring in the bathroom, so I must be quick.

I see headlights from a car beam into the living room window. Grabbing my book bag and running back to my bedroom, I silently close the door. Sweat is running down my face, and my hands are also slimy. I almost drop my book bag on the floor. I walk towards my bedroom window to see if the headlights belong to Stepdad's station wagon. Nightfall is quickly coming in, but I can still see a silhouette of Stepdad coming out of the car. He's staggering towards the front door.

Great! Drunk as usual! That also means he's gonna be loud!

Bang! Bang! Bang!

"Someone let me in!"

Stepdad continues to bang on the front door. Grandma shouts back while walking towards the front door. I can't help but hear everything; they're both so loud.

"Hold on! Keep it down!" Grandma shouts; she unlocks the deadbolt lock with a slam. The door swings open and crashes against the wall. Stepdad's clumsy footsteps thunder in. His loudness and crassness are so rude and selfish that I could feel my heart beating and thumping hard. From the corner of my eye, I can see Chrissy stirring from all the noise. Mom's feet stomp down the hallway from outside my bedroom door.

"Keep it down, you *buto*! The bebe is crying!" Mom screams, holding a bawling Natalie in her arms. I hear Mom trying to comfort my youngest sister. Then I hear a shriek from her. Then a crash, bang, and thud. Natalie's cries turn into high-pitched shrieks while I hear Grandma crying. My body shakes with so much panic, so I jump out of bed. Chrissy bolts straight up and screams.

"No, Gi-Gi! No! Don't leave me!" She holds her arms out, expecting me to hug her. I'm too agitated to comfort Chrissy. Looking around and under the covers, desperate to find her teddy bear. Found it. Handing her the bear as I try my best to calm her down.

"Hold on to, Bear, okay? He's really scared, and he needs you right now. Can you be brave? Hide under the covers with him, okay?"

I whisper in her ear while holding her in my arms. Chrissy's face breaks into a weak smile, and she slowly nods. She lies down, hugging her bear tightly, and sucks on her thumb. Her eyes grow distant, half-closed. Pulling the covers up to her shoulders, I give her a quick kiss on her right cheek.

The mobile home shakes as the commotion outside of my bedroom gets louder. I say a prayer to gather my strength and to get past my fear of facing the chaos in the living room, my talisman is warming up, glowing under my clothes. My blood boils because I'm not looking forward to seeing what I'm about to see.

Quietly walking out into the hallway and the living room, I see Mom lying on the floor, passed out. She's face up, face bloody, eyes so swollen they look like slits. Grandma, Stepdad, and Natalie are all gone.

The front door is wide open, letting in a cold draft of the night air. I walk back to my mom to check for her pulse on the side of her neck. It's weak but there.

Same crap, different day!

I don't know how to feel about seeing my mother in this typical situation. I used to cry; fearful he might kill her some-day. This is a regular thing; I've become used to it.

I want to pick up Mom and wake her up but think better of it. It's time to call for an ambulance— again.

Maybe I should check on her. She might wake up.

"Ma, Ma, please wake!"

Her head bobs left then right; her eyes slowly open, and she lets out a soft moan.

"Mmmmmmm, What? Where?"

Mom looks drowsy; she struggles to get up on her elbows. Blood gushes out of her nose and her mouth. She coughs, gasping for air. Holding her head up, I prop her back against my body. She continues to struggle.

The footsteps and movement from the front entrance, startles me. My gaze turns to the person standing at the front door.

Mrs. Jenkins continues to knock on the open door. Her face is frozen in horror at the sight of us. Forcing myself to give her a weak smile isn't working. The tears on my face have been streaming since I walked into the living room.

"Hey, Gina! Oh, my God! Do you want me to call an ambulance?"

Mrs. Jenkins quickly runs over to the telephone hanging on the kitchen wall. She doesn't wait for my permission, picks up the receiver, and starts to dial. Mom struggles to breathe, then coughs violently.

"Shhhhh! Ma, we're calling the ambulance. Hang on, okay?" I whisper into her right ear. She struggles to escape my grasp, but her body is too weak. She cries in pain, clutching her stomach with both arms wrapped around her waist.

"Gi! No! No ambulance! …. must find your father … he has Natalie! He-he wants to take her away!"

Mom hyperventilates, and I rub her back to get her to relax. As soon as Mrs. Jenkins hangs up, she walks toward us with a clean, dry kitchen towel. She hands it to me so I can wipe up the blood pouring out Mom's nostrils. Mom hangs onto the towel and puts more pressure on her nose. I tilt her head back gently; her jaw drops down. Her eyelids are both puffy and becoming slits. Mrs. Jenkins crouches down next to us, both curious and horrified.

"I-I couldn't help but hear your stepdad screaming outside, trying to come in. I don't know what to do! I wanna respect your family's privacy, but when I heard Rosaria and May screaming and crying, I wanted to run in!"

She casts her eyes downward, admitting her embarrassment. I reach over to grab Mrs. Jenkins' left hand to squeeze it.

"It's all right, Mrs. J. The ambulance will be here soon. Thanks for calling. It's probably best you stayed out of it. Stepdad can be violent when he's drunk as a skunk." I let go of her hand. Mom is quiet, and her eyes are slammed shut. Hoping there's nothing broken, I shift her weight off my chest. I move her gently to rest against the bottom of the couch nearby, she starts whimpering in pain. She clamps her arms down on her stomach.

He must've punched her there. You've seen it before! It must stop!

"Hey Gi, you there? Hello, hello!" Danae walks into the living room.

"Sorry... hi, Danae, didn't see you come in."

Mrs. Jenkins and Danae's auras were a mixture of pink and blue. Their eyes study me as they both give me a look of pity.

"How long has this been going on?" Mrs. Jenkins' eyes squint, eyebrows furrowed.

Feeling uncomfortable answering that question, I look away.

"He's not gonna get away with it!" Danae's eyes darken and her voice is angry.

Two paramedics who came over to the house a few weeks ago show up at my doorstep. The guy with curly black hair and hazel eyes recognizes me immediately.

"Georgina and Rosaria Trabeck, right?"

"Yes, sir."

He gets down on his hands and knees to check out Mom. Mrs. Jenkins pulls me away so the paramedics can do their jobs. I don't fight her off. Instead, I completely fall into her arms, crying my eyes out. She holds onto me tightly. All I feel right now is pure relief.

So tired of this life, so tired of hurting. I blubber into her T-shirt. She strokes my back gently. I haven't had any adult get this close to me; for now, I need this.

I cried all I could, so I let her go. Danae gives me a few sheets of toilet paper to blow my nose and wipe off my tears.

"Thanks, Di." She gives me a reassuring smile.

"I couldn't find any tissue box, so that's the best I could do."

"Doesn't matter. It's all the same to me." Mrs. Jenkins and Danae both smile.

"Not to break up this moment, but do you know where your stepdad and grandma went? Are Chrissy and Natalie here?" Mrs. Jenkins asks, her eyebrows furrowing, pupils wide, showing concern.

"Chrissy is sleeping in my bed. I-I think they took Natalie. I didn't see what was going on, but there were struggles. Mom was trying to keep Grandma or him from taking Natalie."

"Do you have an idea where they might have gone?"

Sadly, I could only shake my head.

"Can't we call the police and tell them that your Stepdad kidnapped them? I mean, c'mon! There's something we can do, right?" Danae asks; she keeps her gaze on her aunt.

"No, Di, we can't. They would only tell us this is private. Cops can't intervene. I oughta know. I've run into many women trying to run away from their abusive husbands only to receive another call from a relative that the woman dies at the hands of her abuser." Mrs. Jenkins' grim look bothers me.

"For God's sake, this is the '70s, man! We're fighting for equal rights. This isn't fair at all!" Danae shouts in frustration, then crosses her arms.

The curly-haired paramedic comes up to us quietly.

"Sorry to interrupt, but we're ready to take your mother to Waitborne Hospital emergency center. I take it you know where it's at?" he asks, keeping his gaze on me. I nod my head, "yes."

We look past the paramedic to see Mom strapped on a stretcher with an oxygen mask and tank in tow.

"I've been listening to your conversation and can safely assume this is an altercation between your parents, right?"

"Yes, but I didn't see what took place. Mom taught me to stay in my bedroom with my little sister when this happens. It's for our safety."

I'm tired of putting on any more acts of denial. He nods his head to let me know he's been listening. He finishes writing in his notepad and puts it away.

"I will ensure Gina will be at the hospital to see her mother. We don't know the whereabouts of her stepfather yet."

Mrs. Jenkins mentions to the paramedic. He nods and turns around to help the other guy pick up Mom on the stretcher. They hoist her out of the house and into the back of the ambulance. The lights flash bright red and blue in the dark, distracting the neighbors. Mrs. Jenkins closes the front door and gives me a look of exhaustion.

"Gina, I want you and Chrissy to spend the night at my place. You both have school to go to in the morning, and I can watch Chrissy. We'll sort this out tomorrow. I'll check to see if I can work with local police and the air force base about your stepdad. Let's get some rest tonight, okay?"

Feeling exhaustion take over me, I only agree by nodding my head. Danae puts her arm around my shoulder.

"Let's get Chrissy some clothes for you both and your book bag. We gotcha! I already made a bed for the Cookie Monster sister!" She beams a big smile as we walk toward the hallway. Mrs. Jenkins follows us to my bedroom.

It only takes a few minutes to gather Chrissy's diaper bag filled with clothes and training pants, plus a tote bag with my clothes, toiletries, and school books.

Fortunately, Chrissy is asleep; she only stirs in Mrs. Jenkins' arms.

I lock the front door with the key Mom gave me for emergencies. We walk quietly in the night towards their home. The night air feels so clean and cool. Even with the crickets chirping, which usually calms me, it only reminds me that life has no comfort.

CHAPTER FOURTEEN

NEVER AGAIN

"Gi-Gi, where are you? Gi-Gi, help me!" Chrissy cries out, with her arms stretched out to me. I'm trying to get to her but can't! Everything around us is hazy, like some faraway place. Tears stream down her face. Her pajamas are wet with urine. She's on her hands and knees, looking around for her teddy bear. I try to run towards her to scoop her in my arms. Instead, I hit face-first into what feels like a glass window. Does she see me? Maybe I can call out to her.

"Chrissy! I'm right here. Can you see me?" I'm screaming desperately for her. Fists are banging furiously against this glass window—that's what it feels like. Chrissy looks around as if she can hear me but can't see me somehow.

There's laughter from a distance yet so close it sounds like a woman's voice.

"Ha, ha, ha ... hello, Gina ... it's me, your lovely half sister, Ravanna. I want to let you know about my new plaything! Isn't she cute? So don't worry about her, she's in my care!"

I can hear Rav's smug voice but can't see her either. Feeling my blood boil, my talisman hot and glowing, and my aura turning from a cornflower blue to maroon red, I keep banging my fist against this transparent wall.

Even though my aura can separate from me and divide into strips, they hang in the air with no place to go. Everything around me is white, smoky like I'm living in a light bulb. Running from one side to another proves fruitless. I could run forever in either direction, but I would only wear myself out. Trying my best to figure out where I'm at is a lost cause.

Yet I hear Chrissy crying non-stop; it just tears at my heart. I've always sworn to protect her and keep her away from harm. I plan on keeping it that way.

"How 'bout you leave my sister alone and face me like the coward you are, Rav! I know you sent the banshee to come after me!"

A puff of white smoke appears before me. The smoke transforms into a long figure with long, flowing, fiery red hair, emerald, green eyes, and a defiant smirk who is wearing a beautiful emerald-studded gown with sparkly studs at the seams.

She floats above me with her transparent dragonfly wings, trying to intimidate me. The air around me is still. Her hair flows around her face like a draft of wind.

"Yes, Gina, you're in a bubble, and your little sister there happens to be in her bubble. You see, this is the price you pay for killing my banshee. If you had just cooperated, nobody else would've been involved."

Rav's voice purrs like a cat who just ate a mouse. Trying to contain my anger, I focus on my aura to keep away. I need some answers.

"So you're saying that letting the banshee tie me up and drag me back to the Other World so you can turn me in for ransom is me being a hero to my family and friends? Boy, what a crock! Let me ask you this: Are you missing your talisman too?" Rav's face contorts to an angry scowl.

"What in Behemus are you talking about, little sis?" Rav crosses her arms in front of me.

My aura rests around my feet, waiting for my command. Feeling even more confident, I proceed to entice her.

"So get this, I found Irra's talisman not too long ago. Now she's at total capacity. Lucky you, 'cause otherwise, who knows where you would've ended up if she did have her full powers when she threw you out of our timeline."

She floats around me, sizing me up and down. She could scare me into telling the truth or admit I was bluffing.

"I don't believe you. Prove it!" *Rav's eyebrows raise, her lips tightened to a thin line.*

"Don't have to. Call her. I dare you!"

My talisman warms me, and she notices the light behind my T-shirt. She floats away. Unsure about whether I can glide toward her, I took several steps to reach her.

Returning the smirk she gave me earlier; I can't help but feel arrogant.

"I can't, I tried, and besides, what does my missing talisman have to do with you? I may not be as powerful as you, but I can hurt the ones you love. It's working, isn't it?" *Rav beams a big crocodile smile.*

"I can help you get your talisman back, and if we ask Irra nicely, we can get to the bottom of it. Or are you scared of your sister?" *She laughs maniacally, then stops. The smile leaves her eyes.*

"Yeah, right, I don't believe you."

"On the other hand, if you hurt or kill anyone of my family or friends, all bets are off. You'll have me to contend with! So, I'm giving you a count of ten to let Chrissy go. She has nothing to do with you!"

It feels good to have this power for once in my life. I look down at my aura, all maroon-red ribbons coil below my feet. I focus on them to attack Rav. The ribbons stretch out, rapidly reaching for Rav. Her smile drops, her eyes grow big as saucers. She lets out a shriek.

"Aww! No!"

The ribbons are too fast for her. Instantly, each ribbon wraps itself around her body, mouth, and ankles. In fractions of a second, she's bound and floating in midair. Her emerald green eyes turn to a brownish green. I drift closer to her and rise just above her, looking down.

"Here's the deal: Return Chrissy, take off any curses you might have put on Danae, and tell me where my stepfather's location is. As soon as you can do that, I will let you go. And, no, I will not go back to the Other World with you; that's your problem."

I smile confidently at Rav's face. God, that's so satisfying, and knowing I have power over a Fae, I'm winning for now.

Rav's eyebrows are raised, and a tear rolls out of her left eye. I focus on the aura wrapped around her mouth to release, so she can speak.

"I will leave Chrissy and Danae alone. I have no idea about your stepdad. I-I don't know what you're talking about."

"The teddy bear is not with Chrissy. You have something to do with that. You were that guy we ran into at the hospital. Don't tell me no, because I eventually recognized his aura signature. It belonged to you! You didn't figure I could see a Fae's aura, either. I take it you don't have that ability. So don't give me any jive! You planted the teddy bear as a homing device so you can keep tabs on my family." I'm practically spitting the words in her face.

"I couldn't let Irra know I was around. I found my way back. I wanted to destroy your family as you destroyed mine. You're not equipped to handle Fae powers as long as you're half human; it's pure abomination! But I know you can give up your talisman. If you do, I will call off the bounty on you." She searches my face for a reaction.

"I'll still have my aura abilities. You can't take that away from me. As much as you try to deny me, I'm here alive and well. So, get used to it! How 'bout you get this through your limited mind: I did NOT destroy your family. Take that up with our father." My voice is hoarse with anger. I let an aura ribbon swarm around her face. Her eyes grow big with fear, and her mouth falls open, giving a frightened animal look.

"So what's it gonna be, Sis? I've already killed your banshee, and I have no remorse whatsoever. I don't have any problem snuffing you out too! I could care less about creatures from the Other World. Tell me Stepdad's location, and I'll spare your life."

She closes her mouth and looks away. I let the rest of my aura ribbons, still wrapped around her body, tighten their grip. She moans in discomfort. Sweat breaks out on her forehead, and she grits her white teeth over her lips, drawing pinkish blood. I focus on my aura's constriction around her chest until she screams

"S-stop! I-I can't breathe! Please don't kill me. I'll help you find your stepfather," she pleads while struggling for air. Her face is a paler shade of light green and becomes almost white. I focus as much as possible to relieve her by letting up on the constriction.

"So, speak! You have thirty seconds!" Rav lets out a deep sigh of relief, bows her head, then looks up at me.

"For a moment there, you sound exactly like our father. He had no problem stealing, lying, and killing other Fae, not humans. I find it so repulsive that he would couple with a human woman like your mother." Rav spits out her words with pure disdain, trying to make me feel worthless. Growing impatient with her delaying tactics, I can't take any more of her babbling.

"You just wasted ten seconds of your thirty seconds!" She gives me a look of contempt.

"Fine! Use a tracking spell to find your stepfather. Recite these words: cuidich mi le bhith a l'org! Say it three times and close your eyes; you will see the location in your mind's eye." Rav looks defeated and turns her head away in shame.

"You act as if you've done something so wrong. I am half Fae, and it's high time I learn this part of my heritage." A smirking Rav laughs uncontrollably.

"You've got what you wanted. Now let me go!"

Feeling paranoid that she might retaliate as soon as my aura lets her go, I hesitate for a few seconds.

"How do I know you're not gonna get back at me? I want to see proof that you're not holding Chrissy anywhere. I want to see her!"

A smile grows on her face, and Rav lets out a quiet laugh.

"I don't have Chrissy. This is all but a dream, dream, dream ..." She fades from my view as I step back, recoiling from her words. My aura is no longer bound to her as she disappears completely.

I feel a push, a nudge when all I want to do is sleep forever. Whoever is shoving me is about to get punched in the face.

"Gi, yo! Wakey-wakey, girl!" Danae's voice hovers over me. She shakes my shoulder as I roll over to the other side of the bed. Thinking I got away from her, pushing and shoving to wake me, I feel another warm body as I roll over to my left. That's when I bolt straight up from my fight to go back to sleep.

"Chrissy? Is that you?"

I pull down the covers to find her sleepy body. She rolls from her left side and onto her back. She mumbles something and sticks her left thumb in her mouth.

"Sleepy, leave me alone." Chrissy moans, rolls on her right side, and sucks her thumb. I let out a sigh of relief. I wanted so much to hug her, but that would only wake her up. So, I take a good long look, no scratches or bruises on her arms and legs. Someone put on her favorite pair of yellow pajamas with the cute yellow bear on the front.

Unfortunately, the pants part is soaking wet. I'm sure it has everything to do with Rav. Her right arm stretches out to reach for something; it's the teddy bear. My heart sinks to see it here in the same bed as us. I need to figure out what to do with that thing and distract Chrissy enough to get rid of it.

"Hey, you okay?" Danae asks. I turn my gaze in her direction; she gives me a confused look.

"Just a bad dream. I thought I lost Chrissy, too." Danae sits on the bed next to me and studies me for a while.

"Just really worried about my baby sister." Danae's face softens, her eyes water, and she smiles at me. Yes, that smile everyone gives me when they feel sorry for me.

"I'm not feeling sorry for you, but I do know what it's like to suffer losing a loved one. We're gonna find Natalie. Aunty and I will see to it!" Danae pats my hand, gets off the bed, bends down to pick up my tote bag, and throws it at me. It lands on my lap.

"So, get dressed, breakfast is ready, and see you in a few!" She quickly leaves the room. Looking around me and admiring the decorations of this guest room, it's nice to see delicate rose-printed patterns on the white curtains and matching bedcovers. A couple of rose pictures in white frames are hanging from opposite sides of the room.

The full-size bed that Chrissy and I are sleeping on feels soft and comfortable. Whoever decorated this room tended to favor roses. I'm puzzled about who would pick such flowery decorations. Just from my experience as their friend, they're both so tomboyish, with Danae being so athletic and Mrs. Jenkins a retired cop; neither comes across as choosing feminine designs to decorate their home.

Snapping out of my thoughts, I jump out of bed with my tote bag in hand—time to do some cleanup, hair brushing, and clothes changing, maybe a quick shower. I can't remember the last time I was able to shower, so here I go.

I need a hot shower, clean clothes, and teeth brushing to start my day. I quietly stow away my tote bag back in the guest room without disturbing a sleeping Chrissy and close the door gently. The smell of bacon, toast, eggs, and freshly brewed coffee tempts me to head directly toward the kitchen.

"There you are! Pull up a chair, gotta plateful of food ready for you, Gi!" Danae, already seated, points at the empty chair next to her. Mrs. Jenkins is leaning against the counter nearby, waiting for her percolator to brew some coffee.

"Good morning, everyone!"

Mrs. Jenkins smiles and winks at me. The percolator starts whistling with steam from its spout; she unplugs it and pours some black coffee into her empty cup. She sniffs the aroma rising from her cup, then drinks it happily.

"Ahh … I need this right now! It's gonna be a long day, girls."

Mrs. Jenkins pulls out a chair across from us. Danae and I nod as we shove forkfuls of eggs with bacon in our mouths. She watches us happily finish our food.

"Aren't you hungry, Mrs. J?" Mrs. Jenkins pushes the scrambled eggs around on her plate. She looks tired and worn. The bags under her usually sparkly blue eyes now make them look dull. She gulps some more coffee, holding the cup against her face.

"Not hungry. I'm worried about the whereabouts of your stepfather and grandmother. He doesn't seem like a stable person. There's so much anger in him. I've seen it before and am concerned about Natalie's well-being. She's only a newborn."

Mrs. Jenkins barely mumbled her words. Danae and I had to lean closer to listen carefully.

"Do you have any idea where they might be?" Danae asks me after she finishes drinking her orange juice. I give myself a few seconds to think of the possible places he would take Mi Ma and Natalie.

"Well, he only goes to the air force base for work from 7:00 a.m. to about 5:00 p.m. on most days, but lately, he doesn't come home until after 7:00 p.m. I don't know where else. I don't think he has friends outside the base other than, than..."

My voice trails off to a mumble. Mrs. Jenkins' eyes widen with interest as she puts her coffee mug on the table. Danae looks curious and confused, staring at me with furrowed eyebrows. They both lean in closer.

"Was there someplace else? I didn't hear the last part." I could feel my cheeks heat up with embarrassment.

"I-I don't know if I should say anymore. I-I think my mom would be ashamed if you guys knew about, about..."

I'm trying to avoid their intense stares. Danae grabs my left hand gently and smiles at me. Her aura is soft yellow and pink hues mixing.

"Hey, Gi! It's us. We're not only your neighbors. I like to think we're closer to being family. Whatever you say is safe with Aunty and me." I gently pull my hand away. For some reason, I still feel uncomfortable about being touched right now.

"I-I appreciate that, and I'm grateful for you helping my family and me. It's just that Stepdad had a thing with Robert's mom." I blurt it all out just like that. I can see Danae's mouth open and jaw dropping at the corner of my eye. The pupils of her eyes widen as the yellow specks of her hazel eyes dance around with light. Even Mrs. Jenkins looks surprised; her lips pressed tight into a long, thin line. Danae jumps in loudly, almost startling me.

"You mean that Mrs. O'Malley had an affair with your step-dad! Geez, Louise!" Danae's face and voice both express shock.

"Di!" Mrs. Jenkins, annoyed with her niece, shakes her head in disbelief and pauses for a moment. She gazes somewhere in the distance.

"I'm not making it up. I saw it with my own two eyes. Something I didn't want to see, especially after he hurt Mom enough to send her to the hospital." I feel the sweat on my upper lip as I wipe it off with the paper napkin.

"Gina, I'm so sorry you had to witness this terrible situation, but on the one hand, you've given me some vital information that can help us find him. My heart goes out to your mom." Mrs. Jenkins' voice sounds full of remorse. And, of course, that look of pity again.

Wait! Mom doesn't know anymore, and neither does Robert's Mom! Irra practically erased their memories. Think! Before Mrs. J says anything to Mom!

As much as I felt relieved to confess to Mrs. Jenkins and Danae, I've painted myself figuratively in the corner.

"Uhm .... maybe we don't talk about Robert's mom and my stepdad's thing with her to my mom. She's sensitive about it, and I'm afraid she will be more upset with me by telling you two. Can we keep quiet about that?" Danae puts a finger to her lips, and Mrs. Jenkins nods in agreement.

"Mums the word, little lady! But maybe I can drive by Phyllis's house and stake it out quietly. I promise I won't say anything to her." Mrs. Jenkins reaches over to pat my hand.

"Thanks, Mrs. J, I trust you. If you don't mind, I need to get Chrissy out of bed so she can have breakfast, too. And-and she might have wet the bed," I say with so much regret and shame. I can't take any more sad, pitiful looks, so I pick up my plate and utensils to put them in the sink. Danae grabs my items from me, looking a little insulted.

"Gi! You're the guest. I'm the host, so let me take those from you so you can see if Chrissy is awake. Go on! Aunty can make her some eggs, too."

"Hey, Gi-Gi, don't worry about Chrissy wetting the bed covers, there's a mattress cover, and we've got a washer, so no biggie. Just bring her out for some food."

Mrs. Jenkins' aura is a mixture of pink, light blue, and some green. She looks tired and apprehensive about what I don't know. Maybe she's being a cop and an adult, so she wouldn't feel comfortable talking to a kid like me about her feelings and concerns.

"Thanks, Mrs. J! You know Chrissy, she'll be here in two shakes."

Our heads turn to a sleepy Chrissy standing at the edge of the hallway with her left thumb in her mouth, a teddy bear wrapped with her right arm, and fully dressed.

She has a troubled face as she furiously sucks on her thumb. For now, I'm proud of her dressing without being told and with practical clothing: her short-sleeve, yellow T-shirt with a bird puppet on the front and a pair of blue jeans. Her little, white tennis shoes look odd worn on opposite feet. She pulls out a chair and sits down patiently with an adorable smile on her round face. Her hair is still messy, but I can tell she made some attempts to brush it.

When the sun shines on her hair, warm chocolate and sandy brown highlights are in her medium-length hair.

Mrs. Jenkins walks into the dining room, smiling at Chrissy, holding a plate of scrambled eggs, cut-up bacon, toast, and a plastic cup of milk.

"G'morning, Mrs. J!" Chrissy beams a smile, with one of her front teeth missing.

"Good morning. Miss Chrissy! Here you go!" Mrs. Jenkins says with a high-pitched voice, placing the plate of food in front of her. Chrissy's eyes grow big, and she beams a wide smile. She gently puts her teddy bear in the chair next to hers and picks up her fork. She stabs chunks of food onto her little fork, grunts like an ape, and shoves the huge chunks in her mouth.

Danae and I go back to the table to sit across from her as she chews away.

"Dang! You're one hungry little girl!"

Danae says, smiling at Chrissy, who swallows her food and then picks up her plastic cup of milk. She sips happily while swinging her legs back and forth under the table.

"Hey, Cookie Monster, so proud of you for dressing yourself!" She puts her cup down and stares at me. Her smile drops from her face, then she leans to her right to grab the teddy bear. She immediately sticks her right thumb in her mouth.

"Did you sleep okay?" Chrissy shakes her head "no," takes her thumb out, and gives me a frown.

"You didn't save me! You let that-that bad fairy girl take

me!" Chrissy shouts while pointing her right finger at me. I tried to play it off like she was joking.

"Sounds like you had a bad dream. I wasn't there, you know."

It's never easy trying to reason with my three-year-old sister. She shakes her head left to right, swinging her legs violently back and forth under the table.

"I heard you, Gi-Gi! You were yelling at that fairy girl!" Danae and Mrs. Jenkins are both motionless in their chairs.

"Dang, that's one heck of a dream, but you know that's all it is. You can't use a dream to get mad at your sister, sweet pea." Danae's voice is soft and soothing. Mrs. Jenkins sits next to Chrissy, putting out her right hand to stroke her semi-messy hair filled with static electricity.

"It'll be okay. We're all here, and you're safe now, Chrissy." Chrissy swipes off Mrs. Jenkins' hand from her hair angrily. She stands up in her chair and points at me.

"You! You need to stop this bad fairy girl! She wants to hurt me!" Chrissy screams, tears running down the side of her face. I get up from my chair to hug my sister, but she slaps my hand away and screams some more.

"I want my mommy! I want my mommy!" Mrs. Jenkins tries to hug Chrissy, but she is only pushed away.

"It's okay. She's frustrated with so much, especially for a three-year-old."

Pushing back the worn-down tears, I decide to get some fresh air. Walking towards the front door, I leave Mrs. Jenkins behind with Chrissy to calm her down.

The air outside is fresh and cool, an excellent start to calming my nerves. The front porch was just the spot I need to gather my thoughts. Danae is right behind me and immediately sits on the rattan chair across the couch I stretched out on. She pulls out a book from underneath the seat cushion.

Relieved to see her read a book instead of talking to me, I rest my head against a couch pillow as I stretch my legs across the couch. I take a deep breath and slowly let it out. My eyes wander beyond the porch and towards the grass area of the front lawn. There's a movement amongst the bushes just ahead. I close my eyes again, hoping for someone to be there.

Telly, are you there?

I open my eyes to see Telly's head rise above the bushes. He pops out from between the leaves.

"Come over here!" Telly mouths these words while motioning me to come over.

"*Telly, is that you?*" My mind is asking and hoping he answers.

"*Yes! Young lady, can you get away from the girl? I need to speak to you.*"

"*Meet me at the tree line in the back. There's a large rock with a "GT" painted in red letters. I'll see you there.*"

"*Okay, see you there.*" I no longer hear him talking in my head, so he must've left for the large rock.

CHAPTER FIFTEEN

TRACKING SPELL

Danae is fast asleep with a book over her face. That's a good sign for me to sneak away. I could use Telly's help in tracking Stepdad.

Looking through the screen door, I can see Mrs. Jenkins on the phone while Chrissy is sitting quietly, trying to finish her breakfast.

I step away from a snoozing Danae, down the porch stairs, and several steps into the tree line. I walk into the cool forest area for a few minutes to where Danae and I started our trek into the wetlands the other day. I looked around for the rock with the red letters and used it as a starting point for our trail.

It's handy since the rock is about the size of a football and flat on the top. I finally catch Telly lying on it with his hat over his face, arms on his chest, and hands together. His snores remind me of a toy train puffing out a small roar of smoke. So, taking another step with my tennis shoes, cracking a dry leaf, and kicking up pebbles along the way startled him to sit straight up.

"Huh? Oh, hey there, Gina! You alone?" Telly brushes off

the dust from his tunic.

I shake my head with a "yes," he raises his right arm and signals for me to sit on the ground next to him.

"Why are you here, Telly? Do you know what's going on?" His eyes scan the area around us, and he looks weary.

"Well, to be honest, I've been watching over your home as per Irra's request. Did you say you see signatures, and if so, have you seen Rav's lately?" Telly asks, looking awkwardly at me.

"Yes, she talked with me in my dreams last night. So, what?" I say calmly, shrugging my shoulders. Telly's eyes grow big and shiny, and he leans forward.

"You did? You saw Rav? Do you have any idea where she might be?" His curious gaze is annoying me.

"Sorry, I was too concerned about my litter sister, Chrissy, being taken hostage by Rav. And yes, she's been stalking my family and home through a teddy bear. She gave me a tracking spell to find my baby sister Natalie who's been kidnapped by Stepdad and Grandma." He sits back, studies my face, and frowns.

"So she's here. What can I help you with?" He relaxes on the stone surface and sticks a blade of grass in his mouth as he rests his head on his left hand while crossing his right leg over his bent left leg.

"I need you to help me find my baby sister, Natalie. Rav gave me a tracking spell. Will you help me?" I ask while scratching my arms and swiping away the bugs biting me. Telly waves his right index finger in a circle, then blows at the bugs. They all fly away at his command. He sits straight up, keeping his gaze on me.

"What will you pay me? Got any more of that chocolate cupcake snack with the cream filling?" Telly's eyes shine, and his lips crack in a slow smile.

"Whatever you need, so are ya gonna help me?" I feel skeptical and question how much power does Telly have? Telly picks up on my doubts and continues smiling.

"I'm here to teach you how to use your power, m'lady, and that's what I aims to do."

"What are you talking about?" Telly's aura tells me he's losing patience with its orange and tinge of red streaks hues. He gets up on his feet and stands up to talk to me. He stops for a few seconds to take a deep breath, then proceeds to give me instructions.

"Okay, put your hands together as if you are about to pray, then close your eyes. Take a deep breath and let it out slowly. Clear your mind of lingering thoughts until you hear silence around you." Telly motions for me to close my eyes. As the words travel into my ears while I close my eyes, I feel heat and electricity between my fingers.

My talisman heats up, and I feel its glow warming my chest. Telly's voice trails off. Pushing any thoughts out of my mind was easy; I could also feel my heartbeat slow down and my pulse almost stop. Telly's voice comes back and startles me.

"Shhhh, now recite the tracking spell you were given. Say it several times until you see the people you're looking for." I try to open my eyes but can't; they are slammed shut. So instead, I focus on recalling what Rav said to me.

C'mon brain! It's in there. What was it? Cuidich ... something. Yes, there it is!

"Cuidich mi le bhith a l'org ... cuidich mi le bhith a l'org ..."

Silence surrounds me; I can't hear the birds chirping or flying overhead, nor dogs barking or crickets ... nothing but silence. Then I remember to recite the spell again.

"Cuidich mi le bhith a l'org ..."

I can feel my body floating, but not physically. I am traveling through a white void for what feels like forever in a dreamlike state, then voices. They sound familiar but are still too far away to recognize whose. The air around me feels thick until a vision appears before me.

It's Stepdad and Grandma sitting at a table drinking coffee. Little Natalie is sleeping in her bassinet.

"We need to leave now. They will come after us," Grandma May says, sounding desperate as she grips her coffee mug tightly between her hands. Her knuckles are white, and she is gripping the cup to her mouth to take small sips. She looks tired and much older than the last time I saw her. The bags around her eyes have grown more extensive, and her face is much looser with skin hanging down. She hasn't slept well or at all.

Stepdad gets up from the table; he pulls out his wallet from the back pocket of his air force fatigues pants. He opens his wallet to pull out a few dollars to give Grandma.

"Here, if you need more formula for the baby and to get more groceries, there's a supermarket just down the road by the base."

Stepdad puts his wallet back in his pocket. Grandma stares at the handful of money on the table as if she's never seen money before.

"She's sick, and we need to take her to the hospital, son."

Grandma says, her face covered with so many worry lines when she frowns. Stepdad is about to leave but turns around, tired, annoyed, and losing his patience. His bloodshot eyes stare directly into Grandma's face as he walks quickly to the table and leans down on her.

"Then take care of her! I have to report to work or be charged for AWOL. Do you understand?" He shouts into her face as Grandma leans back, her eyes big as saucers.

"Wh-what's AWOL? Can't you just quit? I can hide you. It's no problem." Grandma's voice trembles as the words spill out of her mouth. He slams his right fist on the table next to her, and she lets out a yelp of fear. She holds a shaky hand in front of her. He raises his right hand just above her head to strike down on her just like he used to do to Mom. Then he stops, puts his arms down, and stares at her.

Grandma starts crying in her hands. He takes a step back, pulls out the chair he was sitting in just a few minutes ago, and plops back down. He tries to reach for her hands, but she slaps him away and bawls her eyes out.

"Look, Ma, I'm in the air force. I signed up for six years of active duty and must fulfill those obligations. They will send the Military Police to find me if I do not report to work. I will be reported as absent without leave. That's what AWOL stands for, and it's punishable. I could end up in a military jail. I will report to my commanding officer and ask for leave, meaning put in as many vacation days as he will allow me to take. As soon as I get approval, I will call to let you know. Okay?"

Stepdad looks over towards Natalie, stirring from his yelling and slamming. Grandma wipes her eyes and nods her head. She gets up from the chair to walk toward Natalie's bassinet. She picks up my baby sister to cradle her gently in her arms and hums a calming lullaby to soothe Natalie.

Sweat beads emerge from Stepdad's forehead as he backs off. He looks disturbed and scared and looks around the motel room. It's modestly furnished with old furniture: faded-wood armchairs and a couch with rough-looking, burnt-orange cushions. The television is black-and-white but turned off. The dinette table they were sitting at has four aluminum chairs with red plastic cushions in a kitchenette area with a mini-fridge, a small sink, and a two-burner stove and oven.

His eyes continue to scan the room until he looks in my direction.

Can he see me?

I'm frozen in place as he continues to stare into my area. My heart races as his eyes grow wider with panic; he takes several steps back. His mouth falls open in shock; he keeps backing away from my direction. Grandma May watches in horror at Stepdad's behavior.

"Y-you look like you've seen a ghost ...you okay?"

He shakes his head at her comment but doesn't say anything; he focuses on me. I move closer to him to see if he sees me or senses my presence. The sweat from his forehead burns his eyes as he furiously wipes his face with the back of his hand.

He gasps and runs out of the motel room. He stops outside his motel door. I move towards him, flowing through walls to follow him.

I look around to find the motel's name on a sign outside the parking lot. "Waitborne Inn" in big black letters on a giant whiteboard.

My eyes scan the parking lot and back to the motel room that's shows a number 115 on the door.

Good to know! Not surprised Grandma would pick such a trashy place; she can be extremely cheap when it comes to spending her money.

Stepdad is still freaking out while looking in my direction. He fumbles around with his car key, trying to fit it into the lock, then drops it. I keep looking for his and Grandma's auras, but it's not visible to me for some reason. I'm sure it's more to do with the tracking spell.

Using my finger to point at the keys, they float up mid-air. Stepdad backs away instantly, trips on his feet, and falls on his rear end. The hard concrete landing isn't pleasant, but he continues to run from the floating key chain.

"Get away from me, you! You! Freak!"

Stepdad keeps his gaze on the keys. I put my fingers down by my side, signaling the keys to fall to the ground. The black aura cloud that constantly hangs around his neck doesn't seem visible right now. Curiously, I whisper a few words to see if it works.

"Black cloud aura, show yourself!"

It appears around his neck and moves around. His eyes look like giant golf balls, and he grabs at his neck maniacally. Bloodcurdling screams fly out of his mouth. He gets down on his knees, clawing at his neck. Strips of blood seeping from torn skin appear around his neck, chin, and chest.

The black clouds increase in size as the aura completely covers his neck. It's funny how it looks like a turtleneck collar without the sweater. Stepdad writhes on the ground with so much noise and struggle. Even the patrons staying at the motel come out to see what's happening.

Grandma May burst out of their motel room door with little Natalie crying in her arms.

"David! David! What the hell!"

Grandma looks helpless and runs back into the motel room. Stepdad continues to wallow in pain as I focus on the black clouds to choke him little by little. His bulging eyes look in my direction again even though his face is turning blue, and his tongue hangs out of his mouth. He swallows hard, reaching for the sky above him with his right arm.

"Please, p-please stop!" He gasps between words, fighting to breathe. Watching him in so much pain, so much misery, is so satisfying. I feel like the cat who toys with a mouse before ending its life.

Do you want to kill him? Will it make-up for what he did to you, Chrissy, and Mom?

Must think more about that. Right now, he's paying for it, which makes me feel okay.

Within fractions of a second, I'm pulled away from this vision. I am returning from my dream, only to hear Danae's voice.

"There you are, Gina! You had me so worried!" Danae rushes out from behind the trees and forest vegetation. I look in her direction and then quickly look back to find Telly. He's gone.

Trying to recover from being pulled out of the tracking spell to this reality has taken its toll. Exhaustion sweeps over me, the sweat soaking through my clothes, and now my teeth are chattering.

"I-I had to get some fresh air … just stressed." Danae puts out her right hand to help me get back on my feet. I gladly accept. After she pulls me up, I quickly brush off the dead leaves and dirt sticking to my bottom.

"Let's get going, Gi! Aunty has questions about where your stepdad might be and needs your input."

Danae takes significant strides, walking back to her home. My bones are too tired to catch up with her, and my heavy, sweat-soaked clothing isn't helping either. She continues walking and doesn't look back. We reach her home; Mrs. Jenkins is sitting on the couch on the front porch. Chrissy is playing with some toys next to her, frowning at me.

"Oh good, you're here, Gina. Listen, Officer Banedridge will be here in a few minutes to ask you questions. Can you do that?"

"Sure thing, I might have an idea where they might be, and hopefully, we can catch up to them."

I approach the front porch step and don't stop to sit down with the rest of them. Danae plops herself on one of the nearby armchairs next to her aunt.

"I-I need to change my clothes, sweated through these, and now I'm freezing. Can you give me a few minutes?"

"Sure, hope you're not coming down with something. It looks like you just broke through a fever." There's a look of concern on her face, but it's not necessary.

"I was feeling anxious and worried, but I'm okay now. I'll be right back!"

Not wasting time, I race to the guest bedroom and dig out another set of clothes and a comb from my tote bag.

As soon as I step into the bathroom to change, there is a tapping on the window glass. It's a crow with bluish-black feathers perched on the windowsill outside. This is way too weird even for me. Walking up to the windowsill, I'm hoping it will fly away as soon as I open it, but it doesn't.

Instead, Telly jumps off the bird and stands with his hands on his hips. Rolling my eyes, I pull the window up, revealing the screen.

"Telly! Your timing couldn't be any worse. You need to

leave!" I say, feeling invaded by him standing on the sill.

"I need to tell you that you came close to killing your stepfather if I hadn't pulled you out of the tracking spell. Is that what you intended to do? I'm concerned for you, Gina!" Telly's eyes look watery, and his aura is a light purple with tinges of darker blue.

"You came back to tell me this? Are you serious? The answer is 'no!' Okay? Please leave!" I slam the window closed on him. He stands there, looking confused. Pulling the curtain closed gives me a little more privacy. I can hear the crow back on the windowsill and Telly voicing a command to take off.

Now I can take a deep breath. I am not wasting more time since Mrs. Jenkins is waiting for me.

As soon as I finish dressing and combing my hair into a ponytail, I rush to the kitchen fridge to rummage for food. I find no sweet treats until I look through the pantry and find a box of dried cereal with colorful charms shaped from corn and extra sugar. I take a bowl from a nearby cabinet and pour the dry cereal to the brim. I run back to the bathroom windowsill, open it, push out the screen, and put the bowl on the outside of the windowsill. I promised Telly payment, and that's the best I can do.

Walking back onto the porch, I notice Officer Banedridge sitting in an armchair across from Danae. He's sipping on some coffee offered by Mrs. Jenkins. They are talking amongst themselves.

I quietly sit next to Chrissy on the couch. Fortunately, she looks tired and ready for a nap. She leans her head against my right arm and starts sucking her thumb. I'm so relieved to see her depending on me for comfort, so I gently move my arm away so her head can rest on my lap. She falls asleep quickly.

"Danae, can you put Chrissy in the guest room so she can nap quietly?" Danae nods and gets up immediately to pick up Chrissy gently, and she gives me a quick smile. Chrissy stirs a bit, but happily rests her head on Danae's left shoulder as

Danae carries her back into the house. Looking back at the officer and Mrs. Jenkins, I feel like I'm in some hot seat.

"Hey, Gi, you're not in any trouble. I've asked the officer here to help us locate your stepfather and grandma."

"Well, all I can tell you is that I overheard them speak just before they left. There's a good chance they could be staying at a motel near the air force base. Grandma usually pays since my stepdad never seems to have enough money."

I avoid the officer's intense stares; his aura looks olive green with some mustard yellow, almost reminding me of little Natalie's mushy green poop smeared all over her rear end from a diarrhea episode. Officer Banedridge clears his throat to get my attention.

"Do you know that for sure? It would be beneficial to know which motel," he says. The lines on his face look deeper than when I talked to him last. He pulls out his pocket-size steno pad and clicks on his pen. He leans forward so he can listen closely.

"It's more likely the Waitborne Motel; we've stayed there before when we first arrived from the Philippines when Stepdad got his new assignment. In case you didn't know, he's in the air force."

He continues to scribble into his notepad. Mrs. Jenkins squirms in her seat, picking up her coffee and taking a long sip to calm herself down. Her aura changes from pink to red to blue. She must be feeling anxious. Officer Banedridge gets up and puts his notepad in his top front pocket.

"Thank you, Miss Trabeck. I will check out the Waitborne Motel. Oh, by the way, do you know anything about Mrs. O'Malley finding a crunched-up fender in her backyard?"

I shake my head left to right, feeling thrown off by such a question.

What's this gotta do with me?

He stands staring at me, waiting for my response.

"Does the fender have anything to do with my stepdad? I don't understand."

Mrs. Jenkins gets up and picks up both empty coffee cups. She's trying to hide from shaking, but almost drops one of the cups. I reach over to help her.

"Mrs. Jenkins, let me help with the cups."

She happily hands me the cups and smiles. Officer Banedridge takes out his notepad again and scribbles some more.

"I'm just curious, that's all. Well, I better go. Got some errands to do."

The officer puts his notebook away and then rummages through his back pockets for his car keys.

"Would you mind taking them to the sink while I talk to Officer Banedridge? Please tell Danae to watch over Chrissy. You and I are driving out to the Waitborne Motel. Okay?"

I nod my head "yes" and walk back into her home, leaving her alone with the police officer. They murmur to each other, keeping their voices low. As I place the cups in the sink and turn around, Danae bumps into me.

"Why do you keep doing that? You almost made me pee my pants!" Danae lets out a giggle while I make a funny face.

"So, what's the happening, Gi? We gonna get Natalie?" She beams with excitement. My smile drops, hating that I must break some bad news. Danae takes a few steps back to let me get to the front door so I can go back outside.

"Umm ... your aunt wants you to stay with Chrissy while I ride with her to Waitborne Motel. I hope they're staying at this place." Danae stops smiling and shrugs.

"No biggie, got some homework to do, anyway. Hey, just letting you know that Aunty called the school to excuse you for a family emergency."

I completely forgot about going to school today. There's too much happening at home. Now I'm worried about whether I will have a family after things calm down. If anything ever calms down. *Sigh* ...

"Yeah, I appreciate your aunt doing that. I hope we can catch up with my grandma at the motel today."

Mrs. Jenkins pokes her head back into the front door. "Hey, lady, you ready?" She sounds a little too excited while she gives us a painted smile.

"Yes, ma'am, I'm ready." I join Mrs. Jenkins at the front door while Danae gives me a quick wink and closes the door behind us.

EMERGENCY CENTER

We reach the Waitborne Motel parking lot close to 1:00 p.m. I'm unsure if Stepdad is there since the station wagon is still in the parking lot.

I notice something I've completely overlooked for a while now. The station wagon's front fender differs from the rest of the car. It's all gray with no paint job, while the front end of the vehicle has been replaced with an olive green paint job and the rest of the body is in its original tan color. My eyes are glued to the car as Mrs. Jenkins parks the Bronco.

What was Officer Banedridge up to when he mentioned the fender?

"Hey, I'm going to the front desk to see if your stepdad is renting a room. Can you wait in the car? I should only be a few seconds."

I close my eyes and try to remember the room number in my vision. That's right; it's room 115. Feeling Mrs. Jenkins' fingers tapping on my shoulder, I open my eyes to her staring at me with concern.

"It's room 115. Let's try that!" She gives me a confused look.

"How do you know that? Okay, let's see if you're correct!" She takes the key out of the ignition after she puts the Bronco in park. I can't help but smile; she is listening to me. She's one of the few adults who treats me like I am more than some dumb child.

"I have a good feeling Grandma will be answering the door." She shrugs and follows me after we get out of her car and lock the doors. All rooms have doors facing the parking lot, so we don't have to enter the front office's main entrance.

Room 115 is at the very end of the whole motel. Mrs. Jenkins rushes past me to knock on the door. She knocks a few more times. I can see Grandma peeking between the blinds and slipping out of sight.

"Are you sure this is the correct room number?" Mrs. Jenkins asks nervously, her eyes darting everywhere, then she keeps her gaze on me.

"Mi Ma, it's me, Gina, your skarbie!" Mrs. Jenkins bangs on the door again. That's when we both hear a baby screaming at high volume. The door finally opens, and Grandma is standing before us, haggard, with a screaming Natalie in her arms. My baby sister is beet red in the face, her eyes sunken.

I quickly place a hand on her forehead; it's hot. Grandma hands her over to me, tears running down her face. The front of her red house dress is covered with baby vomit, and the smell tells me she's been wearing it for a long time.

"She's very sick! We must go to the hospital. Something's wrong with our Natalie!"

"Okay, May, grab your stuff so we can take you and Natalie to the hospital. Your daughter-in-law is there now." Mrs. Jenkins follows Grandma inside the motel. Grandma grabs her items that are scattered all over the motel room.

"Give me about five minutes to change into something cleaner." Grandma picks out a couple of clothing items from her tote bag. She quickly runs to the bathroom and closes the door.

I grab Natalie's diaper bag and bassinet. I gently place her in her bassinet. Unfortunately, her diaper is stinky. I rummage through the bag but, couldn't find a disposable one. Grandma must've used them all.

Fortunately, there's a handful of cloth diapers. I quickly take off her soiled, one-piece pajama. Her poor bottom is messy with runny poop, so I have no choice but to wash her in the kitchen sink.

She continues crying even though her tears dried up long ago. This can't be good. I do my best to sit her in the sink with warm soapy water and quickly use a hand towel to clean all the crevices. Little Natalie stops crying when I get her into a dry, clean diaper and another one-piece pajama.

I gently wipe off the dried tears, snot, and slobber from her face. Mom taught me how to swaddle little Chrissy when she was this young, so I did the same for Natalie. It was such a relief to be able to calm her down. I am able to find a pacifier and stick it in her mouth; that should stop the crying for a reasonable amount of time. Natalie falls asleep in no time. I hum softly as I pick her up and place her in the bassinet.

Looking around for some cans of formula in the kitchenette and in the fridge, I have no luck finding any. All the baby bottles are empty and piled up in the sink.

I look again in the outer pockets of the diaper bag and find one can of formula plus a clean baby bottle.

That's a relief!

Grandma comes out of the bathroom in clean white blouse and black slacks. Her auburn hair is put up in a quick bun. She still looks tired and weary. She smiles quickly while putting her stuff away in her tote bag. The two ladies are waiting for me to get Natalie's things together. To keep it quiet, I signal them to go ahead so Natalie can sleep peacefully.

As soon as we load up in the Bronco, Mrs. Jenkins starts the engine. I sit in the back with my sleeping sister in the bassinet.

Grandma is in the passenger seat, quietly looking out her window. Her aura emits a combination of green, mustard yellow, and a tinge of red. She's keeping to herself; I can tell she's worried about something and maybe hiding something too.

"Mi Ma, how are you doing? Are you sick too?" I lean in from behind her to see if she will answer me. I keep my right hand on her left shoulder; that's when she lightly taps on it with her right hand and gives me a weak smile. Her eyes look haunted and distant, and the circles under them darker.

"I am okay. I don't know how you found us, but the timing couldn't be better. I'm too worried about Natalie." She hangs onto my hand and squeezes it, then lets it go.

"We'll find out about Natalie soon enough and hope it's just some bug she can get over with proper medicines from the doctor. Is Stepdad at work? How come the car is still in the parking lot?" I ask, trying my best not to sound too excited, but curiosity has gotten the best of me.

"Your FATHER was able to call a co-worker to come to pick him up, and he's filling out paperwork for some vacation time. I left a note at the motel so he could take the car to pick us up." Grandma closes her eyes and rests her head back. I can tell that my constant staring at her is making her uncomfortable.

What is she hiding? She's not looking too good, with pale skin and cold, clammy hands.

Mrs. Jenkins gives me a quick wink; she's been listening to our conversation.

"We're almost there, and this will allow us to visit your mother, Gi! May, there is a minor emergency center you and Natalie can go to and see a doctor on call. That's probably where you need to start. They should be able to contact your family doctor afterward." Mrs. Jenkins pulls up into an empty parking space close to the emergency room section of the hospital. I am feeling nervous and anxious since I must pick between walking with Grandma to take Natalie to see a doctor or going with Mrs. Jenkins to visit my mom.

Do you trust Mi Ma right now? Something is going on with her, and Natalie is sick! How well was she able to care for a baby? Don't let her out of your sight!

"Mrs. Jenkins, can we at least walk with Grandma and Natalie to make sure they both see a doctor first? I'm sure Mom will understand, especially when she finds out Natalie is sick and can't do anything about it." I ask, hoping Mrs. Jenkins will agree.

"You know what? That makes a lot of sense! Let's get you squared away, May! You should be proud of your granddaughter for being such a smartie! She can think on her feet like no other kid," Mrs. Jenkins says, smiling at me. Grandma doesn't object, but she also doesn't have any reaction to what was told to her.

Her silence hurts. I don't know anymore. Does she even love me? I'm beginning to think Grandma only likes the idea of a family on her terms. We're nowhere near the loving and supportive ones she sees on television.

Her aura changes from pink to red, then maroon and deep blue. Grandma's face looks pale, waxy, and covered in sweat. She crosses her arms in front of her chest like she's trying to brace herself from a fall. She leans forward and moans.

"Mrs. Jenkins! Something's wrong with Grandma! Can you get help?"

Unfortunately, Natalie starts screaming too. Mrs. Jenkins leans to her right to look at Grandma closely.

"May! May! You all right? Talk to me."

Mrs. Jenkins' eyes grow big as she puts her right hand on Grandma's left shoulder. Mi Ma can't answer; her face falls on her lap, and she continues to moan in pain.

Growing impatient waiting for Mrs. J, I jump out of the car and run straight to the emergency center. Fortunately, it isn't too far; I am already at the intake desk.

"Please, please! My grandma is having a heart attack, and

my baby sister is hot with a fever! We're in a silver Ford Bronco in the parking lot."

I can't help but feel panicky and probably look sweaty too. The lady behind the desk doesn't waste any time; she picks up the phone to call for orderlies to come out.

"Okay, sweetheart, the orderlies are here, and they'll follow you to the Bronco." I nod and wait for them. Within seconds, two tall guys come out with a rolling cart.

"We're ready. Go ahead."

They follow right behind me as we run to the Bronco. The passenger door at Grandma's side is wide open; she's hunched over. Mrs. Jenkins is holding Natalie in her arms. The swaddling was taken off, so Natalie cries, kicking and screaming.

The orderlies walk over to Grandma. Thankfully, she was not unconscious, so she can move off the passenger seat. It's heartbreaking to see my grandmother, who's typically a loud, strong, and vibrant woman, look so pale, weak, and speechless.

One of the orderlies helps her onto the rolling stretcher. She gladly lies back and closes her eyes. A stout nurse with dyed blonde hair tied in a ponytail and wearing thick-rimmed eyeglasses comes out. She quickly listens to Grandma's chest with a stethoscope and asks some questions. Grandma cooperates and answers them. The nurse tells the orderlies to take her to one of the exam rooms.

She comes back to us and breaks out her stethoscope again. Little Natalie keeps kicking and screaming in Mrs. Jenkins' arms while the poor nurse listens to the baby's heart.

"Oh my! She is burning with a fever! You both need to follow me to the emergency room so I can page a pediatrician."

Mrs. Jenkins and I both nod our heads. Poor Natalie's face is beet red again, and she is crying uncontrollably. Her stomach area is hard as a rock while I try to swaddle her. Mrs. J takes the bassinet out of the car so we can gently place Natalie in it. Luckily, the bassinet has built-in handles, so Mrs. Jenkins and I grab a handle with each of us on opposite sides.

We follow the nurse into the emergency center and place the bassinet on the stretcher. A younger guy, slim built, with combed-back, sleek, brown hair and brown eyes, walks up to the bassinet. He pulls a stethoscope from his white lab coat pocket and undoes the swaddling. Little Natalie looks weak, her cries are feeble, and her breathing labored. She lets out a low moan and then closes her eyes. Both the nurse and pediatrician look panicked. They whisper to each other; the nurse nods and picks up a nearby phone. Two more nurses and a couple of orderlies arrive within seconds. The first nurse tells us to wait in the lobby and they will come for us.

"What's happening? What's wrong with my baby sister?"

Mrs. Jenkins puts her right arm around my shoulder as we stand still, waiting for the nurse to answer. Two orderlies come over to push us out of the way as another set of people shows up with a rolling stretcher and a bunch of machines.

"You need to leave now! There's nothing you can do here! Please fill out the paperwork at the intake desk so we can get the baby admitted to ICU," the nurse yells and signals the orderlies to escort us out of the examination area. There are so many people gathered around my baby sister. This is all too much. I want to stay and watch everyone. I'm afraid for her. Mrs. Jenkins grabs my hand and pulls me away.

"C'mon, Gi, we gotta fill out some paperwork and call your stepdad. This is getting serious. Your baby sister is counting on us now. Let the doctors and nurses do their job, okay?"

Her eyes look watery, her voice shaky with concern. She swallows hard and stares at me. I nod my head as tears stream down my face. She doesn't waste any time pulling me away from the buzzing crowd surrounding my sister. We walk out into the hallway; my feet are on autopilot, moving and following Mrs. Jenkins. The front desk nurse already has a clipboard of papers. I walk up to the front desk, grab the clipboard, and look through the documents.

Fortunately, most of the paperwork is filled out. Grandma May gave out some info with names and phone numbers, including Stepdad's work number.

"I'm gonna call Stepdad's work right now." Mrs. Jenkins takes the clipboard from me and nods her head.

"May I use your phone? My Stepdad is stationed at Waitborne Air Force Base, and I need to contact him."

The nurse behind the desk nods her head. She waves for me to come around the front desk and grab one of the phones nearby. There is a black desk phone sitting on an empty desk. I pull up a chair and grab a pen and paper nearby just in case I must take notes.

There was a box of tissues, so I grabbed a couple of sheets to blow my nose. My whole world is falling apart in front of me, and now I must look for my stepdad.

Keep it together, Gi! There's nobody else you can lean on. Eventually, Mrs. J will have to worry about Danae and their own lives. Take it easy.

My brain is scrambling around, I can't seem to remember his work number. All I can remember is his commanding officer's phone number, so I dial it. The line rings just once, and somebody picks up.

"314th Squadron, Waitborne Air Force Base Supply Depot. This is Sergeant Thomas. How can I help you?"

Feeling tongue-tied for a second, I find my bearings again.

"Uh ... yes, sir, this is Georgina Trabeck, and I'm trying to find my stepfather, Airman First Class David Trabeck. There's an emergency at Waitborne General Hospital. My mother, grandmother, and now my youngest sister are all admitted. He is needed to fill out paperwork and for the doctors to talk to him."

The sergeant paused a bit; I can also hear paper rustling.

"Sorry about that, miss ... It seems he left on emergency leave. That's all I have. Would you like for me to leave him a message?"

"If he does come back, please let him know that Rosaria Trabeck, May Trabeck, and Natalie Trabeck are all patients of Waitborne General Hospital and to check in at the emergency intake desk for more information."

I hang up; I don't feel like listening to him repeat the message. Putting the phone back in its cradle, I look over to where Mrs. Jenkins is waiting on the other side of the intake counter. She seems curious and waits for me to walk closer to her.

"Hey, did you get a hold of your stepdad?" she asks anxiously. She motions for us to sit by a set of cushiony chairs in the nearby waiting area. Her attention is all on me, waiting for me to give her an answer.

"I talked to some sergeant who picked up the phone and told me that my stepdad went on emergency leave. So, I left a message just in case he returns to work." She grabs my hand, squeezes it, then lets it go.

"It'll all work out. Maybe he returned to the motel and saw the note. He's probably on his way here. Let's hang on to that for now." She's trying to sound reassuring, but her eyes are full of worry. I grab the clipboard from her to see if I can fill in the empty spaces that Mrs. Jenkins didn't. She pulls the paperwork from my grasp and looks at me sternly.

"Hey! Remember, you're still a kid! Let your stepdad take care of this. It's his responsibility, anyway! Could you do me a favor and get us some snacks?"

She rummages around in her purse to pull out a five-dollar bill. She hands it to me. I shake my head. She grabs my hand and shoves the bill in it.

"Now, go! Remember the gift shop? It shouldn't be too far from here. I'll take an orange soda pop and a bag of chips and get something fun to eat. You look like you could use some food in you."

She waves me off and goes back to looking at the clipboard. I get up slowly, feeling light-headed. I search for a clock on a wall somewhere. There's one hanging just above the intake desk; it says 12:30. No wonder I can't seem to think straight.

I asked one of the nurses for the gift shop's location, I was told to go to the hospital's main entrance and find the signs. Simple enough. I proceed to my search and walk into the hallway leading me to the hospital's central area. It still surprises me to see many people, doctors, nurses, technicians, and everyday people walking around.

The whole place is buzzing with so much activity. The hospital intercom is constantly paging a doctor or a nurse to report to surgery or an exam room. The hallways are filled with people bumping into me or even shoving me.

Seeing people with their kids or elderly members rushing from one floor to another only reminds me of my situation. My mother, youngest sister, and now grandmother are all patients at this hospital.

What happens now? You think Stepdad even gives a crap about us?

I can take care of Chrissy at home.

So, what happens when you have to go to school? Who's going to drive to the grocery store for food? What about your science fair?

I wish I could stop time and go somewhere to gather my thoughts. It's all happening at once. My feet drag along the shiny, just-buffed floors. Instead of taking a direct path, I ride the elevators and walk around each level. I wander from one hallway to another and take a deep breath.

The number of auras surrounding me makes me dizzy. I return to the elevator again to take another floor, and this time I stop at the second floor. It's quiet, and not many people walk past me.

The sunlight beams brightly through the windows as I pass by. I stop to look out the windows; the parking lot is crammed with many cars.

My eyes search for the station wagon. That's when I notice

a familiar face in a black uniform with a gold badge on his left chest. He's walking into the main entrance of the hospital. His facial expression is blank, and he scans the area. His aura is a tinted red with some brown hue.

Is he looking for somebody? Maybe he's gonna arrest someone but was rushed to the hospital for an injury?

Whatever it is, he's not here to visit a sick friend or family. He stops walking and checks out one of the parked cars. It's the station wagon parked close to the emergency center. He walks around, looks inside, and grabs the driver's side door. It's locked, so he takes out his notepad and starts writing something.

He looks around again, then puts his notepad back in his front pocket and walks towards the emergency center.

He's looking for Stepdad.

I rush back to the elevator. I tap the number "1" button for the first floor, and the door slowly opens. Nobody is on but me, so that's a good thing.

As soon as the elevator descends and opens to the first floor, I run out to follow the signs for the emergency center. Panic hits me as my feet pick up my pace. I'm not allowed to run down this hallway, and there are too many people.

Trying with all my might to avoid wheelchairs pushed by others, baby carriages, and stretchers driven by hospital people rushing to get to the surgery or intensive care, my feet pick up the pace.

I see Stepdad standing at the intake counter of the emergency center. He is in his green fatigues uniform with his olive green baseball cap on his head. His back faces me as he shouts angry words toward the nurse behind the counter. She doesn't look impressed with his rantings.

"All I'm asking is the whereabouts of my mother and my baby daughter! Why is that too much to ask?" Stepdad shoves the clipboard of paperwork toward the nurse. The nurse is a large-set lady with flaming red hair in a giant beehive do. Her light blue eye shadow is so thick that it overpowers the rest of her face. She's also wearing frosty, pale pink lipstick over her thin lips. I must admit that the makeup isn't doing her any favors. The scowl on her face seems so permanent.

"Sir! Calm down! I will get the information to you as soon as possible! I just got on my shift," she shouts back, then turns around and mumbles something to herself. I can tell she wants to avoid his confrontations because he won't shut up.

Feeling a tap on my shoulder, I turn to see who it is. Mrs. Jenkins looks down to give me a nervous smile.

"Hey, Mrs. J! Did Stepdad see you? Or are you ..."

"Just waiting for him to calm down so I could talk to him, but he seems like he's off the rails or something." I can tell she is tired of this ordeal and ready to go home.

"Hey, Mrs. J, you've done so much for my family and me. Thanks for everything! I'll fill him in on the information. You don't need to be here. I'll make sure Stepdad returns to your house to get Chrissy if that's okay with you."

She gives me a concerned look, and that's when I remember to get the five-dollar bill out of my jeans pockets and hand it to her.

"Oh, hey, you didn't buy yourself any food? Are you sure? And besides, with your stepdad on a short fuse, I don't think I should leave now!" Her eyes turn a darker blue while frown lines surround her mouth area. I grab her right hand and shove the five-dollar bill back to her.

"Seriously, I'll be okay. I'm sorry I didn't buy anything. I thought I saw Officer Banedridge looking at the station wagon in the parking lot. He's here too."

Her eyebrows raise, and her aura turns bright orange; I certainly piqued her curiosity. She takes the five-dollar bill and shoves it in her purse.

"Huh! I wonder what he's up to?"

"I don't know, but he did enter the emergency center entrance. That's all I know."

I feel a strong tug, and I'm pulled away from Mrs. Jenkins. Stepdad's strong hand grips my left shoulder tightly, causing pain. I wince under his grip and try to pull away.

"Let go of me!"

His bloodshot eyes grow big as saucers, lips pursed tightly as he takes a couple of steps closer. Mrs. Jenkins jumps in between us; she stares at him boldly.

"Dave, this isn't the time or the place. If you wanna pick a fight, how about you do it with an adult instead of a helpless child?"

He takes a step back from her, lips still pursed. He casts a dark look at Mrs. Jenkins and then over to me. I've seen that look too many times before, usually right before he raises his belt or a hand to strike me.

My heart hardens; I dare him to strike Mrs. Jenkins or me right here in public. Would he do something so reckless?

You know the answer to that question. Take a big sniff! He smells like he fell out of a beer factory or something!

The room is silent; others stop what they are doing to watch us.

"Mrs. Jenkins called the ambulance for Mom and drove Grandma and Natalie to the emergency center. I'm thankful for her because Grandma might have had a heart attack, and Natalie has a high fever!"

Mrs. Jenkins puts her right arm around me and stands next to me. A nurse calls him to the counter.

"Mr. Trabeck! We have all of the information you need." She waves for him to approach the counter. Before he turns around, he walks up to us.

"This isn't over! You think you have an ally here? Guess again!" Mrs. Jenkins' face twisted in pure anger. Her aura turns a deep red.

"You lay a hand on her, and you will answer to the authorities for child abuse! I've heard and seen enough of your actions!"

Stepdad's reaction is something I'd never seen before: surprise. He's speechless, sweat beads on his forehead and above his lips. He backs away from us slowly, never taking his eyes away from me.

He glares menacingly, warning me that this is genuinely not over. My knees shake uncontrollably and, feeling light-headed, I fall forward. Mrs. Jenkins moves her arm from my shoulder to my chest to keep me from falling.

Not understanding what's happening to me, I'm grateful for her holding me up. She smiles at me and holds me tighter.

"You're going to eat some decent food. Your blood sugar must be low. That's why you're feeling faint, little lady!"

"I'm okay. I'll sit down and wait to see if I could walk with Stepdad to see Grandma and Natalie."

"I don't think so! He looked like he was about to kill you! There's no way in hell I'm letting that-that m-man near you!"

"Then, what should I do?"

She grabs my right hand and pulls me away. We walk down the hallway and away from the intake counter.

"First, we're gonna go to the cafeteria and get you something to eat! You're a growing girl about to hit puberty and thin as a rail!"

Her words are stern and final. Since my stomach has been growling at me for the past couple of hours, and if it could talk, it would agree with Mrs. Jenkins about the cafeteria thing. We follow the signs directing us toward food.

CHAPTER SEVENTEEN

BLACK CLOUD AURA

Lunch at the hospital cafeteria does the trick. I pick meatloaf, mashed potatoes, green beans, and a salad. Mrs. Jenkins finds my ravenous appetite entertaining. Now to finish off my dessert of apple pie a la mode.

"I'm glad you ate some decent food. You look so much better!" She gives me a quick wink. Unfortunately, it wasn't the same for her. She went through a few cups of coffee and small bites of her chef's salad.

Something catches her eyes while she's looking over her shoulder. Her smile drops, gaze steady as Officer Banedridge approaches.

"Hello, ladies! May I join you?" Officer Banedridge asks. His voice sounds tight, and his aura is a light orange with a hint of green.

Good thing you finished your lunch because he's hunting for some information, right?

Mrs. Jenkins gestures for him to sit at the empty chair opposite us. Unfortunately, our square table has four chairs, with two available chairs. His fake smile is so apparent when he sets his tray down and takes a seat. He looks squarely at me, intensely, which bothers me so much.

I don't know why. I want to finish my apple pie a la mode, but I can't pick up my fork. Sweat seeps through my clothes; my talisman is heating up under my T-shirt.

"Something wrong, Miss Trabeck? You look sad."

He picks up his coffee and takes a long gulp, never taking his eyes off me, and I wonder why.

"Since you ask, why are you here? It's certainly not to visit with us," I say, rolling my eyes and returning his rude stares. He cracks a genuine smile, but it just gives me the creeps. It's too broad, too wide, and perfectly toothy. The smile isn't genuine because his eyes continue to bore through me as if I have something to hide.

Well, you do, don't you? Maybe he knows about Stepdad's violence, or perhaps it's the station wagon?

"You don't waste any time, do you? I had a feeling you're sharper than you let on."

His tone is amused and only makes me squirm in my seat. I can't eat anymore, the company has made me lose my appetite, and that's a shame too.

"If you both will excuse me, I'm done eating and need to go to the bathroom, please." Mrs. Jenkins' reaction was that of sheer surprise and confusion.

"Whoa, wait a minute! I'd appreciate you finishing all of your food. I thought you were hungry?" Officer Banedridge continues to sip on his coffee cup. Mrs. Jenkins gestures for me to sit back down. Since she's supported me and is a good friend, I decide to listen.

"How 'bout this? I will finish all my dessert since I'm still hungry, but I won't answer any of your questions until after I finish eating. Can we do that?" I emphasize, looking directly at Officer Banedridge. He nods his head and looks at Mrs. Jenkins. She sits back, looking relieved.

"Look, officer, if you have any questions for me, we can

talk after lunch or at another table if this can't wait. We both had a long day, and it isn't over yet. Three of Gina's family are in critical care at the hospital."

"I'm sorry to hear that, and I will respect your request, Ms. Jenkins," he said, putting down his coffee cup. He picks up a Danish with his right hand and takes a big bite.

We sit for a few good minutes quietly eating our food. That's such a relief for me. I'm glad I didn't throw my dessert away because it was so delicious. I still must finish my steamed green beans and my tossed salad. I haven't been a big fan of vegetables lately, so I eat those last. It drives my poor mother crazy how I refuse to eat my desserts last.

I wonder how she's doing. I miss her so much right now!

They are both staring at me, and I didn't even realize it. Mrs. Jenkins' eyes look dark and tired, with heavy shadows under them and only getting darker. Officer Banedridge's gaze continues to be intense while the left corner of his lip twitches every few seconds. He leans forward, ready to fire off a barrage of questions.

"Is your stepfather here, Miss Trabeck?"

I can't believe he's asking this. Didn't he see my stepdad not too long ago?

"Of course. What's this all about?" Mrs. Jenkins grabs my left hand and squeezes it. Her eyes tell me it will all be okay; even her aura is a soft peachy pink. She cares and inspires me to stay strong even though all I want to do is run away from these questions.

"Well, I have to investigate an event that took place last year, and I just learned that your mother is not available to answer any questions for now."

My patience grows thinner as he slowly drags it out.

Can he be any more dramatic? I feel like I'm on one of those TV cop shows where the detective goes through a montage of questioning the perpetrator into a guilty plea.

I shrug my shoulder in response to his statement.

"I haven't seen my mom since the ambulance hauled her off, so we both must wait for her to recover. I'm sorry I can't be of any more help. How 'bout you tell me the room number and floor she's on? I'm sure you already found out." The officer's eyebrows raise while he cracks a smile.

"I knew you're brighter than the average twelve-year-old, probably due to living with an alcoholic stepfather, right? Okay, why don't we all go up to the fifth floor, room 517, to see if she's awake?"

He picks up his tray of empty dishes and cup, and Mrs. Jenkins follows suit. We all go to the nearby tray rack to put our trays in an available slot and walk toward the cafeteria exit. Even after 2:00 p.m., many people are still piling into the cafeteria to buy their meals.

We all proceed to a nearby elevator. Officer Banedridge pushes the "5" button on the panel and waits. The elevator door dings and opens. Like robots, we all step in at the same time. Mrs. Jenkins' face is frozen; Officer Banedridge avoids looking at me as I stare intensely at him.

When the elevator dings again and opens to the fifth floor, we all step out into the quiet corridors of this floor. Our footsteps echo through the hallways as we get closer to my mother's room.

The door is propped open, and we see my stepdad sitting on the left side of my mother's bed. Her bed frame is set up at a 45-degree angle with pillows to hold her up. She looks dazed, staring out into space. There's an air tube in her nose and an IV line going into the vein at the crook of her left elbow. Stepdad's back was facing us, so he didn't notice us stepping in.

Mom's aura is a troubling array of gray, with tinges of red and blue. Her head faces our direction, and that's when Stepdad turns around to see us. His bloodshot eyes are weary, angry, and wet.

Was he crying?

"She's dead! My mother is dead! And I blame you!"

"Dead? What are you talking about?"

It's shocking to hear this news! He's got to be lying!

Officer Banedridge steps in front of me to block him. Mrs. Jenkins grabs me and shoves me out of the way. Stepdad stumbles into the officer's arms as he screams and kicks like some spoiled brat not getting his way.

My eyes focus on the black aura cloud that's been hanging around his neck. I will for it to tighten slowly, and his eyes grow big with fear. He slaps the officer's hands away and shoves Mrs. Jenkins, who tries to approach him, against a wall. The back of her head hits the wall hard with a thud. Her eyes turn glassy; her mouth gapes open as she slides down to the floor with her back against the wall.

"Mrs. J! No!" The words fall out of my mouth; my lungs burn as I scream. Two nurses and a couple of orderlies rush in. I run straight to Mrs. Jenkins to see if she's all right, but a nurse pushes me aside.

"Please stand aside; we need to help the lady."

Tears run down my face. I'm feeling so helpless. I switch to anger and towards something I can control, and that's to hurt HIM. Both orderlies struggle to contain Stepdad as he goes into a frenzy, fighting them off as well as Officer Banedridge.

I focus on the black cloud aura again and finish the job this time. My talisman heats up and bursts into bright light flames through my T-shirt. My aura separates from me and glides towards Stepdad. I continue to focus on the black cloud tightening around his neck. He screams, grasping at the black cloud but never touching it.

"No! You're gonna kill me!" He struggles to breathe; his gaze is directed at me as he chokes from the black cloud aura's tightening grip. My aura divides into several strips, each grabbing onto an arm or leg. He loses control of his arms as my aura strips slam him to the ground. Even the orderlies and Officer Banedridge stand in confusion and horror. Everyone around Stepdad stands watching him scream on the floor, struggling to get up.

"Get her away from me! She's-she's a demon! The devil!" he screams like some crazed lunatic. For the first time in my life, I finally have control. Control over him and the power of this situation. I let the black cloud tighten until his face turns blue, his tongue hangs out, and he is frothing at the mouth. The nurses scream in terror, watching but turning away. Even Officer Banedridge yells in horror.

"Somebody do something! He's, he's choking to death! C'mon, man!" he yells at one of the orderlies and shoves him toward Stepdad. I can't help but smile as my aura keeps him down on the floor. I hear a weak voice calling my name from behind me.

"Gi, Gi, you gotta stop! Stop!" Mom yells in a weak but raspy voice. My attention turns towards Mom's bed, tears running down her face.

Is she serious? Of all this time, he's hospitalized her over and over again?

"No more, not this way! I'm, I'm s-sorry, Gi!" Mom struggles to get out of bed, but her IV line pulls her back.

Stepdad stops gasping for air; his eyes slam shut, and his head falls to the floor.

I release the aura strips that kept him on the ground and allow myself to ease up on the black cloud aura. It fades out. All that's left is my stepdad's unconscious body, limp and lying on the floor. A nurse rushes toward him with a stethoscope, listening to his breathing and heartbeat. She runs to a phone on the wall and shouts for more personnel with a crash cart. Within seconds, a group of people rushes in with a rolling stretcher and machines. Stepdad is hoisted onto the stretcher while people gather around him to revive him. After a few more minutes of hooking him up to every cord and hose, they get Stepdad breathing. They also leave just as quickly as they came in to haul him off elsewhere.

Everything will be better once you finish the job, right?

*There's no other way; he will kill you! Mom knows, though ...
she knows you have powers!*

Mrs. Jenkins comes over to me, rubbing the back of her head.

"Hey, Gi-Gi, you okay?" I nod to let her know I am. Walking towards Mom's bedside and sitting next to her, I grab onto her right hand.

"Sorry, Momma! He's not gonna hurt any of us anymore," I say with a confident smile. I lie next to her and wrap my right arm over her chest. She clings to my hug and starts to cry; we both hold on to each other.

I'm so tired; I don't want any more of this! I want to be with my family and have an everyday life.

"Do you tink he was right 'bout Granma being dead? Where's my Natalie? She okay?" Mom asks weakly, her face twisting into a prune of worry. I hug her tighter; it bothers me to feel her rib cage. I answer her question as best as I can.

"I- I don't know about Grandma, but Natalie has a fever, and the doctors are taking care of her here at the hospital. It will be okay, Momma." I'm not sure if I believe what I say.

Mrs. Jenkins stays in the room, sitting on a nearby chair to watch us. She looks exhausted and ready to pass out in her chair.

Officer Banedridge leaves the room; he follows the group that hauled off Stepdad. Mom sits up and loosens her hug. I let her go so she can adjust, but I stay on the bed next to her. I look around and notice a pitcher of water, a cup, and a box of tissues by her bedside table.

I grab a handful of tissues to gently wipe the tears from her face. It looks like she's lost more weight; she's practically shrinking in her hospital gown. She smiles weakly at me and gingerly takes the tissue from my hand.

"Tank you, my *magunda*. I'm so sorry, so sorry, Gi." Tears trickle down her face; she wipes them away. She starts to mumble a few more words in Tagalog.

I miss talking to her in our language. I hated the school for forcing us to speak only English at home; it was part of their program to eliminate my Filipino accent. Teachers would complain that my accent was so thick that they couldn't understand a word I would say.

That's a bunch of crap!

Mom took it to such literal extremes that she stopped speaking Tagalog several years ago. She even stopped cooking my favorite Filipino dishes at home. She wanted me to be a complete American girl who spoke only English.

She was only trying to be a good mother; that's all she tried to be. So, I decided to speak Tagalog again, and she didn't object.

"Momma, the police are asking about the front fender of the station wagon. What's going on?"

"That's all you're worried about? I have a concussion, and it isn't good. And you want to know about the car? He crashed it." Mrs. Jenkins sits in her seat, looking confused because she can't understand Tagalog.

"I'm sorry, Momma! That police officer came here to ask you questions. I think Stepdad did something horrible, like drunk driving and possibly killing someone. That's what I think! I don't want you to get in trouble with him! Do you see what I mean? I hope you're not protecting him."

I'm pleading for her to listen to me. Her face freezes, her eyebrows furrowed tightly. She frowns as she recalls something that happened last year.

"Your father had to pull extra duty before Christmas Eve; he had to drive to the Columbus army depot to deliver some supplies. It took him a couple of days to drive back and forth. He went drinking with his co-workers right before he left Columbus after his final delivery. He called late at night, saying he would come home on Christmas Eve morning, but he didn't. He came home on Christmas Day late in the evening. I was so mad at him. Remember? We waited so long to open our presents!" Her voice takes on a hostile tone; I nod in agreement.

"Did he say anything to you about what happened?" She sits quietly; more tears run down her face.

"I don't remember any ting!" Mom answers in English; it is disturbing for her not to recall anything about that situation. She lies back against her pillow, exhausted from our conversation and what happened earlier.

I can't help but think about Irra's actions when I asked her to help me with my mom's face-off with Phyllis. Irra must've wiped out the memory of what occurred on Christmas Eve. I want to find out what happened and don't know where to go.

Mom picks up a remote pad with buttons attached to a cord near her bed. The head portion of her bed goes down so she can roll over and sleep. She doesn't say anything else. It's her telling me she doesn't want to talk to me anymore. Mrs. Jenkins gets up from her chair and walks toward me.

"Hey, Gi, we need to get back to my house. There's nothing more we can do here, and your mom needs her rest." She faces Mom and puts her hands on Mom's shoulder lovingly.

"Rosie, hey, lady! I'm gonna take Gina back to my house! Okay? Chrissy is also staying with us. Just rest, and let the doctors and nurses take care of you. I'll come back tomorrow to see how you're doing." Mom turns to face her and holds out her arms to Mrs. Jenkins, who gives her a quick hug.

"Tank you Lau-ra! I will neber furget jour kindness!" Mrs. Jenkins pats her on the back.

"No problem! I love your daughters. They're good cookies!"

I give Mom a quick hug. "I love you, Momma!"

Mom doesn't move, her face blank, eyes staring off into the distance. She can be so hot and cold with me.

Mrs. Jenkins and I step out of Mom's room and into the quiet hallway. I make sure to close the door behind us. Mrs. Jenkins studies my face for a few seconds.

"Hey, it's all right. I had an emotionally unavailable mom, too. Don't give up on her; she needs you more than you know."

Wow! Hard to believe Mrs. J had to suffer through a sad past.

"I'm sorry to hear that."

We walk towards the elevator. Mrs. Jenkins shrugs her shoulders and acts like it's no big deal.

"We can talk about it someday. We should head back to have some supper. Can you wait here? I think I see Officer Banedridge walking by."

We both see the officer coming out of one of the rooms.

"Wait here. I'll only be a few seconds, okay?"

He had already noticed her and waits for her to catch up. He nods in my direction with a frozen face. His aura is a muddy brown with tinges of yellow, green, and peach.

Something's up! He's worried about something!

Mrs. Jenkins says something, and the officer puts a forefinger to his lips, signaling to keep her voice down. They whisper to each other as they walk farther away from me. I decide to walk back to Mom's room but think better of it.

An orderly run out of one of the rooms. He runs towards the nurses' station just twenty feet away. I lose sight of him after that, so I follow him. He calls out to one of the nurses to call security.

"He's escaped! Code green! We need security now!"

A nurse grabs a phone and calls; she chatters and hangs up. She nods at the orderlies, who tell visitors on the floor to leave; one of the patients escaped. Officer Banedridge overhears the commotion and returns to the room that the orderly had left.

That must be Stepdad's room! No!

Mrs. Jenkins runs towards me, looking scared.

"Gina! We need to leave this floor. Your stepdad took off!"

"He didn't go back into Mom's room. I would've seen him!"

Where the heck could he be? I know he screamed about

Grandma May being dead, but I'm having a tough time believing him.

It's too much, and he's lied before!

"Well, I'm not taking any chances of him finding you. He's not stable at all!"

Mrs. Jenkins grabs my arm and pulls me towards a nearby elevator. My heart races, then drops when I realize what she means.

You know that if he catches you, your goose is cooked!

"If he does, I'm ready! I'm sick and tired of living like this!"

Mrs. Jenkins stops and looks at me. A look of concern is all over her face.

"Sweetheart, you can't mean that? You're no match for him! C'mon, we need to get outta here!"

Alarms go off in the hospital; now my heart is racing. I can't believe the stupid stunt Stepdad is pulling. A nurse comes over to us; she looks annoyed.

"Ladies, please take the stairs. All elevators are turned off for now!" she shouts while walking by Mrs. Jenkins, who rolls her eyes. We walk past the elevators toward the other side of the hallway. We reach the door with a sign saying "Stairs" and open it.

We look down the stairwell and hear footsteps rushing up to our level. I hear a familiar sound, that breathing, and cursing under his breath. He mentions my name, calling me the "b" word, and how much he wants to deport me.

"Mrs. J! He's down there! Let's go up!"

She nods and starts racing up the stairs. I follow right behind her. My legs are already burning; my lungs feel like they're exploding. The footsteps below are gaining on us. My knees wobble, and I'm out of breath.

You can't stop now!

"How much longer, Mrs. J?"

Mrs. Jenkins is slowing down to a walk; she leans forward, breathing hard.

"It's, it's another flight of stairs, and we'll be at the roof-top!"

I can't help but worry about being on top and having no-where else to go.

Oh, God! When will this nightmare end?

We reach the door to the rooftop; I push through it. A blast of cool air hits my face. It's windy up here, and there's nothing else on the rooftop except a big square with a giant red cross painted on the helicopter pad and a cluster of industrial-sized air conditioners just opposite the square.

"We're at the helipad where helicopters drop off patients for emergency care."

Mrs. Jenkins looks worried because there's no place else to run. There's a dark area just behind the air conditioner fan units. I immediately run towards the units, and Mrs. Jenkins runs behind me. We crouch down and sit quietly.

The fans are on right now, so it masks any noise we are making, and we feel relieved to hide and catch our breaths. Mrs. Jenkins is soaking in her sweat and leaning against a nearby wall. I keep looking past the air conditioner units and listening for footsteps. A door slams, footsteps run around, and the fan units stop. It's dead silent.

"Where are you? Come out, you demon spawn!" I move closer to Mrs. Jenkins and lean against the wall. She puts her arm around my shoulder.

Stepdad won't shut up!

"Come out, come out, little piggy! You know I'm gonna send you back to the PI. I didn't want you! You know!"

"What does PI mean?" Mrs. Jenkins asks under her breath. Stepdad hears her somehow and starts running towards our hiding spot.

"It means Philippine Islands. He thinks he can deport me," I whisper back. Then I grab her hand to run away.

"He's gaining on us! We need to get away!" Her face freez-es in place while she's staring over my head. He's there; I can hear his heavy breathing that reeks of stale beer. Mrs. Jenkins shoves me behind her.

In a split second, she falls over me. Her body lands on me as I fall back against the wall. The back of my head hits the wall; I start to see black. Disoriented and nauseous, I can still see Mrs. Jenkins falling to her knees. Stepdad reaches over her and grabs me by the neck.

CHAPTER EIGHTEEN

STEP-DADDY ISSUES

Finding myself on the floor coughing uncontrollably, I slowly get on my hands and knees, trying to catch my breath. I must've passed out. I can feel my back aching; I must've hit the concrete hard while blacked out. Just a few feet away, I see Stepdad grabbing his midsection, hunched over. Mrs. Jenkins must've regained consciousness. She rushes over to me.

"Oh, thank God! Can you get up? I managed to kick him in the back and punch him in the stomach! Let's go!"

I nod my head, too weak to speak yet. My knees are too shaky, but I try to get back on my feet. I feel like throwing up; the nausea isn't helping. Mrs. Jenkins wraps her arms around my waist to hoist me onto my feet. That is when she falls forward, taking me down with her. She collapses over me, and I scream as her weight crushes me.

"Mrs. J! You're crushing me!"

My body slams on the concrete below me. A shot of pain races from my knees to the rest of my legs. Mrs. Jenkins screams along with me; she tries to roll off and get up on her feet again. Instead, she's pulled up by the back of her hair. She lets out a scream of pain.

Stepdad pulls her off me and throws her against an opposite wall. Her body collides against the wall. She lets out a big "Oomph" and falls on her hands and knees. She's trying to get back on her feet but looks dizzy and disoriented. Taking a few more breaths, I manage to find more energy.

"C'mon, aura! Show up! Focus!"

It takes a few painstaking seconds, and I can see the black cloud aura around his neck. I immediately focus on it, tightening around his neck. He gags and screams.

"No! You demon spawn!" He grasps his neck, but he can never touch this aura.

"Stop calling me that! I'm so tired of you hurting the people I love and me! YOU'RE THE MONSTER!"

My aura pulls away from me and separates into four red strips. They immediately wrap around each of his wrists and ankles. He screams in sheer terror, so I focus on making the black cloud aura tighter around his neck.

He can't grasp anything!

Finally! Got him pinned down; he can scream all he wants!

My anger is surging through me. I'm tired of crying, living in fear, and being used as a punching bag.

Time to put an end to all this!

"How does it feel? I'm in control! I control whether you live or die!"

Tears run down his face, and he gags and gasps for air.

"I didn't kill Grandma May! She had a heart attack! You will not blame me for her death!"

The rage in me wants to hurt him in every way I can imagine. My aura strips squeeze out the blood flow to his hands and feet. My legs grow weak, running out of energy, and my focus on the black cloud aura is starting to waver.

No! You can't give up; he will kill you if he gets back up!

The thought of losing my energy scares me. Sweating profusely through my clothes, I focus on my aura strips and the black cloud aura. I need answers, so I loosen up the grip of the black aura around his neck.

Stepdad is still on his back and turns his head to the left to cough for a good while. I can tell his throat is raw, and he rests his head on the ground.

"I need answers right now. What's up with the station wagon? Why is the front part a different color from the rest of the car?"

He avoids my question. That's fine; I can make him answer me.

"Did you hear me? Did you hit someone with the station wagon during your trip to Columbus? Were you drunk driving?"

He laughs to himself at first, but then it becomes louder and boisterous. I know he's trying to get on my nerves, so I smile at him. He stops laughing and spits in my direction, but I'm too far for it to reach me.

"As soon as I'm out of this, I'm throwing your butt back to the Philippines. You'll be begging on the streets where you belong!"

There's so much hate in his voice. I always knew he didn't like me, but to throw me out on the streets? My cheeks are burning with so much anger.

Since I've been able to relax my attention on my aura strips, I now have a little more energy to focus on the black cloud aura tightening around his neck. He gasps again, then gags from his saliva.

"You're not answering me. I'm the only one who can spare your life! And I'm not gonna repeat myself! Tell me!"

His face is turning blue, and his eyes are begging for mercy. It felt good to stand over him, smiling big and bright. Then I let the black cloud aura loosen up again so he could breathe more.

"Please ... Please ... okay ... I hit something, all right? I-I don't even know if they're dead or alive. I can't get in trouble."

"Does Mom know?"

He takes a couple of deep breaths. He mumbles something, then shakes his head.

"What was that?"

My energy is diminishing again, and the grip around his neck is loosening even more. He wiggles around and pulls his left arm out of my aura strip wrapped around his wrist. He struggles to get his right arm out of the aura's grip.

My focus tightens down on his right arm and his neck again.

"I said NO!"

He succumbs to the tightening aura. It's taking all my energy to keep my aura grip on Stepdad and pin him to the ground.

I'm startled by Mrs. Jenkins' hand on my left shoulder. Stepdad quickly jerks up from the aura grips; he struggles to get back on his feet. Mrs. Jenkins pulls me back and drags me towards the rooftop door. Officer Banedridge rushes through the rooftop door, pointing a pistol in Stepdad's direction.

"Freeze! Mr. Trabeck!"

Two orderlies crash through the rooftop door with a stretcher. Stepdad had no other choice but to lie back down. The two orderlies rush towards him and hoist him on the stretcher. They make sure he is strapped down securely. Officer Banedridge steps up to Stepdad, whose hands are up. The officer puts his pistol back in his holster and slaps handcuffs on Stepdad's wrists.

"Wh-what? Am I under arrest?"

"We have a physician waiting for you to examine you for any damage and treat you as necessary. You will be in my custody for questions about a fatal car collision. I will allow you to call your commanding officer and an attorney."

The officer says with a monotone voice, while giving Stepdad a stern look.

"This is a bunch of crap! She's the one who hurt me! You

saw it!" Stepdad screams, sounding hoarse and pointing at me. Officer Banedridge gives him a disbelieving grunt. Stepdad gives him a dirty look.

"Mr. Trabeck, I recommend you keep quiet. I'm this close to pinning more charges against you!"

Stepdad mumbles to himself, then looks at me.

"This isn't over!" He threatens in my direction as the orderlies carry him away to the door. Smiling back at his threats was all I could do. Mrs. Jenkins surprises me when she stands before me and yells back at Stepdad,

"You lay a hand on her. I swear you won't be around to see Natalie's first birthday!"

I gently grab her hand to calm her. She tightens her grip.

"Mrs. J, did you hear anything he said when he was on the ground?"

She looks around and waits for the officer to leave with the orderlies and Stepdad. She turns back to me.

"Yeah, I heard everything. I'm so sorry you and Chrissy had to live with such a troubled parent. It's over now. Your stepdad will be accountable." Her blue eyes soften and her face slowly breaks out into a small smile.

"I'm ready to go back to see Danae and Chrissy."

"Me too! Let's go!"

We leave as quickly as we can. The ride back will be a relief.

Chrissy spends all evening clinging onto me; she's been listening to Mrs. Jenkins describe the day's event to Danae. She didn't get into any gory details, but enough to keep Danae from asking further questions. Danae's puzzled look tells me she isn't satisfied with vague answers.

We have a quiet evening dinner, and everyone calls it a night. Mrs. Jenkins drags herself to her bedroom. Chrissy falls asleep without any hassle.

I can't sleep right now, even though I'm exhausted. If it wasn't for Mrs. Jenkins' generosity, I don't know where Chrissy and I would end up. Negative thoughts float in my head. I try so hard to fight them off, but tonight it's not working.

There's no point in falling asleep; I've been tossing and turning for three hours now. Chrissy stirs while I try to slip out from under her arms and legs, so I stop. She eventually rolls off me and to the opposite side of the bed.

I slip out without disturbing her. She mumbles something in her sleep, then sucks her thumb. I wish I could turn on my lamp, but that will wake my sister. I rummage around in the dark, searching for my sweater, finding it slung over the chair in front of the desk. I manage to slip out of our guest room, close the door quietly, and enter the hallway.

There is someone in the living room because I can see the bluish glow of light emanating into the hallway. So, I stop to take a peek from the shadows. I'm hoping it isn't Mrs. Jenkins. We've had a long day, and I don't want to upset her by not being able to fall asleep. Taking another step to get a better view, I'm relieved to see it's Danae watching TV. She's stretched out on the couch, holding a bowl of popcorn with an open can of soda on the coffee table. Padding into the living room, Danae first doesn't notice, but then she realizes my presence. Some popcorn falls out of the bowl as she jerks up.

"Oh, my God! I thought you were Aunty! Gina, you sneak!"

The TV's glow reflects her face with a big smile. I signal her to scoot over so I can sit next to her and share some popcorn.

"Good job on the popcorn! There's lots of butter, too." Danae lets out a giggle and reaches over to grab her soda.

"I'm glad you're here. This movie is kinda creepy."

She leans against me while we share the popcorn bowl. It's a black-and-white movie; the main character had too much make-up for a believable vampire. It is cartoonish to me.

"I don't know how it could be creepy. This show looks corny, and I like scary movies!"

I make fun of Danae's choice in movies; she sticks her tongue out. I can't help but laugh while popcorn flies out of my mouth. It feels so good to have a friend. Danae eats more popcorn, then sits up to look at me.

"Hey! Why are you awake? I thought you'd be exhausted from what happened and all." I stop eating any more popcorn.

"Yeah, I thought I was gonna pass out too, but I'm over-tired. Got a lot on my mind, you know what I mean?" I prop my feet on the coffee table since no adults are around. Danae nods in agreement.

"I know what you mean. We should be doing some home-work but dog-gone it! I don't feel like it, ya know?"

"Hey, got any more soda? I'm getting thirsty."

"Yep, there's plenty in the fridge. Aunty doesn't want us to drink anything with caffeine in it. Otherwise, we can't go to sleep."

"No problem, I love fruit flavor sodas anyways."

I'm in the kitchen, the fridge door is open, and I'm check-ing out the soda flavors. There's orange, grape, cola, and lemon-lime. I love lemon-lime, so I grab a can and close the fridge door. Danae scoots over again so I can sit next to her. She checks out my soda can and gives me a thumbs-up.

"Hey, I don't feel like watching TV anymore, and besides, I got a ton of questions to ask. You okay with that?" I hesitate for a few seconds, then nod.

"It's all right. I didn't feel like watching some corny movie in black-and-white anyways. You need to pick better movies!"

She elbows me in the ribs; I flinch and laugh. Danae gets up to turn off the television. The living room becomes pitch black. I hear Danae stumbling around, trying to find one of the lamps on either side of the couch. She manages to find the lamp to my right and turns the knob. It isn't a bright light, but it is enough to see each other. We sit in silence; I want to finish the popcorn, so that's where my attention goes. Danae watches me for a while.

"I'm so sorry to hear about your grandmother and everything else going on. Aunty told me a few things about the accident last year. She was the one who pointed out the station wagon to Officer Banedridge." Danae's eyes search my face for a reaction. Learning about this piece of information feels too weird.

"Why would she do that? I'm confused."

She shrugs her shoulder. I suddenly lose my appetite for the popcorn; now I'm burping up my soda. Danae burps louder. We both laugh out loud. Just realizing we're making too much noise, I put a finger to my lips. Danae looks embarrassed, then giggles quietly.

"Yeah, I wondered why Aunty is so obsessed with your stepdad's car. She starts digging around when she sees a smashed bumper in Phyllis's backyard. She doesn't know how it got there. So, Aunty brought it to Officer Banedridge to examine it."

Danae stares out into space. I'm still confused about why Mrs. Jenkins would be so interested in the bumper.

"So what's up your aunt's bonnet to dig around? I still don't get it." Danae hesitates, takes another breath, and goes on explaining.

"She found out about the bumper when she snooped around in Phyllis's backyard after your Mom said he was in Columbus for a couple of days last year. That's all I know."

Danae is starting to look bored and tired of our conversation. So, I get up from the couch and take the bowl of popcorn. I motion to her to ask if she wants any more. Danae shakes her head and gives me her empty soda can. So now I get to throw things away and put the dirty bowl in the sink. Danae gets up to join me in the kitchen.

"You tired? If not, I thought we could hang out in the backyard and look at the stars. Whaddya think?"

"Maybe being out in the night air can help me sleep. Let's do it."

Danae raises her right hand; I return her high-five. Danae runs back to the living room to grab an Afghan blanket and a few little pillows. I wait by the front door until Danae reaches me.

We quietly step out onto the porch. The crickets are loud this evening; their chirping comforts me. The cool night air feels good, and Danae gives me the blanket. We find a soft grassy spot in the front yard, so I lay out the blanket. Danae throws the pillows on the blanket; we lie down, propping our heads on the pillows.

Looking up at the night sky, I spot a shooting star. Closing my eyes, I make a wish. I've never done that before, but it can't hurt with my luck. Danae is lying beside me, looking up as well. Moving my head to look at the empty, dark mobile home next door just makes me sad. That's my home; nobody is there. Danae notices and pats my arms.

"It'll be all right, Gi. Your Momma and baby sister will be home real soon. You'll all be home soon."

"Thanks, Di! I don't know about my stepdad. Honestly, I don't want things to be back to normal. I can't live like that anymore."

"Yeah, Aunty told me what she saw in your Mom's room and on the hospital rooftop. She was saying he was acting strange like he was being pinned down. And he was gagging or choking on something. What's up with that?"

She crosses her legs and yawns for a few seconds. Her aura is a cool, light blue. She must be getting tired.

"My stepdad is an alcoholic. He gets blackouts and sorts. I hope he gets help soon. That's the only thing I could think of," I say, feeling bad that I had to lie to my only friend. Danae is silent, then glances at me.

"So I have a strange question. Do you believe in magic?" I turn my head to see if she is smiling and joking.

"Are you serious? What's that gotta do with anything?" Danae seems serious and is now looking at me.

"I've seen some things that are hard to explain, like with Mrs. Young during lunchtime and when Robert and his bullies choked on something right after they attacked us. This time it's your stepdad! And to be honest, I don't know what happened to me in the woods." Her voice trails off, then she yawns loudly. I don't know if I'm ready to tell her.

"I don't know what to tell you. I-I don't have any answers."

"For the first time since I've met you, I knew you're intelligent and honest. This time I'm having a hard time believin' you, Miss Georgina! Somethin's up!"

I wish, I wish I could just come clean! If I tell her about my gift, will she laugh at me? Will she think I'm crazy? It wouldn't be too far from the truth since I live with an abusive Stepdad. His hitting and punching probably knocked some marbles loose in my head.

"Do you believe that certain people were given a gift, and it's not superhuman strength, psychic abilities, or anything like that? How would you feel about knowing someone who can see others through a different vision that a normal person doesn't see?"

I choose not to smile when talking to signal her that I am serious. I want to see her reaction.

"It's funny you should mention this to me. Just before my parents got into that accident last Christmas, I remember my mother telling me about having gifts. She said everyone has a gift they are born with. How one uses that gift makes a difference. We all can acknowledge our gift and use it to benefit the greater good. If we ignore its existence or use it for revenge or selfish gain, it's like spitting in the face of the Great Grandmother who thought you deserved it. It's a great responsibility to carry that burden, but it can also be a great reward."

Danae seems much older than she appears this evening. I can see her mother say those exact words. It's still very cryptic to me right now.

"What do you mean by Great Grandmother? I take it

you're not talking about a relative, right?" She has a pensive look while staring up into the night sky.

"Mom never forgot about our tribal spirit. I hold it close to my heart. I've even tried to find books and magazines to learn more about my mother's heritage so I can continue it in my life. There's not much written about the Shawnee tribe, so I had to rely on people she knew from the reservation. Great Grandmother is the ruler, much like the Father God in Christian religions."

I wish to meet her mother. She sounds like a lady worth knowing.

"You miss your mom, don't you? I hope she'll wake up from her coma soon. I'm sure she's missing you."

I reach over to grab Danae's hand. I squeeze it tightly; she squeezes back.

"Yeah, I miss her like something fierce. Aunty wants to find this driver who hit my parents so badly. She's practically obsessed with it."

Danae lets go of my hand. She closes her eyes and takes a deep breath. We both lay looking up at the stars in the sky. I wish I could make out the constellation, but I never really paid attention, even though it's such an exciting subject. The more I concentrate on seeing recognized star patterns, the more I'm brought back to Danae's words. Her aunt is obsessed with finding the driver who killed her father and put her mother in a coma.

Think about it, Stepdad was in Columbus before the Christmas holiday. He confesses he hit someone that horrible night. Officer Banedridge and Mrs. Jenkins find out about the station wagon with different paint jobs and the fender in Phyllis's backyard. Connect the dots, stupid!

Sitting straight up on the blanket, something snaps me wide awake.

Oh my God! Stepdad is the drunk driver who killed Danae's dad and put her mother in a coma.

He crashed into them and probably drove off. That's got to be an illegal thing to do. Who would be so selfish and cowardly to drive off knowing he hurt someone? Wouldn't he at least try to see if he did? Wouldn't it be better to try to get help and do their best to save that person's life instead of leaving them behind to die?

Guilt washes over me like a bucket of cold water. I can't even look at Danae right now. It's bad enough that I have to hide my aural reading powers and being half Fae, but how do I even tell her about Stepdad?

"Hey, you okay? You look like you just stuck a finger in a light socket."

She gets up to look at me. I'm shaking so badly now that sweat beads form on my nose and forehead.

"I-I don't know how to say this, but I think Stepdad is the drunk driver who hit your parents and drove off. He-he even confessed it to me earlier today on the rooftop. He said he hit someone or something. I-I don't think my mom knows about it," I say, feeling like I am going to throw up. She stares at me quietly, searching my face. Tears are running down my face; my nose decides to leak out too. She gets up and grabs both pillows. She doesn't say anything but starts to tug on the blanket I'm still sitting on. I get the hint to get off so she can pick it up.

"Danae, say something! Please, can we talk?" I plead with her while following her back to the front door. She pushes it open and then turns around.

"I don't know what to think, Gi. I think it's time to turn it in, okay?"

Her watery eyes bore into me. She's trying her best not to cry, but it's too late. The tears streaming down her face are too much for me to bear. She goes inside, sniffling, and throws the pillows and blanket on the couch. Her brisk walk towards the hallway to her bedroom is enough to hint that she is done for now. There's nothing else I can do but watch her close the door to her bedroom. I wait for a second, then hear a "click."

The sound of someone locking her door is the sound of my best friend locking me out of her life.

ABOUT ATMOSPHERE PRESS

Atmosphere Press is an independent, full-service publisher for excellent books in all genres and for all audiences. Learn more about what we do at atmospherepress.com.

We encourage you to check out some of Atmosphere's latest releases, which are available at Amazon.com and via order from your local bookstore:

Icarus Never Flew 'Round Here, by Matt Edwards

COMFREY, WYOMING: Maiden Voyage, by Daphne Birkmeyer

The Chimera Wolf, by P.A. Power

Umbilical, by Jane Kay

The Two-Blood Lion, by Nick Westfield

Shogun of the Heavens: The Fall of Immortals, by I.D.G. Curry

Hot Air Rising, by Matthew Taylor

30 Summers, by A.S. Randall

Delilah Recovered, by Amelia Estelle Dellos

A Prophecy in Ash, by Julie Zantopoulos

The Killer Half, by JB Blake

Ocean Lessons, by Karen Lethlean

Unrealized Fantasies, by Marilyn Whitehorse

The Mayari Chronicles: Initium, by Karen McClain

Squeeze Plays, by Jeffrey Marshall

JADA: Just Another Dead Animal, by James Morris

Hart Street and Main: Metamorphosis, by Tabitha Sprunger

Karma One, by Colleen Hollis

Ndalla's World, by Beth Franz

Adonai, by Arman Isayan

ABOUT THE AUTHOR

Toni Yap is an immigrant, and US Army Veteran married to her Veteran husband of over 27 years. She has three adult children. She currently lives with her husband and three cats in Snohomish, Washington.

Milton Keynes UK
Ingram Content Group UK Ltd.
UKHW010839271023
431440UK00004B/262